Christmas With the Kingston Girls

Deb Stratas

Producer & International Distributor
eBookPro Publishing
www.ebook-pro.com

CHRISTMAS WITH THE KINGSTON GIRLS
Deb Stratas
Copyright © 2024 Deb Stratas

Edited by Adi Kafri

Website: debstratas.com

ISBN 9789655754735

Christmas With the Kingston Girls

*A Festive and Uplifting WWII
Historical Fiction Novel*

DEB STRATAS

ReadMore Press

DISCOVERING THE NEXT BESTSELLER

Sign up for **Readmore Press'**
monthly newsletter and get a
FREE audiobook!

For instant access, scan the QR code

Where you will be able to register and receive
your sign-up gift, a free audiobook of
Beneath the Winds of War
by Pola Wawer,
which you can listen to right away

Our newsletter will let you know about
new releases of our World War II historical
fiction books, as well as discount deals and
exclusive freebies for subscribed members.

Christmas With the Kingston Girls

A Festive and Uplifting WWII Historical Fiction Novel

DEB STRATAS

ReadMore Press

Sign up for **Readmore Press'**
monthly newsletter and get a
FREE audiobook!

For instant access, scan the QR code

Where you will be able to register and receive
your sign-up gift, a free audiobook of
Beneath the Winds of War
by Pola Wawer,
which you can listen to right away

Our newsletter will let you know about
new releases of our World War II historical
fiction books, as well as discount deals and
exclusive freebies for subscribed members.

Dedication

Christmas With the Kingston Girls is dedicated to all the readers of my Kingston Sisters books. I am so grateful that these brave women in World War Two London have captured your hearts and enthusiasm. If you want to read more about Tillie, Maggie, and Katie – Christmas With the Kingston Girls is for you. Please enjoy with my deepest thanks for your support.

Chapter One

A WHITE CHRISTMAS

1938 – Alice

"You do the talking, alright?" Maggie asked. "You are so much better with words than I am."

Tillie nodded, turning toward the townhouse.

"I'll start, but we must present a united front or I shouldn't think we have a chance." They dashed up the stairs, eager to be out of the cold.

"Girls, is that you? I'm in the morning room," Mum called from upstairs.

They hung up their winter things and joined her.

"Oh, it's nice and snug in here." Tillie rubbed her hands together. "It's still snowing like mad. I've never seen anything like it. It's rather lovely."

"Mum, do you fancy another cup of tea? I can stick the kettle on." Maggie hovered by the door.

Something's up, Alice thought. *These twins are being too agreeable by half.*

"No, I'm good, luv. But go on if you two need a bit of warming up."

The girls looked at each other.

"No, we're fine," they said in unison.

Tillie perched on Mum's armchair, whilst Maggie took a seat on the sofa.

"We've something to ask you," Tillie started unnecessarily.

"I hadn't guessed," Mum said, raising her eyebrows. Albeit she had the same warm brown eyes and wide smiles as the girls, that's where the resemblance ended. Where they were tall, blonde, and willowy, she was short and comfortably round with brown-grey curly hair.

Tillie took a steadying breath.

"Mum, you know how much we've loved working at Pops' office. We've learned ever so much about figures, and accounting, and typing."

"And answering telephones and greeting customers," Maggie added.

"Yes, you've both done well at the firm. Pops and I are both proud of how quickly you've learned, and taken it all on board. But that's not what this little chat is about, is it?"

"Not exactly. You see, Maggie and I have been talking about doing something different, a new direction. Something just for us." Tillie inhaled slowly.

"And what would that be?" Mum asked. *Oh dear, what have these girls cooked up?*

"We love being around people and helping them. We want to be out in the world. We'd like to become Lyons Corner House Nippies," Tillie finished in a rush. Chewing her bottom lip, her eyes never leaving her mum's.

"Those waitresses in the black and white uniforms? In central London – near Coventry Street?" *What? Working in a restaurant? My girls? What in the world are they thinking?*

"Yes, but they're called Nippies – because they nip around in haste, serving all manner of foods," Tillie said with an encouraging smile.

"We'd be able to look after each other," Maggie added.

"You've knocked me for six, I'll admit that." Mum shook her head and sat back. "How long have you been thinking about this?"

"For some time now," Maggie held her gaze. "It's what we both want."

"In the event, we've already applied. Our interviews are next week." Tillie held her mother's gaze.

"Good heavens, girls." Take a breath. *They are twenty-one, old enough to make up their own minds. They've always been sensible, and neither had gotten into any serious trouble. But this is out of the blue. And they're still so young…* She sighed. "So, you're not asking, you're telling me."

Tillie flushed from her neck up – a sure sign of discomfort. Just as Maggie paled.

"Sorry, Mum. We wanted to show you and Pops that we're adults now and have gone about this properly." Tillie stood and paced.

"It seems you have done. I'm not sure I'm ready for this, but it seems you two are. If Pops agrees, you have my blessing, I suppose." *Walter will be shattered. His heart is set on the girls following in his footsteps in the company business.*

The girls hugged.

"Mum, you're the best." Tillie grinned from ear to ear.

"Ta, Mum," Maggie said quietly.

"Just one more thing." Tillie bit her lip. "Could you speak to Pops for us? Soften him up a bit?"

Mum paused, then nodded.

"I'll have a quiet word with him after supper, when his belly is full and he's had a tot of brandy with his pipe. But it's up to you to assure him you've thought this through properly."

"We will, we will," they chanted together.

"Right, that's sorted. I think I will have that cuppa. I've worked up a proper thirst." Tillie led her sister out of the room, both wreathed in smiles.

Alice watched them leave, happy as clams. *This is going to change everything. I can't clutch them to me any longer.*

For the rest of the afternoon, they were helpfulness itself – scrubbing potatoes, setting and clearing away the table, and helping with the washing up.

Mum followed Pops into the library after supper. They'd been up there a quarter of an hour whilst Maggie and Tillie roamed restlessly around the drawing room.

"What's up with you two?" Katie stood and smoothed her skirt.

"It's nothing," Tillie said too quickly.

"Bollocks," Katie replied. "But I'm out for a night with my mates, so I'll leave you to it." She poked her head back around the doorframe as she left. "But I know you are up to something."

Tillie resisted the urge to throw a pillow at her sister. Katie was younger than the twins, tiny and dark-haired like their mother, and full of cheek.

The library door opened, and Mum appeared.

"I've done my best. He wants to speak with you now."

"Thank you, Mum." Maggie gave her a smile.

"Let's go, Mags." Tillie pulled her by the hand.

Pops sat behind his desk, pipe in hand. He wasn't an overly-large man, but he had a presence. Somber, he gave nothing away.

"Sit down, girls. I understand you have made a decision. A momentous one."

"Well, not quite, Pops. We've made inquiries, and yes, we've put in applications. But no decisions have been taken." Tillie responded for both of them.

"Corner House Nippies. What has possessed you to pursue such an occupation?" He wasn't making this easy.

"We want something of our own." Maggie set her chin. "A place where we can help people, learn new skills, and be out in the world."

"I see," Pops said.

"It's a respectable place to work. The girls are from different walks of life, but they are well trained with proper supervision."

"And the uniforms are provided," Tillie added.

"Are you not content working alongside Katie and I? You've been with me since you left school."

"We've loved it." Tillie clasped her hands together. "Truly we have. But being honest, we're looking for a bit more adventure before we settle down."

"Not that we are looking to settle down anytime soon," Maggie jumped in quickly. Neither of them was interested in an early marriage or starting a family yet. Good grief, no.

"That's good to hear." A hint of a smile. "Do you think you have the proper qualifications for the post?"

"I should think we have a chance. The notice said they want girls with pleasant personalities, good deportment, nice hands, and the ability to handle crockery nimbly." Tillie ticked off on her fingers.

"And knowing how to do sums quickly. We have a leg up on that score." Maggie said. "And we are mature. Some of the Nippies are only eighteen or nineteen." At twenty-one, the girls felt quite grown up.

"You certainly seem to have the central aspects covered." He sat back. The girls waited, not daring to glance at each other.

"I'm more than a little disappointed that you are surrendering accounting careers. You've done so well. I'll miss you round the office. But you are

of age, and it seems this is what you want. So, if you pass your interviews – both of you, mind – I suppose I'll give my approval."

"Pops, that's ace." Tillie ran to kiss him on the cheek.

"We won't let you down." Maggie pecked his other one.

Mum bustled in with a tea tray.

"All sorted, then?" She set it down on a side table.

"He said yes, Mum." Tillie smiled.

"So I presumed." Mum winked at her husband.

"No tea for us, Mum, thanks. We want to go upstairs and plan our ensembles for our interview." Tillie beamed.

"Thank you both again," Maggie said formally.

"And it's up to you to inform your sister. She'll be proper cross that you are deserting her," Mum called after them.

"We will," the twins cried in unison.

***

"Shall we get on with it, Faye?" Alice turned to the housekeeper.

"Yes, Mrs. Kingston. Just bringing a cuppa to sustain us."

"Right, let's make a start." Alice pulled her pad towards her, pencil at the ready. "We'll do the pies the day after tomorrow? Rather, you will, but I'll help peel the fruit. Let's see – mince, of course. Then, apple, blackberry…"

"Gooseberry?" Faye asked. As the family's long-term housekeeper, she was steady and reliable. She kept to herself but was a treasure.

"I shouldn't think we need it. You've already made the plum pudding and Christmas cake – both are substantial with the dried fruits. Besides, everyone fills up on turkey and the veg dishes. So that's pie day sorted. Let's go to Christmas Eve. We'll be at Shirley's as usual, but she's asked for your famous pineapple upside-down cake. Anything else?"

Faye pushed a stray hair behind her ear.

"Lemon cookies, perhaps?"

"Just right. For Christmas morning, we'll have the full English, of course. How much can you prepare in advance?" Alice was a tolerable cook at best.

"I'm meant to catch the train for my brother's at half-past twelve. So,

11

I'll be here early to sort the breakfast and get the turkey in," Faye said.

"Thank you." Alice sighed with relief. She didn't like to impose work on Faye on Christmas Day, but the food would all go wrong without her. "Once you've got the turkey and stuffing in, the girls and I can manage the veg. And Shirley is a dab hand with the gravy and pulling it all together. Perhaps you could catch an earlier train?"

"Thank you, Mrs. Kingston. I'll see about that." She gave a rare smile.

"No bother at all. We'll need to do a full day at the shops to fetch all the veg, baking ingredients, and all the bits and pieces we need to make the day special. Brussel sprouts, spuds, parsnips, chestnuts, and so on." She snapped her fingers. "We forgot the spirits – three bottles of white wine, two red, whisky, sherry, and brandy. Oh, and a bottle of champagne. One never knows if there will be something to celebrate. As far as the cooking goes…"

"I'll do the bread and chestnut stuffings on Christmas Eve along with whatever veg prep I can manage. And I'll bring out the good crockery, silver, and the linens."

"The girls can set the dining room table. We'll eat breakfast in the morning room, so that will need to be laid as well." Alice made furious notes. "What have I missed, Faye?"

Faye tilted her head.

"I'll speak to Jessie when she comes Monday about ironing the tablecloths and serviettes whilst she gives the house a good once-over. Nothing else comes to mind. We will undoubtedly pick up odd bits when we're at the shops."

"Brilliant." Alice put down her pencil. "I love Christmas, don't you?" It was her favorite time of year. Everyone gathered with warm hearts, slamming doors to shut out secret gift-wrapping, the sounds and smells so dear and familiar. Christmas morning was the most special. Her children, growing so tall, yet eager as little ones for their stockings and presents… It was all so delightful.

"I do, Mrs. K. But not as much as you. Shall I get on with the supper, then?"

"Yes, thank you. You keep us all running smoothly round here. You're a marvel."

Faye said nothing, but Alice could tell she was pleased.

12

***

Kenny banged on the door.

"I need the bathroom, squirt."

"Keep your hair on, and don't call me squirt." Katie's muffled voice came from within.

After a minute, she opened the door.

"Give a girl a chance. I was washing my hair."

He snatched the towel from around her head.

"Well, you are a squirt." He laughed.

At fifteen, Kenny was just the right age to exasperate his older sisters, Katie in particular.

"Well, I may yet grow," Katie pulled up to her mighty five feet, two inches whilst taking back the towel. Kenny snorted.

"You're full grown, squirt. Admit it." He pushed past her into the bathroom, locking the door.

"Brothers," Katie mumbled.

Dressing, she looked at the clock. Bloody hell, she was late again. She was meant to go Christmas shopping with Aunt Shirley to choose gifts for Mum and Pops. Running lightly down the steps, Mum called to her as she passed the drawing room.

"Please ask Aunt Shirley if she needs any more dishes for Christmas Eve, luv. Tell her Faye is happy to add in one or two. And dress warmly. It's snowing again."

"I will," Katie shouted, taking the stairs two at a time. Now bundled up, she opened the door to a winter wonderland. Snowflakes dropped slowly to the ground, dancing as they fell. It had been snowing off and on for weeks, so the street and landscape were covered in a good two inches – rare for a London winter. Delighted, she clapped her gloved hands. Hurrying to her aunt's house, she arrived out of breath with rosy cheeks.

She kissed her aunt on the cheek.

"Sorry I'm late, Aunt Shirley. I washed my hair, but this snow is just making it curl up again."

"That's alright, darling. Come through. Shall we have a cup of tea before braving the elements?"

"No, I think we'd best get on with our shopping. We've got to get to

Oxford Street, find masses of impossibly wonderful gifts, and get home again in all this snow."

Shirley nodded. She was an older version of her sister, albeit with blue eyes. She and Katie had a special bond. Aunt Shirley had always looked out for her, afraid she'd be lost in the spotlight of the older, stunningly pretty twins.

"Let's get on, then. I'll fetch my coat and handbag."

The pair chattered nineteen to the dozen as they navigated the slippery streets and tube.

"What do you think Mum would like? Since I've been working, I've put by some money, so a handmade Christmas ornament or card won't do. I'm seventeen, you know?"

"Yes, quite the young lady. Depending on what you have to spend, I have several ideas. She's been eying a lovely silver brooch at Fortnum and Mason's, but it's a bit dear. You'd probably have to go in on it with your sisters."

"No, I'd like to get her something from just me. I've joined in with them too many times."

"How about a book or perfume?" Shirley asked, stamping her feet.

"Not quite right." Katie frowned.

"Why don't we take a turn through the shops. Something is sure to spark your heart's fancy."

Two hours later, Katie's arms were filled with packages, and she was excited about her purchases. She'd found a lovely silk scarf for Mum in her favorite light blue. For Pops, a new letter-opener. Matching compacts for Tillie and Maggie.

"Even that pest Kenny should like his gift. I hope he doesn't come at me like a pirate."

"He's more than old enough for a penknife, dear. I expect he'll be thankful for it. Now, I don't know about you, but I'm parched. Tea and cakes?"

"Yes, please."

Finding a local restaurant, they gratefully set down their packages for a restorative cup of tea.

"You didn't do any shopping for Geoffrey today. Still looking?"

Shirley laughed.

"I've already bought out half of London, dear. Uncle Thomas says I must stop. I've spoiled him again, dear boy."

As an only child, Katie's cousin Geoffrey got all his parents' attention, but it hadn't turned his head. He was a fun-loving, warm and caring young man, with an eye on the law for his future.

Katie had ordered a Madeira cake and Shirley settled on a bakewell tart. Tea and sweets arrived, and they tucked in hungrily.

"What are you most looking forward to this Christmas, Aunt Shirley?"

"The same as always, luv. Family time. Being together. Christmas carols. Turkey with all the trimmings. All of it. And you?"

"The presents," Katie answered promptly. "I love waking up early to see what's in my stocking, and then running to see the tree shining, with gifts flowing in all directions. But I love the rest of it, too," she amended. "All the family being together and such." She took a bite. "This cake is divine. Oh, that reminds me. Mum asked if you need any more dishes for Christmas Eve. As for me, I just want a load of your sausage rolls." Katie rolled her eyes in delight.

"I don't think so, luv. I've probably got too much food as it is. I do like a groaning sideboard and full table."

"With candles." Katie smiled.

"Plenty of candles," Shirley agreed, lifting a delicate forkful of tart to her mouth.

They smiled in perfect accord.

***

"Are you chuffed for your date?" Maggie sat with a book on her lap, watching her sister.

Tillie adjusted the belt on her green woollen dress and clipped on gold flower earrings.

"Yes and no. I like Colin, and he's been asking me out for ever so long. He rather wore me down. But he's a fine young chap, as Pops likes to say, and he is charming."

"You don't sound too sure. Where is he taking you for supper?"

Tillie shrugged and applied pink lipstick. Combing her curls out one last time, she turned from the mirror.

"He didn't say. It seems a shame to bother with heels tonight. My overshoes will ruin my look entirely. But it's still snowing, and the streets are slushy."

"You still look lovely. Give him half a chance, luv. And have a brilliant evening."

"Ta ra."

In a whiff of perfume, she was gone. Maggie settled back contentedly to her book.

"It is a filthy night out there, sir. But I'll take good care of her. I promise."

Tillie came down the stairs, pinning on her brightest smile.

"Hello, Colin. You are right on time."

"Hello, Tillie. You look smashing."

"Thank you, Colin." She turned to her father. "Pops, I appreciate you greeting him. We'll be on our way." She put on her galoshes, coat, and hat.

"Goodbye. Mind your step out there. It's treacherous."

"We will. Goodnight, Pops."

"Goodnight, sir," Colin echoed.

He closed the door behind them as they hurried into the night.

"I hope he didn't give you the third degree?" Tillie asked.

"Not tonight, but he asked me a few pointed questions at the office today. My family background, prospects, intentions, and so forth."

"Good grief. I'm so sorry." Tillie bit her lip. *Pops, what are you doing? This is just a simple date.*

Colin tucked her arm into the crook of his.

"Don't be. That's his job as a father. I hope I passed muster."

"Where are we going for dinner? I'm starving." *Keep it light. Enjoy the evening is all.*

"How do you fancy Simpson's in the Strand? They are renowned for their carving trolleys."

"That would be brilliant."

"Marvellous. I made a reservation, in the event."

Arriving safely at the restaurant, Tillie checked her things, and they were promptly seated at a corner table.

"It's jolly to see the city decorated for Christmas. I love all the red and green, and the lights. It puts one in the mood." Tillie eyed her surroundings. No expense had been spared to dress the restaurant for holiday dining. And the mix of smells made her tummy rumble.

A waiter in a tuxedo and with a large mustache brought them menus.

"Good evening, sir, madame. How are you this evening?" He presented the menus with a flourish.

"We are just fine, but hungry, mate." Colin scanned the dishes.

"Would you care for something to drink? An apéritif perhaps? Or a glass of wine?"

"Would you like wine, Tillie?" Colin peered over the tall menu.

"Yes, please. A glass of red would be lovely."

"A bottle of red wine, please. Not too dear – medium-range, if you please," Colin ordered.

"Very good, sir." The waiter bowed.

"Oh, and we want the specialty – the trolley dinner, please," Colin added.

"Carving trolley for two? An excellent choice."

Tillie closed her menu. *I guess I'm not having the fish that I fancied. That was that.*

Colin kept up a constant chatter as the waiter brought wine and soup.

Tillie studied him. He was rather nice-looking. Curly brown hair and green eyes. He wasn't overly tall, but had a good build. Maybe his ears were a little large, but that was uncharitable.

"You are getting on well at Pop's? Do you reckon you'll make a career of it?" She sipped her wine, welcoming its warmth.

"I appreciate the opportunity, and your father has been helpful in teaching me the business. I hope to keep learning from him, and rising towards being a fully qualified accountant."

"That's brilliant, Colin. My father doesn't like to talk about work at home, but I can tell he's impressed by you."

Colin brightened, the tips of his ears turning red, which somehow made him cuter.

"Thank you, Tillie. It's bloody marvellous working in the same office as you. I'm delighted you finally agreed to go out with me."

Tillie thought it best not to tell him she might leave before long to work as a Nippy.

The waiter arrived and presented the trolley, which was loaded with meat, veg and gravy. With subdued fanfare, he sliced the roast lamb and offered roasted potatoes, mint sauce, and a range of side vegetables.

"It's delicious. The lamb melts in your mouth."

Colin poured them another glass of wine as the waiter rushed to take over the job.

"What do you make of this Hitler fellow? Do you put any store into the rumblings from the continent?" Colin asked.

"I'm not sure, really. I don't pay attention to that sort of thing. Didn't Hitler sign the Munich Agreement? It's all smoothed over now, I reckon." She fluttered her hand.

"No sense in burying your head in the sand, Tillie. Mister Hitler has eyes everywhere – hungry for revenge from the last war."

On September 30th, Prime Minister Neville Chamberlain had returned from Munich, Germany, waving the momentous piece of paper that Hitler and other key heads of state had signed. The German leader had threatened to unleash a European war unless the Sudetenland, a border area of Czechoslovakia containing an ethnic German majority, was surrendered to Germany. British, French, and Italian leaders agreed to the German annexation of the Sudetenland in exchange for Hitler's pledge of peace.

It was a triumphant moment for Chamberlain, capped by his notable *Peace for our Time* speech and a Buckingham Palace balcony appearance with Their Majesties, King George VI and Queen Elizabeth. The nation celebrated that another Great War had been averted.

Yet, in the background, quiet war preparations were being made. The Air Raid Wardens Service was set up in 1937. The Women's Voluntary Service (WVS) and Auxiliary Territory Service (ATS) drew women into voluntary positions. Gas masks were issued to all British citizens. Even backyard shelters had been distributed. The Royal Navy was ordered to sea. It was all proper ominous.

Tillie speared another piece of lamb, as Colin rattled on.

"If it comes to anything, I'm going to be in it from the beginning. I'll do my duty and fight for our country. I fancy being a RAF pilot."

Tillie was aghast. Surely, another war wasn't coming? And this young man wasn't considering being a part of it?

"Please don't speak of this unpleasantness, Colin. I'm losing my appetite." She put down her fork, the mint sauce turning sour in her mouth.

His head whipped up from his plate.

"Oh dear, am I ruining your supper? I'm so sorry. Women get distressed with any kind of war talk. My mother is just the same. Forgive me?" He gave her a disarming smile.

"Of course, nothing to forgive." Tillie tried to recover her sunny mood. It was just talk, wasn't it?

"I think there's a raspberry trifle for afters. Would you rather have coffee or tea?" Colin attempted to be amiable.

"Coffee, I should think."

The evening lost a bit of its shine, but Tillie was determined to keep up her end. She told some funny stories about growing up as a twin, and the scrapes that Katie always seemed to land in, or produce.

A light snow fell as they left the cozy restaurant. The air smelled crisp and clean. Throughout the tube ride, Colin shared boyhood adventures, and they were back on even footing by the time he'd walked her home.

"Tillie, I've had a wonderful time. You're beautiful and smart. Would you fancy a night of dancing with me? I hear the Café de Paris is a wonderful spot."

"I would like that, Colin. I adore a night on the dance floor."

On the top step of her house, he pulled her into his arms.

"You are bloody marvellous," he murmured, kissing her.

Tillie was taken aback, but let herself be carried away by the kiss. His warm lips sent tingles through her body. It was a lovely sensation.

She broke off the embrace, conscious of being out in the street. Pops would be horrified.

"Thank you for a brilliant evening, Colin."

He stepped back with obvious reluctance.

"I'll see you in the office and we can fix a time for our next date." She heard the excitement in his voice.

"Goodnight, Colin, and be careful getting home."

"Goodnight, Tillie."

***

"We'll be back by half-past six, but won't need any supper. Could you leave a hot pot or shepherd's pie for the boys?" Alice took her teacup and saucer to the sink. "We'll clear away when we return."

Faye turned from the aga and wiped her hands on her apron.

"Very good, Mrs. Kingston. I'll do them up a nice pie and there's half a Victoria sponge."

"That will do nicely. Thank you. The girls are waiting, so we'll be off to our Christmas tea."

"You're welcome and enjoy yourselves."

Alice went to round up the girls, feeling a mounting sense of excitement. The annual girls' Christmas tea had been a family tradition since the twins were little. Each year they dressed up in their finery, travelled to Claridge's in Mayfair, and gorged on dainty delicacies in exquisite surroundings. It was as much a part of Kingston family Christmas rituals as putting up a tree, Christmas Eve dinner with Shirley and Thomas, stockings on Christmas morning, turkey with trimmings, and all the rest. She couldn't wait.

***

"You girls look pretty as a picture." Shirley gazed around the table. Tillie wore a red velvet frock, and Maggie had a similar one in green. Katie looked angelic in an all-white dress with a white fur stole. "So Christmassy."

"We knew Mum would love us in something matching." Tillie smiled.

"I do. Just the like old days. Remember when you used to wear the same style of clothes all the time? So cute." Alice sighed. *I long for those days when the children were young and needed me. They are so grown up now.*

"Yes, Mum," they said in unison.

"And poor me. Stuck with your cast-offs and matching no one." Katie frowned.

"Not true," Alice sputtered. "I often bought outfits for the three of you. And you were happy to have the twin's good-as-new hand-me-downs."

"Mum's right," Maggie said lightly.

Katie shrugged.

"Where's the tea tray? I'm half-starved."

"My favourite sandwich is the salmon with egg. And I do hope there's blackberry jam for the scones." Tillie placed her serviette in her lap, giving Katie an encouraging nod.

"I like the chicken with spiced mayo. And the cucumber with dill cream. I've been thinking of them all week," Shirley said as the waiter brought steaming pots of tea.

"It's puddings for me. That's what I live for. Battenberg cake, fruit tarts, and chocolate cake. The more chocolate, the better." Katie's eyes sparkled.

"Thomas said the newspapers are calling it a Christmas Card scene this year with all the beautiful snow everywhere. It certainly brings the festive spirit." Shirley beamed.

"We haven't had this much snow in – my heavens – I can't remember when," Alice agreed. "We'll have a true white Christmas." The weather seemed to be all anyone could talk about these days.

For the next two hours, the ladies delighted in the afternoon tea experience. Three-tiered trays were loaded with four types of finger sandwiches. Hot scones, clotted cream and jams adorned the middle tray. And the top tier burst with sugary confections of all manner.

A live band played festive tunes in the corner. An eight-foot-tall Christmas tree stood in an alcove, lights twinkling and baubles glistening.

The tables were crowded with animated parties, all enjoying an elegant ritual with friends and family. The smell of freshly baked pastries wafted from the kitchen as the room hummed with excitement.

"I couldn't eat another bite." Katie finally sat back in her chair. "That was delicious, Mum."

"The best one ever," Maggie agreed.

"I could have eaten a half-dozen of those ham and shallot sandwiches." Tillie pushed away her teacup. "And don't give me any more tea. I'm floating."

"I'm proper pleased you enjoyed it as much as I did. Sometimes I think I'm the only one who cares about carrying on traditions."

A chorus of disagreements said otherwise.

"Mum, we look forward to this tea as much as you do," Tillie spoke for the three girls.

Alice could see they meant it. *Don't be mawkish and ruin the mood. Be grateful your girls still want to spend time with you. Enjoy the moment.*

"Don't mind me. Christmas always makes me a little wobbly," she replied.

"In that case, I think we're going to leave you for the shops. Father Christmas needs a helping hand." Tillie picked up her handbag.

"You two can reminisce about us girls in pinafores with enormous bows," Katie joked.

"Thank you ever so much, Mum. It was delightful. And Aunt Shirley, it wouldn't be Christmas tea without you." Maggie pecked her on the cheek.

"Off you go. We'll see you back at home." Mum shooshed them off.

"That was lovely. Thanks ever so much for including me every year." Shirley and Alice could almost have passed as twins themselves. Only a few years separated them, albeit Shirley was slightly taller, with a few more grey hairs.

"We wouldn't dream of doing it without you. More tea?" Alice held up the teapot.

"No, thanks. I've had plenty."

They sat in silence, enjoying the quiet surroundings.

"I wonder where we will be this time next year?"

Alice startled.

"What do you mean?"

"Alice, you can't ignore what's going on around us. War is likely coming – sometime next year, I should think."

"But what of the Munich Agreement? Surely that has a foothold." Alice felt her heart beat a little faster.

Shirley shook her head slowly.

"You've seen the preparations here in town. Thomas and I have had some sobering talks. He claims it's inevitable."

"No. Not again." Alice's hand flew to her mouth. An image of teen-aged-Kenny flashed in her mind. Thomas held a senior government position and was ahead of the public on some matters. He passed on

tidbits when he could, but they'd learned not to ask too many questions. He must know something for Shirley to be concerned.

"Nothing is for certain. There is time. But the signs are everywhere, and I'm petrified for Geoffrey. He is of conscription age, and will have to serve." Shirley paused. "We can't be naïve, luv."

Alice felt a sense of panic. Walter had been injured in the Great War, and still refused to share the horrors of life in the trenches. *Have we learned nothing?* And the thought of Geoffrey and potentially Kenny in the fray was unthinkable.

"I'm sorry if I've frightened you, darling. Nothing is happening tomorrow. We need to put our hearts into this Christmas and make it even more memorable than other years. That's what I intend to do for my Geoffrey."

Alice pulled herself out of the dark spiralling thoughts that threatened to overtake her. She nodded.

"That's the sensible thing, luv. We won't speak of this for now. Christmas is around the corner, and we'll make it splendid." But her smile was not as bright, and the sparkle had dimmed in her eyes.

***

"We're bringing the tree, Mum," Kenny shouted from the front hallway.

"Coming." Alice stood, hearing grunts and murmurs from upstairs.

Seeing snow dripping on the floor with tree needles dropping, Alice resisted the urge to fuss as she followed them into the drawing room.

"Marvellous. I've cleared the corner table. Did you find a large one? The freshly cut tree smells divine." The needles left a pungent aroma that was truly the heart of Christmas.

"The biggest we could find, Mum. What a wonderful morning. It's still snowing, but not too cold. We saw cars skidding every which way. It was ace."

Walter and Kenny wrestled the tree to the table and into the tree stand with the usual stops and starts. The girls shed their coats and hats, piling them on the sofa.

"Turn it a bit to the left," Tillie said.

"Move it more to the middle," Katie ordered.

"Perfect," Maggie said with a smile.

"Right. That's my part finished. You children have at it. I'll tidy up the car, and return it to the garage. Then I'm for the library with my pipe and paper." Walter stood back, huffing a little.

"Thanks, Pops." Tillie beamed at him. "We'll make it beautiful now."

Pops nodded and left.

"I'll fetch some tea and biscuits for you lot." Mum collected the scattered coats.

The Kingston children spent the next hour pulling out much-loved paper chains, baubles, garlands, and lights and trimming the tree. Tillie and Maggie placed them carefully and evenly around the boughs. Katie and Kenny threw tinsel willy nilly, laughing at their older sisters.

"You two never change. We want it to look proper – not thrown together." Maggie took two baubles from an overcrowded spot and rehung them.

"We don't want it to look too posh. Just a family Christmas tree." Katie laughed.

"I decided cocoa would more suit this occasion. And Faye just made shortbread biscuits. Anyone thirsty?" Mum brought in a loaded tray.

"Mum, you're just in time. We are about to put the angel on top." Tillie turned to her.

"I think it's Maggie's turn." Mum smiled.

Maggie removed the cloth-wrapped angel from its nesting spot in the well-worn carton.

"I'll fetch you a chair," Tillie offered.

Maggie placed the delicate alabaster angel with flowing white dress and gold wings on the top branch. She then climbed down and put her hands on her hips.

"There. Now the tree is complete."

Tillie took the tray so Mum could fully savor the resplendent tree in all its glory.

"It's stunning. Our best tree ever. You've done a lovely job." Mum looked at the tree and shining faces of her children and felt a sob rise in her throat. *Hold it together. It's just a tree.*

Katie came to stand next to her.

"I can't wait for Christmas, Mum."

***

The day before Christmas Eve dawned cold and clear. For the first time in days, no snow was in sight. Alice had spent the morning at her sister's house, helping with the Christmas Eve preparations.

Her steps slowed as she walked, thinking of the still-massive tick list at her own home. The front door opened before she could reach for it. Maggie and Tillie stood there, faces shining.

"What in the world?" Alice took a step in.

"Mum, we have the best news. We've been accepted as Nippies – both of us." Tillie couldn't keep it in another second.

"We start in the new year. Isn't it wonderful?" Maggie pulled her mother in.

"My heavens. That is exciting. Well done – both of you."

They continued to chatter as they settled into the morning room.

"We'll do our training together, albeit they will likely post us on different floors so as not to confuse customers or other Nippies. We'll get measured for our uniforms on the first day. But we'll need to buy some sturdy shoes for the long shifts," Tillie rattled off the details.

"We'll tell Pops as soon as he gets home from work. They want us to start straightaway in the new year. Do you think he'll agree to two weeks' notice?" Maggie asked, perched on a wingback chair.

"I'm sure it will work out fine. My heavens, 1939 is going to start out with a bang for you two. Congratulations. We have reason for champagne tonight." Mum beamed, exhaustion forgotten.

***

It was a small crowd on Christmas Eve at the Fowlers. Besides the two families, Shirley had invited a few neighbours, including the Goldbachs, who had been friends for years. Samuel and Ruth had two children, a young man, Micah, and his sister, Hannah.

The party was in full sway when the Kingstons arrived.

"Come through. Geoffrey, take their things please. Happy Christmas."

"Happy Christmas to you, luv. Everything smells wonderful." Alice hugged her sister.

Geoffrey and Thomas entered the small hallway.

"Hey cousins." Geoffrey embraced them in turn.

"Gentle. You're about to crush me." Katie extricated herself. "Your hugs are brilliant, but a tad too tight." Geoffrey was renowned for his bear squeezes.

"Sorry, cuz. I'm just happy to see you all."

Greetings of Happy Christmas went all around as they came into the drawing room. Christmas carols rang out from the gramophone player. Guests milled about in their festive finery, drinking mulled wine, eggnog, and beer. Shirley's long table was filled with hors d'oeuvres of all types.

The young people congregated near the food as the adults caught up with one another.

"Hello Maggie." Micah Goldbach approached her shyly.

"Happy Christmas, Micah," she replied, looking down.

"You look nice," he said. "Would you like some punch?"

"Yes, please, and thank you."

The pair had grown up together and were firm friends. Both tended to be shy, but they shared common interests in music, poetry, and nature.

He returned, handing her a glass.

"I heard you have big news."

Micah was tall and thin, with sandy brown hair and kind eyes behind his glasses. He worked with his father in their small jewelry shop.

"Yes. Tillie and I were accepted as Lyons House Nippies. We start in the new year." Maggie had told him they had applied, so he was not surprised by the news.

"You'll be brilliant," he said. "Was your Pops cross with you for leaving him?"

A frown flashed across her face.

"I think he's more disappointed than he's letting on, but not cross, no. He wished us hearty congratulations, which was sweet of him."

"He would never keep you back."

They talked for a few minutes. As time passed, Maggie was developing deeper feelings for him, but did he feel the same? For now, she didn't let on that she found him handsome, kind, and agreeable company.

"Maggie," he started, shifting from foot to foot. "Would you fancy going for a walk before you get stuck into your Nippy training? Perhaps Boxing Day or soon after?"

"I would love it," she said with a slow smile. "It's so pretty with all the snow."

"Splendid," he said simply.

The revels got noisier as the evening wore on. Some of the younger generation danced, whilst the men clustered off to speak quietly of the political situation. The table emptied, and the punch bowl was refilled many times.

As the party wound down, a loud knock interrupted the merriment.

"I wonder who that could be?" Shirley turned to her husband, who strode to the door. Faint strains of *God Rest You Merry Gentlemen* seeped through the heavy door.

"Come, everyone. It's singers," Thomas shouted.

The assembly moved into the small hallway, peering out into the night. A group of carolers stood bundled up against the cold. Snow danced and fell as a merry backdrop.

"They must be from St. Cuthbert," Shirley whispered to her sister.

The carolers sang two more rousing tunes before launching into a haunting version of *Silent Night*:

"Silent night, holy night
All is calm, and all is bright
Round yon Virgin Mother and Child
Holy infant so tender and mild
Sleep in heavenly peace
Sleep in heavenly peace."

As the voices died out, the Fowler party cheered "Bravo," "Brilliant," and "Happy Christmas." More than one guest wiped a tear at the moving words.

Thomas offered wine and tea, but the carolers refused, intent to move along.

"Wasn't that just a lovely surprise?" Alice enthused. "A perfect cap to the evening." *And a sweet memory. What a perfect night. And we are all together. I couldn't be happier.*

It was a natural break point for the party, so the guests scattered, eager to bring on Christmas in their own homes. The Kingstons tramped back in the snow, Kenny chasing his sisters with snowballs.

***

"Wake up, squirt." Kenny jumped on the bed.

"Bloody hell," Katie cursed, yawning. "I was dead asleep."

"Good thing Mum didn't hear that. Dreaming of sugar plums?" he teased. "Come on. It's Christmas morning. Race you to Mags and Tillie's room." He sprang towards the door.

Katie snatched a dressing gown.

"No fair. You've got a head start."

By the time they'd reached their older sisters' room, the noise had woken them.

"Happy Christmas, you oaf. It's barely gone seven o'clock. You're not ten years old. We could have done with a little lie-in." Tillie was already out of bed, tying the sash on her dressing gown.

"It's Christmas morning. No sleeping in for anyone," he replied, hair sticking up every which way.

"Let's get a move on, Mags. Don't lollygag about," Katie urged.

"Happy Christmas, you lot," Maggie shook her head and followed the three of them out and down the stairs. Not even time to pull a comb through her hair.

Bounding into the drawing room, Mum was already waiting. She'd turned on the light, and sat in her chair, knitting untouched in her lap.

"Happy Christmas to you all. I think Father Christmas has been here."

With quick greetings in return, the four Kingston children sank to the floor, opening their bursting stockings. Walter lumbered into the room and sat next to his wife.

Happy exclamations over oranges, sweets, chocolates, and new socks, scarves, and gloves ensued. They looked like little children as they tried on the clothing and popped sweets in their mouths. Kenny juggled the oranges he nicked from his sisters.

This is the best moment, Alice thought, heart full. *Everyone is gathered and playful, with no squabbling. I wish I could make this last. In no time, they'll scatter to their friends and other interests. But for this instant, they're here and they're mine.*

Walter put a hand on hers.

"Happy thoughts, dear?"

She nodded.

"Quite."

The children tore into the rest of the gifts. Alice had outdone herself – buying new handbags for the girls and a leather belt for Kenny. Between them, the children shared books, makeup and hair accessories for the girls, and even more chocolate all around.

Walter pulled out four large boxes from under the table and passed them to the children. Kenny was the first to rip the wrapping and open his package.

"Skates," he exclaimed. "Smashing."

In turn, the others opened theirs to squeals of glee.

"You've all been sharing the old ones for long enough. I deemed this year a new set for everyone was just the ticket." He beamed.

"They fit," Tillie cried as she pulled one on.

"I had a little help with the sizes." Pops glanced at Mum.

"Oh, I want to go skating straightaway. Thanks Pops, Mum." Katie grinned.

"What a marvellous gift. Thank you." Maggie smiled at her parents.

Kenny hunted for any straggling gifts under the tree and discarded the wrapping, finding nothing.

"Right, well, that's the lot."

"Thank you everyone for the lovely gifts. Kenny, will you clear away the paper?" Mum asked, standing. "I'm going to make a start on dinner. Girls, once you've washed up, please, will you help out? Then we'll get the breakfast looked after. Faye has been busy and needs a hand."

They all nodded, collecting up their gifts to examine more closely later.

"I'll need your assistance with the extra chairs, young man." Walter caught Kenny as he tried to nip away.

"Christmas dinner first, skating after," Mum declared.

***

The Fowlers arrived promptly at noon with more gifts and covered casserole dishes.

"Happy Christmas everyone. I got new skates. Isn't that smashing?" Geoffrey bounded into the house.

"Us too," Tillie said. "I hope you brought them. Skating party after dinner?"

Shirley winked at Alice. Pre-Christmas sisterly talks had brought about this little miracle.

"I did. And it's snowing – again. I hope the ice won't be too mushy."

"We'll bring a broom," Kenny said.

"Come through," Walter welcomed. It was happy chaos.

Walter offered drinks and tea round, whilst the finishing touches were put on Christmas dinner.

"It smells marvellous." Thomas breathed in the aromas of turkey, dressing, and what smelled like home-baked scones.

Alice announced dinner, and they sat at a beautifully set dining table.

"It's grand, luv." Shirley took in the red and white candles, boughs of holly, and sparkling crystal.

"Thanks, sis." Alice gave her a squeeze.

Christmas crackers were snapped and opened. Paper crowns were donned, and jokes read aloud.

Pops carved the turkey to the mouth-watering attention of the group. Vegetable dishes were passed round the table.

"Dark meat for me, please. And may I have the chestnut stuffing and gravy?" asked Geoffrey.

"Don't forget the roast potatoes." Tillie passed the dish.

Between the turkey and trimmings, several vegetables, bread and chestnut stuffings, cranberry sauce, and so much more – plates almost overflowed. There was plenty for seconds, but most everyone was saving room for the flaming plum pudding – the grand finale.

"Happy Christmas to us all. Thank you everyone for the gifts, the company, and for leaving me the leg," Walter toasted. "And to Faye for a wonderful Christmas dinner."

"Happy Christmas," they chorused.

"When can we go skating?" Katie asked.

The table erupted into laughter.

***

Walter removed his dressing gown and climbed into bed.

"You did a superb job, dear. Just a splendid Christmas."

Alice smiled at the compliment. It had been a lot of work and she was exhausted, but filled with joy and contentment.

"The children really loved their skates. They'll get hours of fun from them." She peeled off her own dressing gown and tucked her slippers under the bed before sliding in next to her husband.

"It couldn't have gone better," she sighed. "I hope next year will be just as marvellous. It will all be the same, won't it? We'll all be together at Christmas?"

He paused and turned off the light, kissing her cheek.

"Happy Christmas, dear."

Chapter Two

FROSTY AND FRIGID

1939 – Tillie

"Mum, come quick," Katie shouted from the front hallway.
Alice put down her knitting and dashed down the stairs.

"What in the world?" Mum stared at her youngest daughter, crouched on the rug, patting a yellow dog. She looked as if she'd fallen in a muddy puddle.

"What's happened?"

"This poor thing. He ran into the street. Lucky I was there. I was able to snatch him back before he was hit. The driver didn't even slow down. There, there." The dog shivered.

Tillie came up the kitchen stairs.

"I'm glad you're here, luv. Can you fetch a bowl of water for this lad? He's trembling from his ordeal. Please?"

Tillie nodded and turned to head back down.

"Look at you. Are you alright?"

"I'm fine, Mum. I tripped is all."

"And you just recovered from your broken leg." Mum tsked. Katie had fallen and broken it during the early days of the blackout. She'd just recently had the cast off.

A knock on the door added to the bustle.

"Hello, can I come in?" Colin pushed through. "Katie, are you okay?"

"Come through," Mum sighed. "Join the party."

Tillie brought up the water dish.

"Colin, did you see what happened?" Tillie kissed him.

"Your daft sister didn't even look. She dashed into the road to seize this silly dog. She almost got hit herself."

"Katie, will you never stop and think? You might have been killed!" Mum scanned her daughter for injuries.

"There, there. You're alright. Drink." Katie looked up at Mum. "Do you think we can keep him? What owner would leave him alone like that? I don't want him to be put down."

Since the declaration of war, the government had mounted a campaign encouraging pet owners to put their pets to sleep. There was a rampant fear that food would be so scarce that pets would either starve to death or, worse – be killed for meat. Thousands of distraught but dutiful pet owners took their cats and dogs to the local veterinary offices to be put down. It brought the war home in an abrupt and chilling manner.

"Darling, we can't have a dog, you know that. Besides, he doesn't look too scruffy. I'm sure there's an owner about."

As if on cue, a knock sounded at the door. Mum answered it.

A short, bald man with a ruddy complexion was ushered in.

"Excuse me, Ma'am. Have you by any chance seen a large yellow dog? He ran away from me down the street. Your neighbour said he might be here."

Katie stood, revealing the dog next to her.

"Charlie," he cried as the pooch bounded towards him. "You rascal. Running away like that." Nonetheless, he bent over to give him a pat on the head. "I'm sorry, where are my manners? I'm Horace Barnaby. Thank you for rescuing my dog."

Mum made the introductions.

"Young lady, that was brave of you. And reckless. That car almost hit you," he said with a frown.

"I didn't think," Katie said.

"You're incorrigible." Tillie shook her head. *Oh Katie, heart of gold, but slow down.*

"Would you like a cup of tea, Mister Barnaby?" Mum offered.

"No, thank you all the same. I'm late for an appointment. I must crack on. Thank you again. Come on, Charlie." He tipped his hat and left, the dog trotting happily beside him.

"Katie, when will you think before you act?" Mum sighed.

"I'll make the tea," Tillie said, Colin following behind.

"Sorry, Mum. But I'm alright. Forgive me?" She beamed.

"Alright. But please have a care. With this war on, it's not safe out there."

"Phoney War, you mean." Katie linked arms with her mum. "Let's see what Tillie has scrounged up."

Since September, Britons had steeled themselves for imminent German invasion. Eyes raised to the sky, expecting tremendous gas attacks, killing on contact. Citizens awaited Germans landing by air and sea, literally tramping to their front doors, murdering all within. Hospitals had been emptied of all but the most serious patients. One-and-a-half million mothers, children, and teachers were evacuated to the country. A million coffins had been built to prepare for what were expected to be overwhelming casualties. The Royal Air Force and British Navy were well prepared to launch into battle.

And then – nothing. Aside from a few false alarms and food rationing, life went on as normal. The barrage balloons, sandbags, and nightly blackouts reminded everyone that war was all around them. But England was untouched – so far.

***

"Your sister is something else." Colin nuzzled into Tillie's neck. "She's a danger to herself and others."

"She means well," Tillie said as she sidestepped him to the sink. "She has a big heart and doesn't think before she acts, I suppose."

"You have a big heart, and you don't go 'round chasing dogs and other foolishness."

Tillie didn't know what to say. Colin could be thoughtless at times.

"What time is the film? I've heard that *The Wizard of Oz* is smashing. Parts of it are in colour and all," Tillie changed the subject.

"The early show. We'll have supper out."

"Are you sure you don't want to eat with the family? I'm sure there's loads," Tillie teased.

"Not a chance. I'm only here on a week's leave and I want to spend every second I can with my beautiful girl."

Tillie hugged him.

"I've been counting the days until I could see you again, too. I hate that you're stationed so far away."

"It's part of the training. I always wanted to serve in the RAF and now's my chance. The blokes are terrific. Good lads."

"But you didn't have to sign up before your time. Your call-up papers didn't even come through yet." Tillie hated he was so eager to get into the fight. Why couldn't he have waited? But he hadn't asked her. He'd just signed up on his own. He talked of Katie running pell-mell into danger, but he himself was just as reckless.

"Sweetheart, you know I'm meant to do my bit. Isn't it better to sign up for what you want than being stuck as a soldier or shipped off to sea against your will?"

"I suppose," she replied. "But we're not to talk of the war and ugly things. We're going to have a splendid time together and have fun." She gave a little twirl.

"That's my girl. Perhaps a night of dancing, too?"

"Brilliant," she replied. He was so handsome and full of life. "I'm going to freshen up and then we can set off. Give the gang tea when they turn up, if you don't mind."

***

"So, what did you think, then? Judy Garland was just wonderful as Dorothy."

"It was alright. I'm not as keen on all that singing, I suppose. The Wicked Witch of the West was awfully good, though."

"Those flying monkeys frightened me half to death."

"How would you know? You buried your head in my shoulder the whole time," Colin joked.

How would you know? Tillie mused. *You had your hands all over me. When you weren't trying to kiss me. I could hardly keep on with the film plot.*

"Shall we go for a pint? It's cold but not too nippy for a walk. No white Christmas this year, I expect."

"You're on." Tillie pulled her collar close as they walked hand-in-hand through central London. "And we have no way of knowing. Not a weather report to be had these days." Since war had been declared, radio and newspaper weather reports were banned – the government didn't want to make enemy invasions any easier by broadcasting weather conditions.

"It's nice to see the shops decorated for Christmas," she continued. "It takes away from the signs of war." Taped-up windows and sandbags on every corner were not very Christmassy.

"So many of them are closed. I expect it is from all the people running away to the country."

"They haven't run away," Tillie protested. "The government wanted the mums and children safe from bombing. Some families evacuated together."

"I'm sure you're right, sweetheart. And don't look so serious. Ah, here we are." He stopped in front of a pub, opening the door for her.

He ordered a pint for himself and a shandy for Tillie. She'd refused a glass of wine. Whiffs of stale cigarettes and beer floated over their heads.

"I need a clear head for work tomorrow."

Colin frowned.

"I want to talk to you about that. You're having a lark serving tea and goodwill at Lyons. But when we're married, you'll need to stop working. A proper wife looks after the house and her husband. Besides, I don't want you exposed to all those men."

Tillie had heard this before. Colin was traditional in his thinking, but it wasn't what she wanted. Or at least, she didn't think so.

"It's not as easy as you think. The shifts are hectic – always. And we provide an essential service – good food at a fair price – served with speed and friendliness. I dare you to try a shift – you'd be whacked in no time."

"Chance is a fine thing. I wouldn't go near it." He looked horrified. "And I know you do a brilliant job of it. Surely you understand you'll have to give it up once we're married," he repeated and took a long swig of beer.

Colin had surprised her in the summer with an engagement ring in front of her whole family. She'd been swept off her feet and said yes straightaway. She loved him; she did. But she was also in no rush to get married. Aside from her work as a Nippy, she had her eyes on the future. She might be needed to serve in the war. She likely wouldn't be able to do that as a married woman. But Colin was persistent in setting a wedding date. So far, she'd held him off. But with him about to fly dangerous missions, could she refuse him any longer? Did she want to?

"I love my job," she replied simply. "Let's not look too far into the future. We don't know what 1940 will hold for any of us." She held his hand. "I hear what you're saying, luv. And I promise I'll think about it long and hard."

Colin sat back.

"I suppose I'll settle for that – for now. But this conversation is far from over, Mathilda Kingston."

***

"Do you have another pair of stockings I can borrow, ducks?" Tillie was running late for work, and bustled around their room.

"I suppose so," Maggie replied. "I expect it's useless to ask you not ladder them." She motioned to her top drawer.

Tillie grinned. "I'll do my best." Sliding them on in record time, she straightened the seams and picked up her handbag. "I'm off. See you tonight and say hello to Micah for me."

Before Maggie could reply, Tillie was gone. Maggie sat back in bed with her sketchpad.

After a quiet morning, Maggie prepared for lunch with Micah. She had been delighted when he'd written to say he'd be in London for a few days to sort some family business matters. Since he and his family had moved to France, she and Micah kept up a steady correspondence. He held a special place in her heart, and she truly hoped she held a soft spot in his. But both were shy, and their friendship was developing slowly.

Today, they were going for a walk and then a light lunch. Both loved to be outdoors as much as possible – even in this icy weather. Somehow, it was easier to open up when they walked.

He called for her and spent a few moments with Mum in the morning room before Maggie joined them.

"Hello, Micah. So nice to see you."

He rose to greet her, looking handsome with his gentle presence and kind eyes.

37

"You look lovely."

"Thank you. Am I late? Should we set off?"

"No, I'm a little early. And yes, I'm ready whenever you are. Goodbye, Mrs. Kingston."

"Goodbye dear. And dress warmly, luv. Micah says it's quite cold out."

"I will. We'll be back before the blackout."

Mum's knitting needles clacked together as she nodded.

Donning her warmest wool coat with a hand-knitted red scarf, matching beret and gloves, Maggie hoped she'd be warm enough.

The stiff wind hit them in the face as they opened the door. Bracing for it, they stepped out, Micah holding her arm so she wouldn't slip.

"How is the weather in France? Just as cold?" Maggie puffed into the cold air.

"It's a little warmer, but not much. Living over the shop, I don't have far to go for work."

Maggie kept walking, not knowing what to say. *What's the matter with me? We've been writing to each other for months.*

"And your grandfather? Is his health any better?"

Micah's galoshes crunched on the snow.

"No, I'm afraid not. In fact, he's worse than he let on. Not only is his heart weakening, which is forcing him to slow down, but his mind is failing too."

"I'm so sorry. He must be comforted that you are there to help him."

Micah laughed, but the sound was lost in the wind.

"He is – but he still wants things done his way. I don't mean to be disrespectful, but he's left the business in rather a shambles. Bills have been left unpaid, and the office is a-jumble. Papa and I have been working through it, but Grandfather slows us down. It's his life business, so it's understandable."

Maggie nodded, sure that it was worse than Micah was admitting. Like she didn't admit how bloody cold she was on this frigid day.

"I think we should stop for some hot tea. I don't know about you, but I can't feel my feet."

"Yes please," Maggie said through freezing lips.

They spied a local restaurant and hurried towards it.

"This isn't the place I wanted to take you, but it's far colder out here than I expected. I hope this is alright."

"It's warm and dry – heaven."

They ordered tea and sandwiches, hands and feet slowly thawing as they tried to look out the steamy windows.

"How are you getting on at Lyons? Your letters are full of stories and drawings. Are you enjoying it?" Micah wiped his glasses with his hankie.

"I love it. My sense of order is satisfied with the speedy process from order to serving to collecting the bill. And seeing faces light up when the food arrives always cheers me. Because our prices are fair, our customers are all smiles when they pay up."

"I should hope they are tipping you properly. I bet you are their best Nippy." Micah took in every word, brown eyes intent on hers.

Maggie shrugged as the tea arrived. Too hot to drink, she held the tea-cup in her hands to feel its heat.

"I do just fine. We have some regulars who really brighten our days. Order the same thing at the same time. Rather adorable really. There's a sweet gentleman named Archie who asks for tea with beans on toast every Tuesday at precisely half-past one." Maggie finally shrugged off her coat. She could feel her fingers and toes again.

"Sounds charming." Micah took a sip of tea, raising his eyes to her. "Maggie, there's something I need to tell you. I believe we will stay in France for some time – the foreseeable future, in fact. We can't leave Grandfather, and he's too frail to travel."

"What if the Germans get closer?" Maggie asked. *Oh dear, Micah was far too near Hitler on the continent.*

Micah sat back.

"We hear loads of rumors. Refugees are pouring in from the east for sanctuary. And the anti-Jewish sentiment is growing. I'm uneasy. I can't lie. But I have no choice. You do understand, please?"

He leaned forward, clutching her hands.

Maggie felt a jolt as his skin touched hers. A shiver ran through her shoulders.

"I understand. You must stand by your papa and mama and grandfather. And Hannah. How is she getting on? We miss her." Maggie flustered as warm feelings seeped through her.

Micah relaxed his grip.

"Thank you. She is alright. Misses London and her friends, of course." He looked away, then back at her. "Maggie, there's one more thing."

She waited.

"You surely understand I have feelings for you. We've been friends a long time – but you must know that those feelings are starting to run deeper." He ran a hand through his hair. "But I can't promise more now. I can't even ask you to wait for me. It wouldn't be fair to you."

Although disappointed, she understood.

"We were all foolish to think this war would end by Christmas. It's barely started, and who knows how long it will stretch on? No one can promise anything with this uncertainty. I have my work, and my family. But you will keep writing to me?"

"As long as you keep answering," he answered quickly. "I live for your letters."

"And I yours."

With that, two reserved young people said it all – by saying almost nothing.

***

"We'll get the tree this morning, and then a skating party this afternoon? Brilliant," Kenny said through a mouthful of eggs. "Who's coming with Pops and I?" He looked round the breakfast table.

"Me," answered Katie. "I'm not about to let you choose on your own."

"Sorry, but we're meant to spend time with Colin's parents this morning. We'll join you later for skating." Tillie checked her watch.

"Not trimming the tree with us?" Katie almost shouted. "But it's tradition!"

"Colin is only here for a few days, luv. I have to spend as much time as I can with him. He's already cross that I have to work whilst he's here."

"I'll join you," Maggie said. "I can't let you have all the fun. Micah will also come by later for skating."

"I'm staying put. I have far too many Christmas details to arrange. Shirley is coming by shortly. We'll admire your tree once it's finished. You know where all the cartons are." Mum felt the teapot to see if there might be one more cup in it.

"Righto, that's sorted, then. Drink up. We leave in precisely a quarter of an hour." Walter got to his feet.

Scrambling, the assorted Kingstons readied for the day.

***

By dinnertime, the tree was procured, set up, and decorated with the familiar ornaments, baubles, and garlands.

"It looks splendid," Mum said, entering with a loaded tea tray. "Did you have a hard go at finding one?"

"Ooh, ta, Mum." Kenny moved to snatch a biscuit from the tray.

"Not really," Walter answered. "The selection was not as bountiful as last year, but we obtained a fine tree, nonetheless."

"Indeed." Mum handed round the teacups. "Not too cold for skating, I hope?"

"Not at all," Katie said.

"Right, well, dinner is almost ready. Faye has been simmering a hot stew to fill you up. Finish up here, and we'll be ready."

The girls bundled up the tree wrappings, stuffing them into the cartons.

"We'll take them back to the attic." Walter offered on behalf of his son. "You two give Mum a hand, and we'll be with you straightaway."

Pops and Kenny carried the boxes to the third-floor hallway.

"I'll stand on the ladder — you hand them to me." Pops puffed a little.

"Pops, why can't I join up? And don't say I'm too young. I'm almost seventeen." Kenny had been restless since the war began, eager to jump in and do his bit.

"You *are* too young," Walter replied. "You must be patient. War is serious business, son. If it is still raging when you are eighteen, you'll be called up in due time." Walter placed the last carton in the dusty attic, hoping that day would never come.

"But I'm healthy and the posters all say young men are needed," Kenny persisted.

Walter closed the attic door and climbed down the ladder.

"Let me tell you something I haven't even shared with the girls." He pointed to the stairs. They sank to the top step. "You know I was injured in the last war. My hearing has never fully recovered from the damage in the trenches. In September, I tried to sign up again. I too want to do my bit."

"You did?" Kenny asked, jaw dropping. "What happened?"

"I was refused. Suffice it to say, I'm too old and my injury prohibits my service. It was a bitter pill to swallow, son. But it's not my time." His voice was heavy. "Just like it's not yours. That doesn't mean there's not work for us to do. I've signed up to be an Air Raid Precautions Warden and for civil defence. We'll need you for that."

Kenny nodded, eager for some role. Defence sounded promising.

"Doubtless more jobs will be needed when this war truly starts. You're already registered to be a bicycle messenger. That will be vital work. Vital." He put his hand on Kenny's shoulder.

"It's a job for a kid," Kenny replied, unconvinced.

"Not at all. You'll be delivering important messages for the war effort. We must all work together to best the enemy – even if our efforts don't seem to count for much."

"I suppose," Kenny said, staring at the step.

"Hello, are you lost up there? Dinner is ready." Katie called up the stairs.

"Come on. That's enough serious talk for one day. Are you alright?"

Kenny nodded, but his shoulders sagged.

Walter came slowly down the stairs.

***

"Race you to the end and back?" Kenny dared his sister.

"You're on." Katie whizzed by him, but he caught up easily. "It's not fair. Your legs are twice as long as mine."

Kenny scooped some snow off the ice and threw it at her.

"Too bad. Maybe you'll grow, squirt."

Katie fervently hoped so. She was the tiniest of them all. And hated it.

"I wish there was enough for a snowball fight." Kenny skated round. "It's cold enough for it."

"Remember last year?" Tillie called. "It was a picture-perfect white Christmas."

"Too bloody cold this year." Katie twirled.

They'd made an afternoon of it, skimming across the frozen pond. Colin showed off his backwards skating prowess, then turned around to hold out his hand to Tillie.

"I wish you weren't leaving so soon." Tillie tucked her arm firmly into his. "It feels like you only just arrived." The time had raced by.

"I'm sorry, sweetheart, but needs must. We still have a bit of time left."

"Not enough." She frowned. She really didn't want him to leave.

Micah and Maggie had their heads together at the other end of the rink.

"My business here is almost finished. I'm hoping you'll see me off at the train?" Micah put an arm around her.

"Day after tomorrow? I wouldn't miss it." Maggie snuggled into his shoulder.

"How about a Congo line?" Kenny shouted.

In seconds, they'd all joined in, forming a snake on the ice. Poor Katie was at the end, and after Kenny built up speed, she could barely keep up. As he twisted and turned, others held tight, but Katie lost hold of Maggie's waist, and landed on her behind.

"Are you alright?" Tillie asked as Kenny laughed.

Katie rubbed her tailbone.

"I'm fine. But that's it for me. I'm frozen through. I'm for cocoa." A chorus of agreement signalled the end of the party. "And I'll get you back, Kenneth Kingston. Just wait and see." She pushed him for good measure.

***

Tillie almost ran the last few steps from the underground to Lyons. When would this cold snap end?

Greeting the other Nippies in the dressing room, she disrobed and put on her uniform in record time.

"I don't want my bare skin exposed any longer than necessary." Tillie shivered.

"Too right," replied Dot. "I near froze me ass off getting 'ere terday."

Tillie finished the long double row of tiny buttons, and affixed her cap and apron.

"Right, let's get on with it."

She met Alfie on the way to her floor.

"Good morning, Tillie. Knock knock."

She mustered a smile.

"Who's there?"

"Gladys," Alfie replied, already laughing.

"Gladys who?" Tillie smoothed her uniform front.

"Aren't you Gladys Christmas?" His laugh turned into a full-fledged guffaw.

"Hilarious. Happy Christmas to you, too," she said. Alfie had a bluff exterior but was a kind boss, and his jokes were harmless. "I'd best get to my station."

"Go on, then. There are always hungry customers waiting." He waved her on.

Losing herself in her work, she smiled and served countless hungry patrons. The morning sped by. *Almost time for my break. I'm gasping for a cuppa.*

She approached a single man at a table, pencil poised over her pad. And stopped short.

"Micah! What a surprise."

"Hello, Tillie. How are you? I don't mean to trouble you at work, but I was hoping for a quick word. Any chance of it?"

"Just fine. ta. I'm due my break in ten minutes, but I can't be seen to sit with customers. Could I meet you in the second-floor café?"

He nodded and picked up his hat.

"I'll meet you there."

What in the world could he want? Was it bad news from Paris? Was someone unwell? Surely, he would have confided in Maggie, not her.

A quarter of an hour later, she ran up to him, breathless.

"So sorry, Micah. We've been rushed off our feet today. Everyone wants in from the cold."

"That's fine, Tillie, and thank you for meeting with me. I've taken the liberty of ordering us both tea and cakes."

She sat and gulped her hot drink. Serving was thirsty work.

"Thank you. How can I help?" She waited.

He fiddled with the brim of his hat.

"Tillie, let me start by saying I don't want to compromise you in any way, or have you keep secrets from your sister."

Heavens, what could it be?

"I've told Maggie how difficult life is in Paris now. And I expect it to get worse, I'm afraid. I think difficult times are ahead for Jews on the continent."

Tillie let out a small gasp.

"Is it as bad as all that?" Oh dear, was the family safe in France? Why was Micah telling her this?

"Maggie knows I can't leave my family. Grandfather is too ill to bring back to England, so we will stay for some time, no matter the conditions."

"That sounds ghastly. Is there no chance of you bringing him – even if you take it slow?" Tillie grasped at straws.

"He won't leave," Micah said simply. "It's his home."

"That puts you in a wretched situation." Tillie shook her head. "And it keeps you and Maggie separated – far into the future, I should think."

"None of us knows what's coming or when, so we may yet find a way. But I wanted to speak with you as well – so you understand the seriousness. If you read things or hear dire reports, will you please be there for Maggie? Help her, comfort her? If the worst happens?" He sipped his tea, fingers gripping the cup tightly.

"Please let things not be as dire as what you say. But, yes, I will always look out for Mags. I will cheer her and encourage her. I will be there for her, no matter what. You have my word." She looked deep into his eyes.

He nodded.

"Thank you. That's all I can ask. In my heart, I know we will be together when all of this is over. Like everyone else, we must live with the instability for now."

"You don't have to thank me. She is my twin. We are closer than sisters." She stood. "I'm sorry, but I must get back to my station. Thank you for the tea. And I'll remember all you said."

He stood and nodded.

It's going to come to naught. Micah is painting a picture bleaker than it is. One thing is for sure. He really loves my sister. It will all work out. It must.

***

Alice and Shirley were busier than ever in the run-up to Christmas. Besides the usual planning, shopping, baking, and cleaning, they had both signed on to the Women's Voluntary Service, spending countless evenings in knitting circles and clothing drives.

"Why do we make it so hard on ourselves, Shirl? Do we really need three different pies and a Christmas turkey with all the trimmings?" Alice pushed back a stray curl. They'd been baking all afternoon, and the house smelled of cinnamon and warm fruit. Or rather, Faye and Shirley baked. Alice's cooking was disastrous. She fetched, carried, and tidied up. They'd left Faye to get on with the supper, and were enjoying a quiet moment in the drawing room.

"Alice, how can you say that? It's tradition. And you love every minute. Besides, we know more rationing is expected in the new year. We must eat, drink, and be merry whilst we can." Her smile faltered. "It's just wretched that Geoffrey can't be here. He's never been away at Christmas."

"Don't get wobbly. You've had a letter from him recently, haven't you?"

"Yes, he's finished with his BEF training and off to northern France. At least, I think that's where he is. I'm reading between the lines because of the censors. But I'm a wreck thinking of him in battle. He's too young to be carrying a gun. How could such a kind soul fire at a German soldier?" She stumbled over her words, one spilling into the next.

"I don't know what to say, luv. I don't want him to kill anyone, either. But we must win this war. It's such a cruel spot to be. I'm so sorry you're not having him home for Christmas."

Shirley sighed.

"Like thousands of other mothers. And wives, for that matter. Our young people have so much ahead of them to cope with. Separations, hardships, and probably some heartache. It's all too familiar, isn't it, darling?"

Both women bent over their knitting, lost in their own thoughts.

"Your Tillie will be feeling low tonight. It's always a wrench to see off a loved one at the train – especially when you have no idea when you will be together again." Shirley tsked.

"True enough. Maggie has been moping about since Micah left. I think there's a genuine romance there."

"I'm happy for them both, but their prospects seem dim. I'd never say that to her, but they've chosen a difficult path."

"You're right, Shirl, but what can I do? What can any of us do? They're young adults, and must make their own decisions, as we did at their ages. That's why we need a jolly Christmas. 1940 is sure to be trying for us all."

"Christmas with all the traditions it is then." Shirley smiled.

***

"Was it awful, Tils?" The girls had retired to their room for a much-needed twin talk.

"Rotten. Is there any place gloomier that a frigid train station saying goodbye to your fiancé?"

"If there is, I don't know what. Micah looked ever so handsome as he waved goodbye. It's only been a couple of days, but I miss him dreadfully."

"Did you cry?" Tillie asked, applying cold cream to her freshly scrubbed face.

"I held it together for the most part, biting my lip so I wouldn't break down. Once his train disappeared from sight, I cried a little. You know I don't like to make a fuss, so I kept it to a few dignified tears. You?" Maggie tucked a hot water bottle between the sheets and slid between them.

"Colin always wants a cheerful face to remember, so I dug my nails into my palms to keep the emotion from bubbling over. I'm going to miss him, but I'm so filled with guilt."

"Whatever for? You have done nothing wrong." Maggie halted her bedtime preparations.

"He's been pressing me to get married on his next leave. He's been relentless. I managed to put him off from setting an actual date, but now I feel I should have agreed. I don't want him distracted from his flying duties, thinking about me and how to convince me to marry him." *Dammit, I hate a lump in my throat when I'm trying to speak from my heart.*

"Do you want to marry him?" Maggie voiced the question in the air.

"I do love him. He's dear to me. We get on so well and have so much in common." It sounded a little lame, even to her own ears.

"But do you want to marry him?" Maggie persisted.

"I do want to marry him, but if I'm honest – not right away. We haven't known each other for long, and he's been away at training for several months. Life is so shaky and changeable right now. Do I really want to make a commitment for life?"

"Those are all sound points, luv. Is there anything else? Come on, this is me." Maggie leaned forward.

"He wants me to quit work once we're married. But I love my Lyons post. And you know I'm seriously considering signing on to drive ambulances. We'll all be needed to fight the enemy – across the board. I don't want to be tied down yet. It doesn't mean I don't love him. Now is just not the time." A tear slipped down her cheek, and then another.

"Oh darling, stop feeling so badly about it. You're being honest with yourself. Now you need to be as forthright with him. You owe him that."

"And break his heart? I can't do it, Mags. Oh, my head is in such a muddle."

Maggie threw back the coverlet and hugged her sister. Her own tears fell as the two girls thought of the men they loved, with a future so doubtful that it was hard to be hopeful.

After a good cry together, they wiped their tears and scampered into their beds.

"Aren't we a pair? What a Christmas Eve." Tillie turned out the light. "Thanks for listening and for the advice."

48

"Anytime." Maggie yawned. "Happy Christmas."

"And to you."

***

"Happy Christmas, Tillie. Happy Christmas, Maggie."

Katie plunked on Maggie's bed. "It's time to wake up, sleepyheads." Dead silence.

She shook Maggie by the shoulders.

"Come on, you two. Are you too old to see what Father Christmas has brought?" One eye opened, then the other. Maggie smiled.

"Go on then. Happy Christmas, luv. Let's go, Tils."

Tillie jumped out of bed and donned her dressing gown.

"Happy Christmas, Katie."

"You faker. Right, let's go get Kenny."

"I'm here, waiting for you daft girls. Mum's already put on the kettle. Race you to the tree."

And that's how four thundering young people came down the stairs on Christmas morning.

"Is that a herd of elephants or my children?" Mum smiled. She'd been up early to get the turkey in. For some reason, she was beyond excited about this Christmas Day. She'd never admit it to her sister, but she felt oh-so-lucky that all her children were safe at home, and no one was being shipped out to battlefields unknown. "Happy Christmas to you all. I'll pour the tea whilst you open your stockings."

They sat on the floor like children, oohing and ahhing with the overflowing abundance.

"Chocolate and oranges. How wonderful," Katie cried.

"And loads of sweets." Kenny popped a jelly baby in his mouth.

"Thanks for the nylon stockings, Mum. Wherever did you get them?" Tillie pulled a pair from the toe.

"I'll never tell." Mum laughed.

"And perfume. How extravagant." Maggie held up a bottle of eau de toilette.

Alice had scoured the shops for weeks, going completely overboard on gifts. Like many Londoners, she wanted to make the most of this Christmas when things were still to be had, and rationing had only just begun.

"There's more," Mum said as Pops handed round the bigger gifts.

Mum had gotten sturdy wool skirts handmade for the girls. Matching blouses gave each of them a new winter ensemble. And new trousers and a shirt for Kenny. Tillie and Maggie had gone together on stationery and fountain pens for everyone. Katie gave makeup and nail varnish to her sisters, and a brush and comb set for her brother. He gave them all sweets – typical Kenny.

The girls had reluctantly taken up knitting for the war effort. Mum had urged them to help keep overseas soldiers warm with socks and balaclavas. None of them loved or even liked it, but gritted their teeth and gave it their best go. Between them, they'd knitted a pipe holder for Pops, knobby dishcloths for Mum, and scarves for them both. Aunt Shirley had come to the rescue more than once, but that was their Christmas secret.

"Splendid," declared Pops. "Just the thing to keep me warm on frosty walks to work." He wrapped the grey scarf around his neck.

"And these dishcloths will come in proper handy. You girls are coming on quite well with your knitting." Mum was touched at the effort they'd gone to.

The biggest surprise was the gifts from Pops. He produced large paper-wrapped packages.

"I think you'll find these quite useful."

Katie was the first to rip hers open. It was a long, one-piece suit of some sort.

"What ever is this?"

"Siren suits," Walter said proudly. "They are for the…"

"Shelter," Tillie finished. "I've read about these – you pull it on over your pajamas, dressing gown, whatever, so you can get quickly to the shelter and stay warm during an air raid attack."

"Well, I never," Mum exclaimed, opening her own brown suit. "It will help with modesty, too."

The girls were busily trying on the suits – Walter had gotten various colours and sizes to fit each of them.

"Indeed," he said. "You all look marvellous. And they'll keep you warm."

"Ta, Pops. What a brilliant idea," Maggie said.

"Even mine fits. It's not too long," Katie twirled in her navy-blue suit.

"Thank you everyone. We've all had a brilliant Christmas. Everyone has been so generous," Maggie said.

Thanks echoed through the room.

"Righto, who will help me with a full English breakfast? As full as I could manage, that is." Mum stood.

The girls jumped up to assist, whilst Kenny and Pops were left to clear away the mess.

The day flew by in a bustle of preparation and tidying away of a generous breakfast, followed straightaway with the dinner itself. Shirley and Thomas arrived late-morning, arms laden with veg and other treats.

"Dinner is ready," Katie announced to the boys in the drawing room.

"It smells wonderful." Thomas rubbed his hands together.

They sat and snapped Christmas crackers. Placing the paper crowns on their heads, they read out the jokes and traded the trinkets inside.

"Who hides in the bakery at Christmas?" Kenny asked, reading his joke.

"I don't know, who?" Katie played along.

"A mince spy." Kenny chuckled.

Everyone groaned.

"Your table is gorgeous, Alice." Shirley took in the bone china, newly polished silver, array of crystal, and crisp fabric serviettes. "I love the candles and tree boughs. It smells of outdoors."

Pops carved the turkey and passed generous portions round. Mum served roasted potatoes, parsnips, bread pudding, sprouts, and gravy.

"And your cranberry sauce is the best." Alice nodded to her sister.

"The pigs in a blanket are my favourite." Kenny popped three in a row into his mouth.

"We are lucky to have such abundance this Christmas," Walter declared. "I'm absolutely fit to bursting."

"Too full for plum pudding?" Alice teased.

"Never," he replied.

With a flourish, Alice brought in the pudding, and Walter poured the brandy and lit it. As per family tradition.

"Brilliant," Tillie said.

"I'll get the dishes," offered Maggie.

"A big piece for me, please." Katie smiled.

"And me, too." Kenny rubbed his hands in glee.

Alice looked from child to child round the table. Tillie, eager for life, helpful and kind. Maggie, more serious with a steady nature and a large heart. Cheerful Katie who bounced from one adventure to another, and her boy – Kenny – the youngest, and in this exact moment – the most vulnerable. She loved them all dearly and felt thankful to her toes that they were all within arm's reach. She was feeling a bit misty-eyed, but resolutely put sad thoughts away.

"Right, time to clear this away. The more help I get, the quicker we can go on our family walk."

"I believe that's our cue, Thomas," Walter stood. "Brandy?"

"Just so," Thomas said. "And thank you all for the marvellous dinner. You ladies have outdone yourselves."

"I'll join you." Kenny jumped up. Everyone laughed.

"Not so fast, young man. You're not quite old enough for brandy and pipes in the library. You're on kitchen duty with your sisters." Mum picked up a platter and handed it to her son.

He shrugged.

"I tried," he laughed.

They made quick work of the loads of dishes, leaving a pot or two to soak.

Dressing in coats, hats, and newly gifted scarves, the family trooped outdoors for a brisk afternoon walk.

In a rare show of affection, Walter took his wife's arm as they braced against the chill air.

"Well done, you." He smiled. "All your hard work paid off in a picture-perfect day."

"Thank you, dear. It was worth all the planning and cooking." She watched the young Kingstons scamper ahead – no longer children, but not quite adults.

"No white Christmas, more's the pity," Shirley remarked. "Last year was so magical, with snow-topped trees and the young people making

snowmen." Alice knew she was thinking of her son.

"Perhaps next Christmas, we'll all be together and you'll be scolding Geoffrey for tramping snow onto your nice rug," Alice joked.

"I'd give anything for his messes, piles of dirty socks under the bed and his face covered in jam at the breakfast table," Shirley said, then straightened her shoulders. "But there's a war on, so we must do whatever it takes to win it."

"Just so, dear," Thomas patted her arm. "That's the spirit."

After a frosty and restorative walk, they gathered to listen to the King's message:

"The festival which we all know as Christmas is, above all, the festival of peace and of the home. Among all free peoples, the love of peace is profound, for this alone gives security to the home. But true peace is in the hearts of men, and it is the tragedy of this time that there are powerful countries whose whole direction and policy are based on aggression and the suppression of all that we hold dear for mankind…

At home we are…taking the strain for what may lie ahead of us, resolved and confident…

I would send a special word of greeting to the armies of the Empire, to those who have come from afar, and in particular to the British Expeditionary Force. Their task is hard. They are waiting, and waiting is a trial of nerve and discipline. But I know that when the moment comes for action, they will prove themselves worthy of the highest traditions of their great Service.

And to all who are preparing themselves to serve their country on sea, on land, or in the air, I send my greeting at this time…

I believe from my heart that the cause which binds together my peoples and our gallant and faithful Allies is the cause of Christian civilisation. On no other basis can a true civilisation be built. Let us remember this through the dark times ahead of us and when we are making the peace for which all men pray.

A new year is at hand. We cannot tell what it will bring. If it brings peace how thankful we shall all be. If it brings continued struggle, we shall remain undaunted…

May that Almighty hand guide and uphold us all."

"Just the thing to complete the day," Thomas said. "He is preparing us for demanding days ahead, but in an inspiring way."

"His stutter seems to be improving." Shirley looked up from her knitting. "And I appreciated his message about the BEF. I felt as if he were speaking of our Geoffrey."

"Indeed," Thomas replied.

"I'm off to write to Micah." Maggie stood. She needed a little time on her own.

"I'll help with the pots, Mum." Tillie gave Katie a meaningful look.

"I suppose I will, too." Katie took the hint. "But charades later?"

"Sounds lovely, dear," Mum said.

"And we'll be off," Shirley bundled her knitting into her bag. "He won't admit it, but Walter's after a nap."

The family scattered to their own devices, feeling rather satisfied with the day.

**

Tillie lay in bed, hearing Maggie's light snores. Turning from side to side, she couldn't get comfortable. What would 1940 bring? Could the fighting be kept at bay much longer? Would Colin stay safe in a RAF bomber? Was the Phoney War about to turn into real hostilities? Sleep wouldn't come.

Chapter Three

SNOWY AND COLD

1940 – Maggie

"Another cuppa, luv? With this rain, I'm in no rush to queue for hours." Alice peered out the kitchen window where rain sleeted hard against it.

"I suppose so," Shirley replied, eyes down.

Alice poured her sister another cup, and tried to think of something to cheer her.

"Faye sent us a letter this past week. She is posting us a surprise parcel. We should be getting it any day. What do you suppose it could be?"

Shirley shrugged.

"Christmas gifts, I expect. Does it matter? Does anything matter?"

Alice felt helpless with her sister's grief. Shirley had been shattered when the dreaded telegram boy delivered the news that Geoffrey had been killed in action. Shirley had been inconsolable at the loss of her only child. Thomas did what he could to support his wife, but buried his own grief in his ever-increasing workload.

And it was an unimaginable death. Geoffrey had been posted with the British Expeditionary Forces in France when the Allies had been forced to retreat against advancing German troops. In May, the Germans invaded the Low Countries, taking Netherlands, Luxembourg, and Belgium, surprising the rest of the world. A shocking advance through the Ardennes Forest resulted in the fall of France, stranding thousands of British and French troops in the north. They were ordered to abandon their weapons and tanks and withdraw to Dunkirk Beach for rescue.

Waiting for days, they suffered with no food or water, under constant German air attack.

Back in England, the country rallied to save their soldiers. Mobilizing every available seacraft – military and civilian – the British forces turned the defeat into a remarkable miracle. Despite losing many boats to German strafing, almost 300,000 British and allied troops were rescued.

The BEF had been saved, but almost all of its heavy equipment, tanks, artillery, and motorized transport had been left behind or destroyed by departing soldiers to avoid the Germans getting their hands on them. And more than 50,000 British troops were unable to escape the continent. 11,000 were killed and thousands were captured as prisoners of war.

Private Geoffrey Fowler had been one of the dreadfully unlucky ones. A mate of his had kindly come to visit the Fowlers when he'd recovered from his own injury. He reassured Shirley and Thomas that Geoffrey hadn't suffered, but had been shot and killed on the first day. It was cold comfort for the grieving parents.

Months later, Shirley was still walking through her days in a fog, unable to rouse herself for anything but the most basic of tasks. She took joy in nothing, and hardly slept or ate. Alice was worried sick for her, and hoped somehow the Christmas festivities would be a distraction and not a ghastly reminder of their son and the gaping hole he would leave at the dining table on Christmas Day.

Alice took her sister's hands into her own.

"Darling, it must be grim facing the day without our dear Geoffrey. Is there anything I can do to help?" She willed her sister some strength.

"No, there's nothing." Shirley snatched her hands back. "And don't look at me with those sad, brown eyes. It's easy for you to ladle out sympathy. You have your four children. And I have nothing."

"Shirley Fowler, that's not fair," Alice replied quietly. "I miss dear Geoffrey, too. And our Kenny is off who-knows-where with the Navy. And him not even eighteen. Our Tillie lost her fiancé Colin in that awful air crash. We must carry on, Shirl. Geoffrey wouldn't want you to be miserable forever. Remember how he used to greet everyone with an enormous hug? Summon up that lovely boy. It's no use wallowing. You still have your husband, and we all need you." Alice wanted to shake her sister.

"I suppose you're right," Shirley said dully. "Shall we get on with the shops? Do you reckon they'll have any decent meat?"

The air raid warning went off and the mood changed.

"Come on, Shirl. We've got to get to the Andy straight away." Alice did a rapid calculation as she scrambled to her feet. Walter and Katie were at the office and would shelter locally. Tillie was at work driving ambulance – in the thick of it. Oh dear. And Maggie? Wasn't she on her way home from a WVS shift? She was responsible and would duck into a shelter, wherever she was. With any luck, she'd still be in the tube. *Please be safe, girls.*

"Pick up the shelter kit. Oh, I wish I'd gone to the loo." Alice hastened out the back door, collecting her coat and gas mask on her way. Shirley was right behind her, clutching the kit and the teapot.

Dashing through the rain, they crossed the few yards to the shelter, and in moments, they sat listening to it pelting against the corrugated metal.

"Did you bring the teapot?" Alice asked once they'd settled on the narrow bench. "What were you thinking?"

"I didn't think. I took the first thing at hand. But it's not a bad idea, is it? Would you like a cuppa?"

Alice laughed at the absurdity of it all.

"I suppose I would. There are mugs round here somewhere."

This wasn't the first of the air raids that interrupted their days, and more recently their nights. Londoners were calling it the Blitz – for *Blitzkrieg* – lightning war. Since Black Saturday in September, the Germans had been mounting bombing assaults almost nightly. Albeit the city had prepared with the blackout, sandbags, taped windows, backyard shelters, and barrage balloons flying low to deflect landings and short-range bombing, the city had been battered over and over again.

To neutralize the power of RAF fighters, the daily attacks had been replaced with night-time raids, forcing Londoners underground. The city had eventually opened up the tubes for overnight sheltering, after vocal protests by those – especially in the East End – who had nowhere to go. Whether on a crowded, uncomfortable cement floor in an underground station, or in an unheated, six-foot long and four-and-a-half-foot wide garden shelter with no electricity or bathroom facilities, the nights were long, freezing cold, and filled with terror.

Citizens dragged themselves to their beds when the all-clear sounded sometime in the night or early morning, and went to work like zombies, barely able to function. But they carried on. What choice did they have? They were all intent on one aim – to defeat Hitler with an absolute Allied victory.

Thousands of Londoners had been killed or injured, and many more left homeless. Firefighters and other rescue teams worked through the nights to put out incendiaries and parachute bombs, take the injured to hospital, and restore some semblance of normalcy by morning.

Each day, Londoners prayed their loved ones would stay safe, and their home would have survived another night. The Phoney War was over.

"I don't hear any planes, do you?" Alice asked.

"All I hear is rain." Shirley sat huddled in her coat.

"Perhaps it will be over soon," Alice said. "At least we won't have to queue for the shops."

Shirley raised an eyebrow in the semi-gloom.

"I don't know what I'll manage for Thomas's supper. We're dry – I suppose that's something." She paused. "Luv, I'm sorry for being so low. I know you are doing everything you can to cheer me. I will do my best to brighten up for Christmas. I promise."

"No need to apologize. You have plenty of reason to be despondent. We'll get through this."

The all-clear sounded.

"That wasn't too bad at all, darling. Just ninety minutes today. Let's hope Hitler doesn't come calling again tonight."

But he did, and every night after that.

***

"I stayed in the underground until the all-clear." Maggie ran a hand through her damp, rumpled hair. "Not much fun, but I was safe. You two managed alright?"

"Just fine, luv. I've just made a fresh brew. Do you want it now or after

you've dried off?" Alice was relieved to see her daughter walk through the door.

"I'll have a cup now, ta, Mum. I'm too tired to move." Maggie was exhausted from her shift today. The haunted eyes of survivors raking through glass and rubble to find loved ones was hard to bear – especially as most were found dead, buried under collapsed buildings. It shook her to her core.

"Was it hectic today?" Alice poured her a cup, and pressed the dish of biscuits towards her.

"They had us at Paddington Station again. With all the soldiers, sailors, and flyers leaving, there're loads of families saying goodbye. They all need a restoring tea, sandwich, or biscuit."

Maggie had given up her beloved Nippy role at Lyons some months earlier to work fulltime with the Women's Voluntary Service. She worked in a mobile canteen, taking to the streets to bring a small measure of comfort in emergency circumstances. Mostly, they were called to live rescue sites where firemen, Air Raid Wardens, constables, and ambulance workers needed a calming cuppa during air raid attacks. Rescued civilians also took solace in hot drinks as they surveyed their bombed-out houses, and streets filled with debris, brick, glass, and smouldering fires.

But it was dangerous work, and Alice had been relieved to hear the front door click to reveal her weary daughter.

"Oh, my goodness. I almost forgot. You got post today, luv. I think it's from France. So sorry." She pulled it from her apron pocket.

Maggie fairly snatched it from her mother. *A letter from Micah. How wonderful.*

"Mum, I'm going to take it upstairs to my room. You don't mind?" She was already half-out of the kitchen.

Mum waved her off.

"Take your time, luv. I hope it's good news."

Maggie wanted to savor every moment of this longed-for letter. She placed it gently on the bed, and changed from her soggy WVS uniform into a warm jumper and trousers. She gave her face a cursory wash and ran a comb through her untidy hair before sitting on the bed and picking up the letter. She traced the familiar writing with her finger and put it to her nose, hoping to find a scent of him. But nothing. Slicing it open with her letter opener, she removed the thin pages.

"*Dear Maggie,*

Firstly, I must apologize that it's taken me so long to write to you. We've had rather a time of it here. I'll do my best to explain, in hopes that the censors don't take their scissors to my words.

As you no doubt know by now, France has fallen to the Germans. It was stunning to us all, and many of my fellow Frenchmen are ashamed that they were unable to hold Allied territories. It was such a crushing defeat that many are fleeing – or trying to.

Grandfather took the blow hard indeed, and his heart is weakening at an alarming rate. Conditions in Paris were harsh. Our family is not welcome in a German-occupied zone. I'll say no more than that.

We've journeyed to the Vichy region in the south where Germany doesn't control our day-to-day movements. Grandfather has a small farm here in Toulouse, and we are safer than up north. But we've had to leave our business behind and farming is not my chosen occupation. We are doing our best, and bartering with neighbouring farmers so that we all get by.

It's particularly difficult for young Hannah. Her schooling has been interrupted, and she worries about Mama, who has become frail and fearful.

If there could be any way to bring Hannah back to England, our entire family would be eternally grateful. As a British citizen, she is free to leave if she can obtain transport. I know what you are thinking, little one – that I can escort her home. But I can't leave my parents and grandfather. They truly couldn't cope on their own. Please understand. As much as I long to see you, I must stay with my family.

Please keep yourself safe. The press that is getting through showing the danger and wreckage of the Blitz has us all in distress. You are so brave to be out during the worst of the raids – offering care and aid to those who need it most as they battle for control. I'm so proud of you.

It is peculiar to think of you preparing for a jolly Christmas. I'm sure it must be trying to find gifts and holiday foods to celebrate. I do wish you and your family a Happy Christmas, even in these ghastly times.

This Lord Byron poem, She Walks in Beauty fills my mind with you, dear Maggie. Please allow me to share it with you:

She walks in beauty, like the night
Of cloudless climes and starry skies;
And all that's best of dark and bright
Meet in her aspect and her eyes;
Thus mellowed to that tender light
Which heaven to gaudy day denies.

One shade the more, one ray the less,
Had half impaired the nameless grace
Which waves in every raven tress,
Or softly lightens o'er her face;
Where thoughts serenely sweet express,
How pure, how dear their dwelling-place.

And on that cheek, and o'er that brow,
So soft, so calm, yet eloquent,
The smiles that win, the tints that glow,
But tell of days in goodness spent,
A mind at peace with all below,
A heart whose love is innocent!

Micah xx"

Maggie let the pages slide to her lap as she looked out the window. Wind and rain lashed against the pane echoing the turmoil in her heart. She was almost faint with relief that he was safe. But utter dismay filled her as she considered the terrible conditions under which he and his family were living. The love poem confounded her even further. Was he saying he was in love with her? Did she walk in beauty? Her mind swirled.

***

Tillie breezed into their room, smelling of fire and cordite.

"What a gloomy day. I'm soaked to the skin. I wish it was my night for a bath. Why can't it snow? This incessant icy rain doesn't even make it feel like Christmas. Are you okay?"

Typical Tillie. All brightness and chatter.

"I'm fine. I was stuck in the tube during the air raid. But I think it was a false alarm. Just time wasting. How was your shift?"

"Quiet. Just a few callouts for minor injuries. The daytime shifts give us a pause between the madness of night calls stacked on top of each other. I hope we get some respite tonight. I'm desperate for a good night's sleep." She peeled off her ambulance coat and street clothes, and was down to her brassiere and panties in seconds. "I suppose it's too early for my pajamas? Mum would pitch a fit." She pulled on a woolly jumper and long skirt. "Is it time to do the blackout yet?"

Maggie glanced at the alarm clock.

"Not quite. I have something to tell you." *I need my sister right now.*

"I'm all ears. What is it?" Tillie sank to her bed, picking up her hairbrush.

"I got a letter from Micah," Maggie replied simply.

Tillie gasped.

"Maggie, you never said. How is he? Why hasn't he written in so long?" She was full of questions.

"They are alright for now. They had to flee to the south – to his grandfather's farm in Toulouse. He doesn't write much, but I fear that they are under persecution as Jews. What we've seen in the papers – Hitler despises them. But why?"

"I wish I knew why, luv, but it's an irrational belief. And I reckon we're not hearing the half of it. The papers keep the worst news out to keep our morale from dropping." Seeing Maggie's face fall, she cursed herself. "But look on the bright side. He's written and they're safe in the south. That's cause for enormous relief, darling. Was there another poem?"

Maggie blushed and busied herself smoothing the bed coverlet.

"Stop being such a stickybeak. Maybe there is, but I'm not going to let you see it." *Micah's words are for me alone.*

Tillie laughed.

"I knew it. You can't keep secrets from a twin. Righto, I won't pry then." Her gaze slid to her hands where she checked her nail varnish for chips. "I wish my Colin had left me with a poem or two."

Maggie stopped fussing and sat on the bed opposite her sister.

"Oh, I'm so sorry. You must be missing him so much."

"You know what, luv? I'm a hodgepodge of feelings. His death was such a shock – he was so full of life that I didn't dream he would ever be harmed. I'm grieving for the life that we were supposed to share together. But it's getting harder and harder to conjure his face. The essence of him is fading away, and it makes me sad and guilty."

"Why guilty?"

"Because I'm young, and still want to get on with my life. I'll always miss Colin, and am so sorry that he's gone. His parents are inconsolable. It's so awkward when I go to visit them. It's like they are frozen in time and can't move forward."

"Quite understandable," Maggie said. She was a turmoil of emotions herself. She felt so badly that young Colin was taken in the prime of his life, his plane shot down over the channel. Yet, Tillie seemed like she wanted to forget him, and Maggie didn't know how she felt about that. "Is it that fireman, Trevor Drummond? Is he the reason for your mixed feelings?"

"Maggie, don't take that tone with me. I can't bear it if you disapprove of me. Do I like Trevor? Yes, I do and I'm not going to apologize for that. In fact, he's asked me out for tea. And I'm going. It's just tea. It's hardly even a date." Tillie dared her sister to rebuke her.

"It sounds like a date." When Tillie opened her mouth to respond, Maggie raised her hand. "I'm always going to be on your side. Just take it slow, please. It's only been a few months since Colin was killed. Please respect his memory."

"I will, Maggie. And don't judge me. You don't know what you'd do if you were in my shoes."

Maggie said nothing, thinking of her young love trapped in an occupied country, fearing for the life of his loved ones. *I could never forget him and move on. Never.*

"Let's get on with the blackout, and help Mum with supper. We're bound to be in the Andy tonight." Tillie left the room.

***

"Darlings, thank you for mucking in with me on the Christmas baking and cooking this year. With Aunt Shirley feeling so low, and Faye gone off nursing, I'm feeling at sixes and sevens about it all." Mum frowned over her tick list.

"None of us are any good at cooking, but we'll do our best. Why don't we start with Christmas Eve?" Tillie suggested.

It was another frosty day. The rain beat steadily against the window, threatening to turn into sleet or even snow if the temperature dropped any further. Tillie and Maggie were bundled up in colourful jumpers. The aga spit out a bit of heat – the kitchen was the warmest room in the house. And close to the teapot.

"I don't expect we can count on Aunt Shirley hosting at hers. It's just too much for her," Maggie said. "She's still a bundle of nerves."

Mum nodded sadly.

"We are likely to be in the shelter anyroad. So maybe an early afternoon tea instead? Gracious, it will be quite different from years past. Tillie, are you working Christmas Eve?"

"I'm on morning shift and off on Christmas Day. But back at it Boxing Day."

"Do you think Hitler will give us a break on Christmas?" Maggie asked. "It would be horrid to go to the bother of cooking a Christmas dinner to have it ruined."

"I think we should plan on an early dinner," Mum said firmly. "We've been in that blooming shelter night after night for weeks. Why should he let up on us now?"

"I don't think we can manage a pie day," Tillie said. "None of us can bake worth a fig, and with sugar and butter in short supply..." Her voice trailed off.

Mum sighed.

"Let's cross that one off. Your father will be so disappointed, but perhaps we could try a mince pie?"

Tillie shrugged.

"We can try. What about a turkey or goose?"

"I've put in at the butchers for a chicken – I expect that's the best we can do. I couldn't bear one of these mock goose recipes that the government is suggesting. Not on Christmas Day. Winter veg as usual." Mum looked up from the list. "It's all looking pretty grim."

"I can look for Christmas crackers at the shops. That will help," Maggie offered. "Not likely to find them, though."

Mum nodded and added it to the list.

"I do have a spot of good news – but it's a surprise. Faye said she made a plum pudding several months ago for us. It's in the scullery."

"Brilliant," the twins cried together, and then laughed.

"Yes, Pops will be most pleased."

Mum put down her pencil.

"Let's see. How many are we for dinner? Pops and I, you three, Aunt Shirley and Uncle Thomas. And you invited the Redwoods, luv?" She turned to Tillie.

Tillie shifted in her seat.

"I did, but I'm not altogether sure about it, if I'm honest. I know they are at a loose end, but I seem to have run out of conversation where they are concerned. I know that sounds beastly." Tillie stared down at her cup.

"You know it's the right thing to do. We'll all help to make conversation. They would have been your in-laws. It's the least we can do," Alice chided softly.

"Of course, you're right."

"Maybe Mrs. Redwood can bring a mince pie?" Maggie asked.

Mum made a note.

"Why not? We can use all the help we can get."

Tillie looked at Maggie who nodded.

"Mum, we know you are being ever so brave, but we are all missing Kenny. It's alright to talk about him."

Mum inhaled deeply, fighting for control.

"It's not easy, but I keep thinking about everyone who has lost someone in this wretched war – husbands, sons, fathers. Just look at Aunt Shirley. And the Redwoods. We don't have it nearly that awful. Kenny is fighting for the navy and for our freedom. But it is hard when I worry about him so. Ta, girls."

"Why don't you read us his last letter? That always brings a smile. That rascal," Maggie said.

"Righto, I'll just fetch it." Mum jumped up.

"Well done you, Mags," Tillie said as she rose to put on the kettle.

"We have to keep each other's spirits up, don't we?" Maggie drained her teacup.

"Here it is," Mum came back, holding up the thin blue paper:

"Dear Mum and Pops,

Sorry for not writing more. You know I was never one for sitting still with pencil and paper. My school marks proved that. I know you worry, so I'm dashing off a quick letter before I kip down for the night.

I can't say where I am but I expect it's warmer here than at home. I can picture snow-covered trees and skating like we did last year.

I love being aboard a ship. Some of the lads are still green with seasickness, but I've been lucky enough to give that a miss. The work is hard, but the shifts go fast and then we have a laugh or two in the mess. I've made a couple of good mates, so we tell jokes to keep from being homesick.

Right, that's all for now. Say hi to those rotten sisters of mine. And Happy Christmas to you all.

Kenny xx

P.S. I hope you forgive me for joining up without asking your permission. The navy needs me. K"

"He sounds chipper," Tillie said as Mum folded up the letter and put in her apron pocket.

"And I'm glad he's made some chums," Maggie said as she poured a fresh kettle of water over the tea leaves. He's so young, my little brother. I just want him to be safe. And Micah, too."

"He says it warmer there. I wonder where he is?" Tillie asked.

"Likely somewhere in the Mediterranean." Mum stirred her cup. "So far away. My boy is so far away."

"He's safe and alive, Mum. And he's strong and resourceful," Maggie soothed.

But they all knew that was no guarantee he would stay safe. None whatsoever.

***

"That took longer that I imagined," Katie moaned as they slung their shop bags over their arms. "If the sleet and queues weren't wretched enough, the bus was late. It's not our day."

Maggie fought to keep the umbrella from turning inside out.

"It's bound to get better. And Mum will be delighted with the offal. And extra bit of sugar. How you do it, I just don't know. You just bat your eyes and the butcher or greengrocer gives you his bit put by under the counter."

"It's all in the way you ask. Besides, I'm motivated by hunger. Aren't you famished all the time?" Katie ploughed through the sleet, eager to get home.

Widespread food rationing was taking a toll on the British public. Since 1939, staple items had steadily gone on the ration – bacon, butter, and sugar in January, and some meats since then. It was a necessary sacrifice – as an island, England was at huge risk of having their food supply cut off by German U-boats – but it made daily life difficult and tedious. The meat rations were alarmingly small – especially for the men – and it was near impossible to do any decent baking with the shortages of butter, dried fruits and sugar. Thankfully, neither fish nor vegetables were rationed. Citizens were encouraged to *Dig for Victory*, and they took it to heart. Many grew veg patches on top of their backyard shelters or in allotments. The Kingston's patch was well looked after by Walter.

Surprisingly, these deprivations brought people closer together. Normally standoffish, long queue-standing was lightened by group moaning and recipe-sharing. Britons normally chatted to strangers about the weather. Now, the Blitz and rationing had taken center stage. It produced a camaraderie of 'we are all in this together' that was comforting.

"I try not to think about it." Maggie shifted a heavier bag to the other arm. "Although tea on the ration is particularly disagreeable. I get my fill at the canteen lorry, I suppose."

"Maybe it's because I'm a growing girl. I dream of bacon and real eggs, and creamy puddings."

Maggie laughed.

"Your dream will come true in a couple of days. You'll get your fill of delicious confections at our annual Christmas tea. Hurry now. We're dreadfully late and it's getting dark…"

The air raid siren wailed just as the girls reached the townhouse. Rushing through the door, they called for Mum. Hearing nothing, they ran down the kitchen stairs and out the door to the backyard. Yanking open the door, they were startled to see – no one.

"Mum must be at Aunt Shirley's." Katie flopped onto the bench. "And now we're stuck in our wet things for who-knows-how-long."

Maggie closed the umbrella and the door and joined her sister.

"With nary a cup of tea in sight. And I was working up an appetite talking about puddings. But our siren suits are here. They'll keep us a bit warm."

"Where is everyone, I wonder?" Katie lit the lantern.

"Tillie is at work so she'll be out with Ernie in the ambulance." Maggie crossed her fingers that her twin would remain unhurt.

"Mum is with Aunt Shirley, I expect. Pops was on his way home from the office. I suppose he'll just pop home for his ARP helmet and start his patrol. I'm that relieved not to be on fire watching duty tonight. It's frigid out there with that driving rain."

As well as their normal jobs, Londoners had to take their turns on rooftops around the city. Their job was to spot fires, put them out with stirrup pumps if possible, and report them. It was a lonely job, and these days also bitterly cold and miserable. But everyone needed to do their bit.

"Never seems to stop the Luftwaffe." Maggie sniffed. "They keep coming no matter the weather."

"And we can't even hear them with the rain hitting the metal. It's so bloody noisy in here, I can't even hear myself think."

Soon enough, the crashing, hissing, and booming of distant bombs could be heard even above the din.

"At this rate, we'll eat through this shopping before Mum even sees it," Katie chewed on a carrot.

"At least it's something." Maggie pulled a blanket around her shoulders.

A large cracking noise, followed by a huge thud made the shelter shudder. The girls clutched each other's hands in fright.

"I'm scared, Maggie. That one was close."

"It's alright, luv. It was probably far away." Maggie wasn't sure if she was trying to convince Katie or herself.

A whizzing sound, then a rumble that sounded like thunder.

"I don't want to die. This war is so random, Mags. I'm only nineteen. I haven't even lived yet." Katie fought back tears.

"You're not going to die, luv. They're probably at the docks again. We've hardly been touched here." I've seen my share of bombs and their damage driving the WVS canteen around town. Too many Londoners killed by bombs – direct hits or horribly buried under crumbling burnings. It didn't bear thinking about.

"Why do all the bangs and crashes sound so loud then?"

"I don't know. But let's not talk about it. It doesn't help. So, have you met any nice young men at Pops' office?"

"No, you daft cow. They are all doddering old men. All the attractive young ones are off fighting, you know that."

"I'm just trying to distract you. What do you fancy then? A blond, redhead, dark and mysterious?"

"I'm not quite sure. Perhaps a tall, dark soldier. With a wicked grin and cheeky sense of humor."

"Sounds like you. You're the cheekiest of all of us." Phew, it was working. Katie was thinking of something else.

"Well, I have to be, don't I? I can't compete with you and Tillie in the glamor department."

"Sod off. We're just a bit taller than you, is all. And I'd die for your curly brown hair."

Katie snorted.

"As if. How about these freckles? Fancy those too?"

"Katie, you are wonderful and darling just as you are. And I wouldn't mind a few freckles."

Katie waved off the compliment. As she always did. Maggie wished her sister could see how special she was. *It can't be easy for her – always in the shadow of Tillie and I.*

"How do you stay so calm, Mags? I try to be like you, but I end up making a bollocks of everything, or somehow buggering it up."

Maggie shook her by the arms.

"Katherine Kingston, listen to me. Stop comparing yourself to me, or Tillie, for that matter. We are just normal girls, making mistakes, trying to figure out what we are doing in life, muddling through this war – just like everyone else. Just like you, in fact. We don't have all the answers – hell, I don't have any answers."

Katie let out a small giggle.

"I've got you right provoked. The angelic Maggie swearing. I never thought I'd see the day."

"We must stick together – like the Kingston girls always have. We'll get through this."

"Ta, luv. Right now, all I can think about is that my bladder is fit to bursting."

"I'll sing God Save the King whilst you go."

They had a bucket in the corner of the shelter, but no one liked to use it. But needs must.

In the event, it was two in the morning before the shelling stopped. Two exhausted, hungry, and ice-cold girls tromped into the dark house.

"Tea or bed?" Katie whispered.

"Loo first, then a quick cup of tea. Hopefully Tillie, Mum and Pops will be back by then."

A drowsy tea party followed. Mum came in, then Pops. Tillie turned up after they'd retired to scrape together a few hours' sleep, so the sisters sipped a cup of tea, chewed a biscuit and drifted upstairs to bed.

***

Tillie's tea date with Trevor had gone even better than she imagined. He was kind, listened to her, and it didn't hurt that he was gorgeous. Did she feel a twinge about Colin? Of course, she did. But war was changing how young people viewed relationships. Both Tillie and Trevor had seen their share of pain and death, and had a hunger for life not yet lived. She wasn't ready to rush into anything serious, nor did she intend to compromise herself, but a little harmless fun and flirting with a dark, handsome fireman hurt no one. She'd agreed to go with him to a National Gallery concert in a fortnight or so. But she hadn't told Maggie about that yet.

***

"No tree? It won't even feel like Christmas." Katie had pulled out the cartons of decorations from the attic and was prepared to make a day of it – sorting through the tangled- up lights, putting up the traditional decorations, wreathing and garlanding about.

"Sorry, poppet. Even if we could get a tree – which is nigh on impossible – it wouldn't be the responsible thing to do. We must bear these sacrifices for the good of us all," Pops chided.

"I don't see how a Christmas tree makes any difference towards the war effort."

"Should we divert men from fighting to tramp around the countryside, cutting down trees for us?" Maggie asked gently. "Besides, we can take all the trimmings and strew them about the house. It will still feel festive."

It was the Saturday before Christmas. Tillie was at work and Mum was busy making lists with Aunt Shirley. The sun had peeked out briefly, giving welcome respite from the clouds and rain.

"Pops, can I have yesterday's newspaper? We can make paper chains," Katie asked. He handed it over.

"We can hang some of our glass balls in the dining and drawing rooms. That will make it cheery on the day."

Katie ran for the scissors.

"Have you heard any more from your young man?" Pops lit his pipe.

"He's not my young man." Maggie turned slightly pale. "But no, nothing since the last letter. Now that you bring it up, there is something I wanted to talk to you about."

Maggie had been reluctant to talk to her parents about Micah's letter. It was such a big ask to even attempt a rescue of this nature. And then to have Hannah live with them. The Blitz was trying enough.

"He said that conditions are worsening each day. They are safe at the grandfather's farm in Toulouse but food is scarce." Maggie pushed back her hair.

71

"Go on, dear." Pops leaned forward.

"Is there any way for us to bring Hannah back to England? She is a British citizen, but Micah can't leave his family there. He wants her safe in England and to be able to continue her education."

Pops considered carefully. Maggie was a serious young lady. For her to raise this, the situation must be dire indeed.

"So, we'd need to provide transport for her from France to England – no easy feat. Do they have any family in London? Or anywhere in Britain?"

"No," Maggie said.

"Well then, she'd have to live with us. The girl must be properly taken care of."

Maggie jumped up.

"Do you mean it? I'd look after her as much as I could. Tillie and I could set up one of the box rooms for her. I'm sure she'd be no bother." Her words tumbled out. A rush of gratitude flowed through her. Pops is the best. Maybe Hannah could be helped after all.

Pops held up his hand.

"We need to discuss this with your mother, but I'm certain she'll agree. The Goldbachs are some of our dearest friends. We have plenty of room, and it's the least we can do."

Maggie almost danced for joy.

"But Maggie, that's the easy part. Getting her from Toulouse to British shores is the hard going. I'll have a word with Uncle Thomas. With his connections, perhaps he'll be able to help. At the very least, he'll provide sound advice."

"Pops, you're ace. Thank you ever so much. I know it's not going to be easy."

"What's not going to be easy?" Katie bounced in, balancing a tray. "Mum has sent cocoa and bikkies for sustenance."

"Splendid. Thank you. And nothing is easy these days, my dear.. Now, let's have that cup of that cocoa." He winked at Maggie.

***

"Why do we bother pinning up our hair at night when this relentless rain turns us into soggy messes?" Tillie removed her hat, lank blonde hair falling to her shoulders.

"Would you rather have this frizzy jumble to deal with?" Katie replied, fluffing her dark matted curls in vain.

"I can't believe you two are whingeing when we're about to have a delicious Christmas tea." Mum snapped open the menu.

"Sorry, Mum," Katie mumbled.

"So sorry. I'm just that tired. But this is a smashing treat. And look at the marvellous decorations." Tillie looked around the stylish restaurant.

"That's better. Shirley, which manner of tea do you fancy?" Mum turned to her.

"Earl Grey, I should think."

"What about the lavender one you like so well? We're splurging today," Mum coaxed.

"How many Christmas teas have we had here, Mum? It's such a part of our traditions every year," Maggie asked.

"Goodness, I've never counted. Let's see. We've been doing this since the twins were about ten, I should think. Is that right, Shirl?"

They were all doing their best to cheer Aunt Shirley. Although she had dressed up for the day, she still looked haunted and afraid, eyes darting about.

"That sounds about right. And young Katie begged to be included. But she wasn't allowed until she was – what? – eight or so?"

"The youngest is always so spoiled. We had to wait till our tenth birthdays," Tillie said.

"I couldn't let you have all the fun without me," Katie objected as the waiter hovered. "It's awful being left out as the youngest all the time."

Mum ordered the usual afternoon tea tray – pots of tea, elegant sandwiches, clotted cream and jam with scones, and at the very top – a myriad of tiny sweet delicacies.

"It doesn't seem to me that you were left out of much of anything," Maggie said, cocking an eyebrow towards Tillie.

"Pushed your way in, more like," Tillie said.

"Now, now, girls. Katie always brings the sunshine and life to any outing," Aunt Shirley said.

They all turned to her in amazement.

"Ta, Aunt Shirley. I'm glad someone appreciates me."

"Remember the time I spilled blackberry jam all over the front of my new Christmas dress? I was so embarrassed," Maggie said.

"It took an age to scrub that out," Mum tutted. "And let's not forget when Tillie sneezed right into her teacup, sending hot tea splashing everywhere."

"You know, I always took these outings for granted. But with the war turning everything topsy-turvy, it's proper special to take time out to enjoy this time together. And I'm not just talking about the salmon sandwiches and Victoria sponges. We are luckier than most," Tillie said.

"Promise me that no matter what comes in the future, that we'll always do this – every year," Mum said. "And no jokes, Katie."

The girls nodded.

"Every year," said Aunt Shirley. "And thank you for always including me. You're bringing me out of my doldrums, one cup of tea at a time."

The waiter appeared with a laden trolley.

"Let's tuck in," cried Katie. "I'm starving."

***

Through all the hopeful planning, the nightly bombing carried on unceasingly. Londoners scurried around in the early mornings, adjusting their schedules to get errands done and meals prepared before Moaning Minnie wailed again. Employers let out staff early so they could make it home in time to get to their shelters before the Luftwaffe began their nightly assaults. Some even learned to sleep during the cold nights below-ground.

The city somehow survived being pummelled. Houses, flats, buildings, monuments, churches, schools – nothing was spared in the onslaught. Fires smouldered as new ones exploded nearby. Streets were rendered unrecognizable with the damage and rubble. More and more people were killed, injured, and left homeless.

Yet, an indefinable Blitz spirit abounded. People gritted their teeth, went bleary-eyed to work and carried on. It was unthinkable that England would collapse and surrender.

Churchill's stirring words after the Dunkirk rescue swirled in their heads:

"We shall go on to the end, we shall fight in France, we shall fight on the seas and oceans, we shall fight with growing confidence and growing strength in the air, we shall defend our Island, whatever the cost may be, we shall fight on the beaches, we shall fight on the landing grounds, we shall fight in the fields and in the streets, we shall fight in the hills; we shall never surrender."

"An orange? But how?" Katie stared at it as if it were a lump of gold.

"Dear Faye." Mum smiled from ear to ear as the girls opened their stockings. "She sent us a parcel with a goose, eggs, and some other bits and bobs including oranges. She said it came from her brother's farm in Shropshire, but I don't know how she managed the oranges."

"I don't care, it's so sweet. Mmm," Katie had already peeled hers and was stuffing the sections into her mouth.

"A goose?" Tillie said. "How marvellous. We'll have to get it in the oven straightaway. How kind of her."

"Let's open our gifts first," Mum said, handing round paper-wrapped packages.

Although the prices were eye-watering, presents were still be had in the London shops. Mum had bought pretty blouses for the girls, and knitted a new hat and gloves for Walter. Bits of costume jewelry and makeup were shared between the girls. Shop candy satisfied everyone's craving for sweets.

"Mum, we made something for you." Maggie brought in a large package.

"Whatever in the world?" Mum asked as she tore off the string, and carefully unfolded the paper. "Why, it's an album.

Katie sat on the floor next to Mum's chair.

"It's a family album. We've taken some of the best photographs and placed them together. And see, here are some of Kenny's drawings from when he was little." Katie pointed.

"We sorted through the cartons and tins of photographs to find the best ones." Maggie smiled. *I hope this flattens the worry lines between Mum's eyebrows – even for a few minutes. She's so desperately worried about Kenny.*

Mum was speechless as she flipped the pages. There was Kenny in a sailor suit – how apt. And with some school mates. And one of the family at Brighton before the war.

"I don't know what to say," Mum said, a catch in her voice. "It's so special and just what I needed. Thank you, girls." She wiped away a tear, hoping no one had noticed.

"Happy Christmas, Mum," they chorused.

"Right, well let's get on with the goose then before the day gets away from us."

The dinner was more splendid than anyone could have imagined. The government had increased the tea and sugar ration just for the Christmas week, and the family had taken full advantage. With Shirley's help, the goose was tender with crispy skin. The sprouts, cabbage and roasted potatoes with gravy rounded out the feast. Aunt Shirley had surprised them all with not just a mince pie, but apple as well. Mr. and Mrs. Redwood had brought a bottle of brandy that they'd set aside and used it to light Faye's plum pudding into a marvellous flaming spectacle.

Each one around the table pushed away their own sad thoughts of those gone or far away, taking joy in Christmas, and couldn't help but be hopeful for 1941.

It was rather stilted having the Redwoods there – still grieving their only son. They left soon after the pudding, full of thanks, yet downcast. Even Christmas couldn't bring a light into their eyes.

"Let's take our tea and brandy to the drawing room for the King's speech." Mum stood from the table. "We'll clear away later."

"And the apple pie," Katie added, picking up the dish.

Pops had allowed a small fire in the drawing room for the occasion, which cheered the room immeasurably.

They sat on couches and chairs, replete and eager to hear His Majesty, King George VI's message:

"In days of peace, the feast of Christmas is a time when we all gather together in our homes, young and old, to enjoy the happy festivity and good will which the Christmas message brings...

War brings, among other sorrows, the sadness of separation. There are many in the Forces away from their homes today because they must stand ready and alert to resist the invader should he dare to come or because they are guarding the dark seas...

To the older people here and throughout the world I would say – in the last Great War, the flower of our youth was destroyed, and the rest of the people saw but little of the battle. This time we are all in the front line and the danger together, and I know that the older among us are proud that it should be so.

Remember this. If war brings its separations, it brings new unity also, the unity which comes from common perils and common sufferings willingly shared...

Time and again during these last few months I have seen for myself the battered towns and cities of England, and I have seen the British people facing their ordeal... On every side, I have seen a new and splendid spirit of good fellowship springing up in adversity, a real desire to share burdens and resources alike.

Then, when Christmas Days are happy again, and good will has come back to the world, we must hold fast to the spirit which binds us together now...

And now I wish you all a happy Christmas and a happier New Year...We do not underrate the dangers and difficulties which confront us still, but we take courage and comfort from the successes which our fighting men and their Allies have won at heavy odds by land and air and sea.

The future will be hard, but our feet are planted on the path of victory, and with the help of God we shall make our way to justice and to peace."

"Quite a stirring message," Pops declared.

"Indeed," Thomas said.

The women were lost in their thoughts.

"Thomas, shall we take our brandy to the library for a Christmas cigar? I have a pair put away. There's a matter I'd like to discuss with you."

Maggie smiled at her father.

Chapter Four

SLEET AND SNOW

1941 – Katie

"Katie, is that you?"

Katie turned, parcels in hand, towards the voice. A young man with a pleasant smile limped towards her. She racked her brain to place him.

"It is you. How jolly to run into you again." He pumped her hand.

"I'm sorry, but I don't remember you." Katie smiled politely.

"Where are my manners? I'm sorry. I'm Sebastian Cole. I was a mate of your cousin, Geoffrey."

Realization dawned.

"Of course. You are the young BEF soldier from Dunkirk. You came to call on my aunt and uncle. How nice to see you." He'd been so kind to visit Aunt Shirley after Geoffrey had been killed. He had shared touching stories of Geoffrey's gallantry as the soldiers had marched towards the coast.

Shoppers bustled all around them. A light snow fell, making it feel Christmassy. But it was bloody cold outside of Selfridge's. She shivered.

"Are you busy at the moment, Katie? Would you have time to spare for a cup of tea?"

She considered. He was a nice enough looking young man. Sandy hair, warm grey eyes and a friendly smile. *Why not?*

"I daresay it would be lovely to get in out of the cold. I've been searching for gifts for my family. But what's left in the stores is outrageously expensive. I'm afraid I haven't gotten too far this morning."

78

"Brilliant," he replied. "Shall we just nip in here? They have a lovely tea room."

In no time, they'd hurried through and been seated at an elegant table. After shaking off their coats and hats, they ordered tea and madeleines.

"Are you quite certain you don't want lunch?" Sebastian asked, placing his serviette in his lap.

"Yes, thank you. My father has given me the morning off to visit the shops, so I'm already on borrowed time. I've a sarnie back at the office. This is just the thing to keep me going."

A waiter dropped off a pot of tea and freshly-baked biscuits.

"What luck to see you again, Katie. How have you been getting on since I saw you last?" He blew on the hot tea and took a sip.

"Pretty well – or as well as one can get on in a war. Thoroughly glad that the Blitz is over, but rationing is dull as ditch water. As you well know. What have they got you doing now that you've recovered from your injury?"

"I'm with the Seventy-Ninth Light Anti-Aircraft Battery at Walton-on-Thames. It's been rather quiet of late. I'm on a forty-eight-hour leave, at the moment. After my shopping, I'm off to see my mum and dad for the day. And you? Doing your bit for Britain?"

"Anti-aircraft? My sister Maggie just joined and is stationed some-where in London. Perhaps you know her?" Katie neatly avoided the question of service. She'd been putting it off for ever so long.

"Afraid not. Ours is a men-only battery. But I've heard wonderful things about these mixed ack-ack units. The women are remarkably effi-cient and so calm under pressure."

"That sounds like our Maggie. And to answer your other question, I'm joining up with the WRENs in the new year. I'd rather choose my own branch of service than be called up as a cook or orderly." She cupped her hands around the warm teacup and sipped it slowly.

"That sounds splendid. I wonder where they will post you." He cer-tainly seemed interested in her.

"I expect something administrative, given my experience. I've been at Pops' firm since I left school. Probably a clerk or answering phones."

He nodded.

"Why didn't you ever ring me after we met?" Katie asked. "You seemed to drop off the face of the earth – or London rather – after your visit."

He shifted in his seat.

"I wasn't sure what to say, if I'm honest. I thought you were ever so pretty, but I knew your family was grieving. I presumed you were just being polite when you gave me your telephone number. And then the Blitz happened. After that, it just seemed like too much time had passed."

"I understand. But it would have been nice to keep in touch. My aunt will be chuffed to know you are in London and getting on so well." And alive, is what she really meant. But no one would say that aloud – not these days.

"I don't suppose you'd ever consider coming out with me for supper, would you? Make up for lost time?"

Katie chewed a biscuit, thinking. *He is a nice chap. I'm young and unattached. It might be fun to go out for a lark. Heaven knows, I don't have much else better to do. This war was dead boring. Besides, I'll be called up in a few weeks and off to training somewhere straightaway.*

"That sounds lovely, Sebastian. But let's do it after Christmas. The run up to the big day is awfully busy." She checked her watch and sat up straighter. "I'd best be off. Pops won't take kindly to me showing up late." She stood and slid on her coat and hat.

"Thank you ever so much for the tea. It was just what I needed. I was feeling a bit forlorn when you found me."

He stood as well, but was too late to pull out her chair.

"My pleasure, Katie. I still have your number. That's for your office?"

"Yes, we don't have a telephone at home. Pops refuses to move with the modern times." She held out her hand. "Happy Christmas."

"Happy Christmas and I'll ring you soon. Smashing to see you again. Please give my best to your aunt and uncle."

Katie collected her parcels and turned. Giving him a backwards smile, she strode out of the tearoom. *That was an agreeable break on a cold day. And a friendly supper won't go amiss. He's rather nice.*

***

80

"This whole Christmas business is hopeless without Faye," Alice sighed. "She made it all look so easy, but the idea of putting on Christmas dinner all on my own is rather daunting. We won't be getting the boost of a surprise parcel with a goose, eggs, and plum pudding this year."

Tillie turned from the sink, tea towel in hand.

"We'll manage just fine, Mum. And you're not on your own. I'm here, and Katie. And we have young Hannah to help. She's a brilliant baker and has offered to take on the plum pudding." She paused. "And Aunt Shirley." They locked eyes. Aunt Shirley hadn't been the same after losing her only son, Geoffrey. It had been over a year now, and she was slowly coming back to herself, but she'd never be the cheery aunt that she'd been before. "She was trumps last year. She's come on loads since then."

"My poor sister. What life has thrown at her. Losing Geoffrey, and then being bombed out of her house. She's had far too much to cope with. But I suppose war isn't fair, is it, luv? Entire families have been destroyed, left homeless, and no one is immune. It's so random." Mum felt the teapot cool to the touch. "Can you stick on the kettle? It's a frosty day."

Tillie nodded.

"At least they were able to rent a house just down the street. That was a lucky thing. Now she's even closer to us. And you are so right about the chanciness of it all. You can be walking along the street when a bomb drops. The person on the other side is blown to bits, and you are safe. Just dreadful." Tillie was remarkably matter-of-fact. "I sure hope Hitler doesn't decide to start blitzing us again. Christmas in that frigid shelter doesn't appeal in the slightest."

The Blitz had ended earlier in May this year. During a full moon and low tide, the Germans sent the largest force yet assembled to raid London. 571 German bombers dropped 711 tons of high explosive bombs and 86,173 incendiaries. This attack would go down as the biggest and last major raid on London during the Blitz. By the end of the night, over 1,400 were killed. Including the injured, the casualty number climbed to over 3,000 people. Many local landmarks were heavily damaged, including the Law Courts, the Tower of London, and the Royal Mint. Not even Westminster Hall and the House of Commons were left untouched — both sustaining devastation and ruin. Shaking London to its core, this raid almost pushed them over the edge. But the Blitz spirit that had prevailed amongst fifty-seven nights of consecutive bombing held fast. It seemed that it would be the last major bomber attack against London – for now – as Hitler turned his attention to the Soviet Union.

In the nine months of the Blitz, 43,500 civilians were killed. Besides London, other major cities were blasted mercilessly, including Liverpool, Birmingham, and Bristol. Most notably, Coventry was hit hard. In November 1940, German bombers dropped 503 tons of high explosives and 30,000 incendiary bombs on the city. 568 people were killed and 850 seriously injured. The medieval Cathedral was flattened. A large percentage of the city's houses and businesses were destroyed. It affected virtually every citizen of the small city.

Londoners survived the onslaught with little sleep and daily hindrances as they resolutely tried to carry on as normal. Many spent the nights in Anderson shelters or underground in the tubes. Emergency workers toiled through the night to put out fires, restore burst water pipes and electrical lines. and clear the streets of debris. Rescue workers faced the grim task of identifying the dead buried under piles of rubble, glass, and brick.

Each morning, bleary-eyed citizens awoke to survey the new damage, praying they wouldn't be homeless. But many were. Muddled and bemused, they stumbled to rest centres, many with only the clothes on their back, as the city did their best to rehome them and restore their identity and ration cards.

It had been a grim period for them all, but a fierce determination to overcome these nightly onslaughts and daily disruptions prevailed. Londoners were united in a common goal – to defeat the enemy, no matter what. Businesses opened with signs *Business as Usual* – despite having had their windows blasted out and almost no stock. People suffered long delays and detours to make it to work, as buses and other transport were delayed, redirected, or cancelled, and roads remained damaged or impassable.

Finally, it was over and residents were able to get back to some semblance of normal. But the prolonged strain took its toll. Nerves frayed, people snapped, and many evacuated the city, hoping for peace in the country. And still the war waged on.

"Do you reckon getting Christmas sorted might be just the thing for her? She used to love all the planning and cooking. Last year she came up aces with a couple of pies, remember?" Tillie hated to see her aunt as a ghost of her former self.

The kettle whistled and Mum rose to fetch it. Tillie waved her to sit back down.

"I suppose you're right. I don't want to push her, though. Maybe we should keep things simpler this year. Without Maggie and Kenny here…" Mum looked out the window.

Kenny had been reported Missing in Action earlier in the year when his ship, *HMS Dainty*, had been sunk. Most of the crew had been lost in the blast and resulting fire, but the entire family held onto a ray of hope that one day he'd be found alive. Not a word had been heard since, and Mum worried for him constantly.

Tillie sat down and refilled the teapot. She put a hand on her mother's.

"He may yet be safe. No news is good news – in this case."

"Do you think he might be found and come home to us for Christmas?" Mum's eyes looked impossibly hopeful.

"Maybe," Tillie said. "But let's not pin our dreams on that, shall we? Let's try to make it as festive as we can for Aunt Shirley and for Hannah, too."

"I expect you're right," Mum's face fell. "Let's get on with the dinner planning. Now, how many will we be on Christmas Day?"

***

"It looks ter be a slow night again, Tillie." Ernie sat back on the hard chair. "Not that I miss ter Blitz, mind, but these nights are bloomin' long."

Tillie looked up from an old magazine.

"Too right. It's just gone ten o'clock, and we're here for hours yet." She yawned. "What are your plans for Christmas?"

"Me missus will 'ave a dinner wiv our girls. Yer know our Trudy is expectin' agin?"

Ernie was a retired London cabbie. Too old for the callup, he was invaluable as an ambulance partner. No-nonsense and reliable, they had become mates since driving together in the Blitz.

"That's lovely. Congratulations. She has two boys, if I'm not mistaken..."

The telephone rang in the office. Tillie stood and donned her tin ambulance hat. The next chit would be theirs.

"Foster, Kingston," bellowed Jasper. "Building fire on Copper's Row. At least four injured."

"That's near the Tower of London." Ernie picked up his heavy coat. His knowledge of the streets was second to none.

"Righto." Tillie was almost out the door already. "Oh, bollocks. It's raining." She stopped mid-stride as the icy sleet mixed with heavy rain hit them in the face.

"Let's get on, Tils. Maybe it will put out the fire by the time we get there."

Tillie climbed in the driver's seat, and they took off. Despite the slow speed limit they were forced to follow, they got to the site in a quarter of an hour. Ernie had been right – the harsh rain had helped the firemen do their work.

Pulling up, Tillie shut off the engine, and the pair jumped out and headed for the cluster of people at the side of the building.

"Hello there. A filthy night, ain't it?" Ernie greeted the firemen who were leading out two walking wounded.

"Ain't it just," a fireman replied in the dark. "There's two more in the back."

"I'll see to them, Ernie. You take these two. If I need the stretcher, I'll call for you."

Hearing his grunt, Tillie sped as fast she could amongst the muck, ashes, and piles of twisted metal and glass. Pointing her torch down, she could barely see a foot ahead of her.

"Ambulance," she shouted. "We're here to help."

"Over here," a man's voice cried. Tillie passed the remains of a crushed outbuilding towards the voice.

Spying two men lying on the ground, she knelt to the one calling out.

"I'm here, sir. Can you tell me what's happened? Where are you hurt?"

"Me arm, me arm. I can't move it. Please 'elp me, miss."

Tillie performed a quick examination.

"I believe it may be broken, sir. Once I determine the extent of this other man's injuries, we'll get you smartly to the hospital for a proper look-see and cast. You may get out of the washing up for Christmas," she added. Cheering up the patients as they worked on them was part of the job. It helped to deal with the shock.

"Do you know this man? Sir? Sir?" She moved to the other bloke lying still as sheets of ice and snow poured on him. No response.

Feeling a slow but steady pulse, she was momentarily relieved. Keeping up a constant patter with the other patient, she checked for broken bones and bleeding. She found none.

"Do you know what happened to this man, sir? Did he fall or was he hit by something?" She felt a large bump on his head.

"I think I saw a beam crash on him as we were trying to escape. The firemen carried him out."

"Alright. I'm going to need the stretcher for him. I'm calling my partner. Ernie. Ernie!" But the sound didn't carry with the wind whipping round and the rain teeming every which way.

"Sir, I'm going to have to find my partner. I can take you with me if you think you can walk, or you can stay here till we both come back."

"I'll stay with Rodney," he replied. "You won't be long, will you, miss?"

"I'll be back in a jiffy, sir. And thank you. It's gallant of you."

Running back down the side of the building, she herself started shivering. *Hold it together Tillie. Those men are counting on you.*

Keeping her torch pointed low, she stepped over mortar and glass, trying to keep her bearings. Wasn't the damaged shed around here somewhere?

Suddenly she stopped dead in her tracks. In front of her was an enormous crater. Flashing her light around, panic clutched at her stomach. Oh no. An unexploded bomb. It had to be. Remembering her training, she stayed rooted to the spot. She didn't want to take a step nearer and blow herself and everyone round her to kingdom come. She fought the hysterical urge to scream. *Stay calm, girl.*

"Tillie, where are yer? Yer've been an awful long time," Ernie's voice called out.

"Ernie, stop. I think there might be a UXB here," she said, voice quavering.

He flashed a light on her face. Her eyes were wide, she was white as a sheet. Rain slashed all around them.

"Bloody hell. Don't move, Tillie. I'll fetch ter firemen."

Within seconds, three men came sloshing through the muck and rain towards her.

"Miss, stay still. I'm going to get you out of there."

"I'm not going anywhere, don't worry," she said, teeth chattering.

"Here's what we are going to do, miss. On my say-so, you'll fall straight backwards. Don't move an inch in any other direction. I'll catch you, don't fret. Just be sure to fall towards me and my voice. Backwards," he emphasized. "Then I'll drag you to safety. Do you understand?"

Tillie nodded, but realized they couldn't see her. She was frozen to the spot. Could she do as he asked?

"Yes," she said. *Please don't let me die today. Please don't let me die today. I'm meant to be married in May.*

"Alright. On three. Just fall backwards. One, two, three."

With a mighty heave, Tillie threw herself backwards as far as possible. The fireman's strong arms caught her and pulled her a few feet back. Covered in a mucky mess of dust and rain, she got shakily to her feet, her entire body shaking.

"Thank you ever so much. I was awfully frightened there."

"The bomb must have landed near that disused shed. We'll get the bomb squad here as quick as we can. But let's get you warmed up. You've had a terrible shock."

"But there are two injured men back there," she protested.

"Tillie, another ambulance 'as come and taken o'er. A cup 'o tea is wot yer need. Ter WVS canteen lorry jus' pulled up. Let's go." Ernie took her by the arm and walked them both slowly to the street. Oh, how she wished Maggie were still a volunteer and would hug and greet her with a warm mug of tea. But her twin was miles away on the ack-ack site, likely stuck out in the icy rain just as she was.

"Are yer alright, Tils?" Ernie was shaken by the events of the evening himself. It had been a near thing.

"I think so, Ernie. But I'll be glad to get out of these wet things."

After a restoring cuppa, the pair reported back to the station, where

86

Tillie was able to towel off and warm up, albeit her teeth still chattered.

"You're off duty for the night – both of you. Good work – those UXBs are all over the city. Lingering gifts from the Luftwaffe." Jasper's voice was gruff but he was relieved they were both safe. They'd lost too many staff during the Blitz.

Tillie took the tube home, feeling exhausted and weak. *I must look a fright, with my soggy hair and no makeup.* She hadn't bother to repair her lippie before leaving the station. *At this point, I don't even care. I just want my bed and hot water bottle.*

Arriving home, she almost wept with relief that the family was already in bed. Time enough tomorrow for explanations. Mum didn't need anything else to lose sleep over.

***

"Darling, what a fright that must have been," Mum said as her knitting needles clicked. "Are you sure you're alright?"

"Right as rain, but rather tired," Tillie replied, huddling into her cardigan.

"Rain, ha ha. Very funny." Katie sat on the morning room floor, listening raptly to her sister's recounting of the previous night's harrowing tale. "You still look chilled to the bone."

Tillie wiped her nose.

"You are lucky, indeed. I don't know how we'll top that for Christmas excitement."

Mum glared at her youngest daughter.

"That's enough." She patted Tillie's hand.

Katie's face fell. *What is wrong with you, you daft mare? Why don't you ever think before you speak?*

"I'm glad you're not on shift today, dear. I've a mind to tuck you back into bed for the day. You look rather done in."

"It's tempting, Mum. But I'm meant to go to the shops with Trevor's mum. She's asked for my help in choosing a gift for him. And she wants to talk about the wedding. Planning, she said."

"Surely that can wait for another day, can't it?" Katie sat next to her sister and gave her a squeeze. *Poor Tils, I need to look after her the way she has always watched out for me.*

"Maybe I'll just have a bit of a lie down this morning and still meet up with her this afternoon." Tillie was feeling the aftermath of the shock and a morning in bed might be just the thing.

"Just so," Mum replied, standing. "I'll bring you some cocoa and a biscuit or two."

"I'll try to find you a magazine that we haven't read umpteen times." Katie also rose. "Let's get a move on, you."

Just then, the post dropped. They had all become accustomed to the thump that meant impending mail. As everyone in the house eagerly awaited news from afar, it was a race to see who could collect it the fastest. Today, Tillie didn't even try.

"A letter for you, luv," Katie waved it in the air. "From Trevor." *This should bring at least a ghost of a smile.*

Tillie's fatigue abruptly faded.

"Here, hand it over. And ta, Mum. Cocoa would be brilliant. Thanks to you, sis."

Tillie ran up the stairs to her room. Mum and Katie exchanged smiles.

"Dearest Tillie,

How are you getting on, my love? It seems an age since I've held you in my arms. Being posted on home soil is almost worse than afar. Within hours I could be by your side, yet I'm stuck here doing fire drills, training, and trying to keep busy.

Not that I'm whingeing, mind. Fewer aircraft fires to put out means less German planes are getting through and our RAF boys can stay put. I'm pleased to put my firefighting experience to use on the airfield now that London life has settled down. I find myself drawn to the engine yard, where the repairs are done. It's something I enjoy doing – tinkering with the aeroplane engines. Working with my hands is quite satisfying. Perhaps after the war, I might pursue it. Who knows?

I'm getting to be quite the champion when it comes to Pinochle. And you'll be shocked to hear that I've even taken up bridge on dreary nights. Perhaps you and I can team up against Micah and Maggie when this is all over. Imagine a pleasant night like that!

I hope you are keeping safe with the ambulance. The thought of you out on fiery, dangerous streets during air raids is more than distressing. The sooner you are Mrs Trevor Drummond and off the streets, the happier I'll be. I know you are careful, and it means the world to you doing your bit for the war effort. Let's hope now that the Americans are in with us, we'll finish this off soon. I can't wait to start our married life together – in more ways than one.

Please keep an eye on Mum over the holidays. She'll be glum that I'm not there, but I'm sure the Kingston family will keep her spirits up.

I'm so sorry that I can't get leave this Christmas. I'm hoping for at least a forty-eight hour pass sometime in January, but one never knows.

All my love, dearest Tillie. Write back soon. I love to receive your chatty letters. It brings your beautiful face closer to me.

Love,
Trev xx"

Tillie clutched the letter to her heart, and then felt a little foolish. Trev wasn't posted that far away and enemy attacks had lessened, hadn't they? He'd be safe. But oh, how I miss you, my dearest love. And how I wish my Mags was here to cheer me up.

***

"Fancy a cuppa at the mess, luv? It's bloody freezing in here."

Maggie snapped her book shut.

"Brilliant," she replied. "This hut never seems to warm up – despite the smoking stove. The coal supply is scanty at best."

Pip and Maggie pulled on their greatcoats and left the other off-duty girls to their knitting, chatting, and letter-writing.

Stepping out into the cold night, they pulled their collars close. It was bone-chillingly cold, but no rain or snow, thank goodness.

"How are you liking it so far, Kingston?" Pip asked as they dashed past more huts to the center of the battery station.

"More than I expected, to be sure," Maggie replied. "I was that shocked when they pulled me aside to work in special forces. I guess we are both not half-bad at maths."

"I'm pleased that you and I had the luck to be posted here together. It's so much better having a friendly face to go through all this marching, physical training, and studying with. And we've only been called out a few times – I'm that relieved, if I'm honest."

"It's funny, Pip. As glad as I am for that, I also want to give it a go. See if I can handle the predictor under pressure. All this waiting around is nerve-wracking."

They reached the mess tent, went in, and found an empty table. Good-natured male teasing greeted them, but they were well used to ignoring it. Women in former all-male territory took some getting used to.

They'd only recently been allowed into anti-aircraft roles in mixed batteries. The army needed able-bodied men in combat posts, and the experiment for women to operate the spotter and predictor equipment was working out even better than expected. They also manned the searchlights. The women were dedicated, hard-working and for the most part – learned fast.

Men still loaded and did the actual shooting of the large anti-aircraft guns. This was in line with the King's express command that no women serve in active combat zones. These were usually older men, or those who had been injured in the previous war and declared unfit to serve in this one. Most were supportive of the new female recruits, but there were always a few who groused about the good old days before women were seen in uniform.

"I'll get the tea in," Maggie offered. Pip nodded as she glanced around the room for eligible soldiers. Putting on her brightest smile, she batted her eyes at a red-haired prospect.

"On the prowl, I see," Maggie commented as she set two lukewarm cups of tea on the table.

"Always." Pip gave her a wink. Or was that intended for someone else? You never knew with Pip. She was young and impatient for life to begin. She found every opportunity to start things off herself.

She and Maggie were like chalk and cheese. Pip had dark curly hair, flashing green eyes, and a lust for life that Maggie only wished she had. The men flocked to Pip, and she basked in every minute of it.

Maggie was blonde with brown eyes – glamorous yes – but shy on the inside. She was just starting to realize how much she had leaned on Tillie to carry them through social situations their entire lives. Now that she was on her own, she missed her sister dreadfully, but was slowly learning to spread her wings.

This friendship with Pip was a great example. Outside of the Women's Auxiliary Territorial Service, she would likely never have met Pip. As a London shop girl, Pip might as well have lived on the other side of the world. The oldest of six, she helped her frazzled mum keep her brothers and sisters in line, as well as doing the bulk of the cooking and cleaning. She actually found the army rather calming after her hectic life.

"Are those rock buns?" Pip squealed.

"Yes – with reconstituted egg and mock cream – but rock buns nonetheless. It's our lucky night."

They sunk their teeth into the unexpected treat. And then, the air raid siren blared.

"Dammit," cried Pip, shoving the entire bun in her mouth as she rose from the table.

"Oh, Pip. We're on. I think my heart just dropped to my stomach." Maggie stuffed her bun into her pocket and shoved her cap on her head.

Within seconds, they were at the gun battery site, along with the rest of the on-call squad.

"And it's started drizzling. Brilliant," moaned one of the men.

The CO turned to him.

"No talking. You know that."

Maggie paid them no mind. She focused all her attention on her predictor machine, just waiting for the spotter to identify and call out the incoming bomber, its location, and projected path.

The unit sat there for thirty minutes with a steady drizzle seeping through even the stoutest greatcoats. Maggie rubbed her gloved hands together to restore warmth. Stamping her boots on the ground, she tried to get her circulation moving – to no avail. She put her mind to blocking out the cold. Micah. She would think of Micah.

She hadn't heard from him in months. Since Hannah had made her escape from France, bringing with her a cherished letter from Micah, not a word had come from the occupied territory. Word about how Jews were being treated were alarming. *Where are you, my love? Are you safe? Please write to me. I'm sick with fear.*

Searchlights criss-crossed the night, scanning the sky for enemy bombers and fighters.

"Come on, you dirty hun. Where are you?" A muttered voice came from the guns.

Pip smothered a giggle.

After another soggy quarter of an hour, the all-clear sounded.

"Thank bloody hell." "Bugger an all." "I'm chilled to the bone."

The crew dispersed as quickly as they'd gathered.

"You were a million miles away, luv," Pip said as they trudged back to the mess. "Were you woolgathering whilst on duty?"

"Just trying to keep my mind off the cold is all. I'm that glad that the all-clear sounded before we saw any action. I doubt my frozen fingers could have worked the predictor properly."

Pip opened the door, and the girls welcomed the warm blast of air.

"Thinking of a certain young man in France?" Pip got the tea this time.

"I haven't heard from him in so long. Do you think he's still alive?" Maggie huddled over the table.

"Hard to know, luv." Pip shrugged. "But chances are you would have heard something by now if he wasn't. Chin up. I'm sure he'll write soon. And with the Americans in with us now…"

"—the war will be over in no time," Maggie finished with a wan smile. She gulped her tea and polished off the somewhat-squashed rock bun. "I hope you are right. I can't take this much longer." Pushing back her chair, she rose. "I'm for bed. I need to get into some dry clothes – everything in my kit, if need be. Will this cold and rain ever stop?" She left abruptly.

Pip shook her head. She'd never seen her chum so upset. Leaving her own half-drunk mug of tea, she hurried after Maggie. She hoped she hadn't upset her with her off-hand comment. *Damn my sharp tongue. I don't want to lose my dear mate.* All round, it had been a nasty evening.

A gentle knock at the door.

"May I come in, Hannah?" Alice popped her head round the door.

"Of course, Aunt Alice." Hannah sat up straight. "I've just been doing my homework."

"I've brought you a cup of cocoa, dear. And a biscuit." The poor dear was so thin.

"Thank you, Aunt Alice." Hannah patted Robbie the cat, who sat contentedly in her lap.

Alice put down the tray and stepped back.

Hannah looked up at her.

"Is there anything else? Do you need help in the kitchen?"

Hannah was nothing if not helpful. Almost too much so. She acted more like a grown woman than a girl of thirteen. An old soul. Too many troubles for a young girl.

"I just wanted to see how you are getting on? I know it must seem strange to you in a new house with relative strangers."

"You've made me most welcome, Aunt Alice. Everyone has. Especially Robbie."

"He's proper taken with you, luv. Maggie will be so pleased that you're fast mates." Alice hovered by the door.

Hannah rubbed Robbie under his chin. He purred contentedly.

"You must miss your parents dreadfully," Alice started. *My heavens, I'm making a mash of this.*

"I do. And Micah as well. He looked after me with so much care when we escaped to the French coast. Even when we had to sleep in barns or once under a tree, he sat up with me all night to protect me."

Thomas had worked with his contacts behind the scenes to organize an escape route for the young girl back to England. Trapped in Toulouse in the south of France, it had been down to Micah to safely transport his sister to the coast and boat rendezvous to take her across the channel. It had taken weeks of planning, and several false starts, but she'd finally arrived on British soil, where Thomas had been waiting to collect her.

It must have been a terrible wrench to leave her parents and brother, but she was safe in England, and the Kingstons were delighted to have her – despite the ghastly circumstances.

"Your brother is a fine young man. Surely, they will all be able to join us soon."

"Do you really think so?" Life jumped into Hannah's eyes.

"We must believe it, dear," Alice said firmly. *Please let it be so.* "Just one more thing. We are having our annual girls' Christmas tea at Claridge's. We'd love you to join us. We're hoping to organize it so that Maggie can get the afternoon off from the ack-ack battery, since she can't be here for Christmas."

Hannah clapped her hands.

"That would be lovely, Aunt Alice. I would love to see Maggie. She's been ever so kind to me."

"Splendid, dear. And please – don't feel you need to hide up here to do your homework. These bedrooms are freezing. There's plenty of room downstairs in the morning room or library. Albeit the kitchen is the toastiest place in the house."

"Thank you, Aunt Alice. I'll be down in a little while. And ta for the cocoa."

"You're welcome, dear." Alice closed the door gently. *That girl needs more than a few extra pounds. She needs cheering as well. We must make this Christmas extra special for her.*

***

"Katie, don't nick all the sweets. Some of us fancy a piece of Battenberg cake or a macaron." Tillie handed her sister a delicate cucumber sandwich.

"It's only once a year, Tils. These desserts are heavenly." She ignored the sandwich and sunk her teeth into a soft macaron. *This is delectable.*

"I've never eaten anything like this." Hannah's eyes widened.

"Have another, dear." Alice motioned towards the three-tier tray. "There are loads to choose from. The hot scones with clotted cream are delicious."

"And jams," added Katie. "Blackberry or strawberry. Mum, can we come here every week?"

"Are you alright, luv? You're awfully quiet." All eyes turned towards Tillie.

"I am feeling a bit wobbly. With neither Trev or Maggie coming home for Christmas, I don't really know what to do with myself." To her mortification, her voice caught in her throat. *Don't cry, you silly girl.*

Mum gave her daughter a broad smile.

"Mum, what the...?" Katie was beyond confused. *What are you up to?*

"I can't do anything about Trev, but I have a little surprise for this afternoon."

Tillie sat up and looked around the elegant dining room.

"Mum, what do you have up your sleeve?"

She saw a blur of khaki in the entrance doorway.

"Mags!" She sprung to her feet and started for the door. But Maggie got to her first and the two embraced.

"Come, sit. You clever thing. You kept this from me." Tillie linked arms with her twin and steered her to the table.

"Maggie, I'd almost given up on you. Were the trains awful?" Mum kissed her on the cheek.

Maggie greeted them all – Katie, Hannah, and Aunt Shirley.

"Sorry, everyone. I've only a four-hour pass, and I've wasted near half of it getting here. There was a stoppage on the line, but no matter. I'm here now." She sunk to her chair and removed her cap.

"Maggie, you look ever so smart in your ATS uniform. I'm proper impressed." Hannah's eyes were glued to Maggie.

"Thank you, luv. How are you getting on? Are you getting my letters?"

"Yes, and thank you. They mean the world to me."

"How's the training? And eat, darling." Katie encouraged her. *How splendid – all the Kingston girls together at Christmas.*

"Pretty well. Rather boring, if I'm honest. We had a false alarm the other night."

"Oh, my heavens." Mum exclaimed before she could catch herself. She already had too many images in her head of her daughter on a live gun site.

"It was fine, Mum," Maggie said with a mouthful of sandwich. "But I don't want to talk about that. I want to hear wedding news. How is the planning going?" She deftly turned the subject away to her twin.

Tillie herself could hardly believe she'd be a married woman in a matter of months. After several tentative dates, Tillie had allowed herself to believe in love again. She admired Trev's dedication to firefighting, his strength, and his kindness for others. And like so many British young people, they didn't want to wait. Each tomorrow was so uncertain that they wanted to seize happiness with both hands today. Maggie had finally come around after initially disapproving of their courtship and was a firm supporter of her future brother-in-law. He made Tillie happy and that was all that mattered.

"Well, not too far along yet. I'm still fussing about what to wear. It's hopeless to think of buying one. We don't have near enough coupons. And I don't want to get married in a day dress, but I suppose I will if I must." She frowned.

"Trev's mum is an excellent seamstress. Perhaps she could run up something for you?" Maggie offered.

"I suppose," Tillie was dubious. "On a brighter note, we'll have the wedding cake from Lyons. Even former employees are given a free wedding cake."

"That's smashing. And will it be a church wedding?" Maggie asked.

"As long as St. Cuthbert's doesn't get bombed," Tillie joked. "It will be small of course, with so many men away and people evacuated. I know it's too soon for you to put in for leave, but you must be my maid of honour."

Maggie nodded and patted her sister's hand.

"Hey, what about me?" Katie asked, pretending a pout. *I hope I won't be left out.*

"You and Hannah will both be bridesmaids, silly. I don't know what we'll do about dresses yet, but there's still bags of time."

"You've got me thinking that we should invite Isla for Christmas dinner, luv. I hate to think of her on her own with Trevor on base." Mum turned to Tillie.

"That's a splendid idea, Mum. She's a tremendous cook, so perhaps we can prevail on her to bring a dish or two." Tillie giggled.

"I see what you're doing, miss," Mum said, raising an eyebrow.

"Righto, I agree wholeheartedly – smashing idea." Katie rubbed her hands together. "Could she sort a Christmas cake?" They all laughed.

And so the girls chattered. *It almost feels like a pre-war Christmas*, Alice thought. *And all my girls are here. For now.* She put everything else out of her mind as another pot of tea arrived.

***

"Is it time yet?" Tillie looked to her father. "I wonder what he'll have to say."

"Almost. Let's turn on the wireless."

Prime Minister Churchill had made a secret trip to the United States to discuss strategy after the Americans had declared war on Japan and Germany following the horrid Pearl Harbour attack. However, news of the visit had leaked out and the nation waited in anticipation for his Christmas Eve broadcast from the White House in Washington.

The family gathered around the wireless, waiting for the noted orator to speak:

"I spend this anniversary and festival far from my country, far from my family, yet I cannot truthfully say that I feel far from home… I cannot feel myself a stranger here in the center and at the summit of the United States. I feel a sense of unity and fraternal association which, added to the kindliness of your welcome, convinces me that I have a right to sit at your fireside and share your Christmas joys...

Here, then, for one night only, each home throughout the English-speaking world should be a brightly-lighted island of happiness and peace…

Let the children have their night of fun and laughter. Let the gifts of Father Christmas delight their play. Let us grown-ups share to the full in their unstinted pleasures before we turn again to the stern task and the formidable years that lie before us, resolved that, by our sacrifice and daring, these same children shall not be robbed of their inheritance or denied their right to live in a free and decent world.

And so, in God's mercy, a happy Christmas to you all."

Katie turned off the wireless as the family looked at each other.

97

"Was that good?" she asked with a frown. "I was expecting something a little more uplifting."

"He's telling us that albeit the war is far from over, we should be heartened by our faithful friends in America and that we will eventually be victorious," Walter said in his halting voice.

"He's also saying that we should enjoy this Christmas, and let the children have joy, so that we can have many happy Christmases to come," Alice added, knitting needles clacking furiously. "It will be marvelous to have a youngster here tomorrow." She smiled at Hannah.

"Are you excited for Father Christmas?" Tillie teased. Hannah was a little old for dreams of a red-suited man coming down the chimney.

"I am," she replied with the ever-present Robbie in her lap.

"Not too early tomorrow, Katie," Mum said.

"But it's Christmas." Katie shook her dark curls. *It's down to me to keep up all the traditions that Kenny and Maggie would want.*

"And a happy Christmas to you, darling," Tillie laughed.

*****

The gifts were even more modest than the year before. Mum had come up trumps by knitting everyone a jumper from pulled apart old cardies. The girls exchanged soaps and second-hand books. Tillie, Maggie, and Katie had somehow found some stationery and a new pen for Hannah, and she was moved almost to tears.

"I can't thank you enough. With paper so scarce, this is ever so precious."

"We knew you wanted to keep writing to your parents," Katie said quietly.

The family had been touched to receive knitted bookmarks from Hannah, with a little help from Alice.

"Mine is red. How brilliant." Tillie smiled.

"And mine is green. Thanks ever so much." Katie hugged the younger girl.

Maggie had sent some chocolate that she'd procured from who-knew-where, and had drawn sketches of the ack-ack-site for everyone.

"Save the paper," Mum said as she rose to start dinner preparations.

98

"What a feast," Walter professed a few hours later. "You've all done splendidly." He sat back, patting his stomach.

"And we'll have eggs for breakfast. Shirl, you and Thomas will be back?"

"Wouldn't miss it. I've put by a bit of bacon to add in." Shirley even smiled.

"Before Hannah's delicious-looking plum pudding, I'd like to propose a small toast." Katie stood with a small glass of wine in her hand. Alice glanced at her husband. *Be careful, darling.*

"Without getting maudlin, I'd like to drink a cheer for those who aren't with us. We are thinking about them – even if we pretend we're not. And to a bright 1942 – and to handsome Americans coming over." She laughed. "To those who aren't with us." She raised her glass.

"To Maggie," started Tillie.

"And dear Trevor." Isla Drummond held her glass high.

"To Kenny." Mum's lip quavered.

"And Geoffrey." Shirley held her sister's hand.

"To Papa and Mama." Hannah's little voice added.

"And Micah," Walter finished. "And to 1942."

They raised their glasses and drank in silence.

***

"Who is for a quick walk before the King's speech?" Katie asked after the plum pudding.

"I'll go." Hannah scrambled to her feet.

"Me too," Tillie echoed.

The elder Kingstons and Shirley and Thomas stayed behind to talk about the impact of America finally joining into the war.

Gathering once again, the family hoped King George VI would round out the day with a rousing speech:

"I am glad to think that millions of my people in all parts of the world are listening to me now. From my own home, with the Queen and my children beside me, I send to all a Christmas greeting…

Christmas is the festival at home, and it is right that we should remem-

ber those who this year must spend it away from home. I am thinking, as I speak, of the men who have come from afar, standing ready to defend the old homeland...

All these separations are part of the hard sacrifice which this war demands. It may well be that it will call for even greater sacrifices. If this is to be, let us face them cheerfully together...

In that spirit, we shall win the war, and in that same spirit we shall win for the world after the war a true and lasting peace. The greatness of any nation is in the spirit of its people. So it has always been since history began; so it shall be with us...

We must all, older and younger, resolve that having been entrusted with so great a cause, then, at whatever cost, God helping us, we will not falter or fail. Make yourselves ready... to offer your very best...

So, I bid you all be strong and of a good courage. Go forward into this coming year with a good heart. Lift up your hearts with thankfulness for deliverance from dangers in the past. Lift up your hearts in confident hope that strength will be given us to overcome whatever perils may lie ahead until the victory is won...

Never did heroism shine more brightly than it does now, nor fortitude, nor sacrifice, nor sympathy, nor neighbourly kindness, and with them – brightest of all stars – is our faith in God...

God bless you, everyone."

They all stood for *God Save the King.*

Chapter Five

CLOUDY WITH FOG

1942 – Tillie

The post dropped. Tillie and Hannah raced for it. Hannah won.

"It's for you." Hannah struggled to smile.

"I'm sorry, darling, that you've had no word from your parents. It must be dreadful." Tillie took the proffered letter and held onto Hannah's hand a few seconds longer.

Hannah nodded. Since the devastating news several months earlier that Micah and her parents had been captured in a Jewish roundup and detained in an exportation camp near Paris, Hannah had lurked around the front door daily, desperate for word from them – any word. According to Uncle Thomas, the conditions at Drancy were deplorable, and she fretted for the safety of them all, particularly her mother who had grown weak and sickly during their time in occupied France. Only the sliver of comfort that Grandfather had died naturally before being seized and treated to harsher living conditions gave the teenager any solace. She wrote letters to the camp, but heard nothing, so it was likely no post was allowed in or out of the deportation camp.

Trailing her hand on the banister, she slowly went up the stairs to her room. Tillie watched, helpless. What could she do for the poor girl? Hannah was holding up as best as could be expected, but this bloody war had gotten to a point where almost everyone was deathly worried about someone. Being brave and carrying on was getting grim.

Drifting to the drawing room, she was pleased to see it empty. It was chilly – Pops only allowed a fire at night to conserve coal, so she sunk to the sofa and pulled a knitted blanket over her shoulders.

Wrestling with feelings of guilt for Hannah against her own excitement to hear from her husband, she allowed herself a thrill to see his handwriting.

"Dearest Tillie,

How are you, my dear love? It is strange to be separated from you yet again at Christmas. Last year was cruel enough, but now that you are expecting our baby, it seems especially awful that we are not together making family memories. Particularly as I'm stationed here in England – you know where. Almost within arm's reach.

How are you coping with your ambulance work? We've talked about this before. I urge you stop soon. You like to keep busy, but I fear for you out with Ernie on dangerous calls in your condition. Please, Tils.

Anyroad, I have brilliant news. Although I can't be home for Christmas, I do have a twenty-four-hour pass. Could you come to me before Christmas? It's not a far train journey, and I've arranged a billet for you overnight. Please say you'll come?

Love, Trevor xx"

"Woo hoo," Tillie shouted to an empty room. *I'm off to Cambridge.* With a broad smile, she jumped up and ran to her room to pack.

***

"Kingston, why are you moping about? You haven't been yourself for weeks." Pip flopped onto Maggie's cot.

Maggie looked up from her tin of letters.

"I told you before. I'm worried about some friends in France. It's hard times under German occupation." Maggie inched a little further away.

"Is it your childhood mate? You have spilled bits about him from time to time. I get the sense he is rather special to you?" Pip persisted.

Pip Murley was Maggie's dear chum and fellow ack-ack gunner girl. They'd met during their original ATS sign-up when they'd both been pulled aside to test further for mathematical and analytical abilities. Both were surprised to pass through the mental and physical testing to become anti-aircraft operators. Sticking together through basic training and an early London posting, they were chuffed to be posted together at Exeter, near the Devon coast. Dark-haired with flashing eyes, Pip was bubbly and full of fun. Always on the lookout for eligible airmen or soldiers, the pair had become fast chums, and Pip had filled in the gaping hole Maggie felt from being separated from her twin.

Maggie admired Pip's outgoing nature which complemented her own innate shyness. Maggie tended to keep to herself, and had shared monosyllabic replies to personal queries.

"Ye-es," she said quietly. "Micah is an old family friend. We grew up together, and share a love of books and music." Maggie's eyes shimmered, thinking of her tall, serious young man. "We've been writing to each other."

"Micah." Pip pounced. "A name at last. Tell me more about this elusive Micah."

Maggie shifted uncomfortably.

"There's not much to tell. Our families lived near each other, so we spent holidays together growing up. He's a bit older than I am. His family owned a jewelry shop in London before – before the war." Maggie stumbled.

"And now? Is he serving overseas? You are that eager when the post comes in."

Maggie's face fell.

"No. If I'm honest, I'm not quite sure where he is. He and his family moved to Paris to help his grandfather with his business. After the occupation, they fled to Toulouse to work on his grandfather's small farm. His health failed and he succumbed several months ago." Maggie stood and went to her small dresser, opening the drawer and fussing with the already tidy contents. "I got a telegram from home a while back saying they had all been part of a roundup and taken to a transport camp outside of Paris. That's all I know." She turned to her friend; eyes clouded with unshed tears.

Pip gasped.

"How ghastly. So – they are Jewish?"

Maggie nodded.

"What will happen to them?" Pip asked.

"I don't know. Possibly they'll be sent to a work camp – somewhere. I'm desperately hoping that it's all some horrid mistake and they'll be released. Micah is British-born." Maggie turned away, wiping a tear.

"Oh, luv, how awful for you. And you've been keeping it to yourself all this time? I'm sure it's all just a huge muddle – with France being occupied by the Germans, it must be a frightful mess over there. It will be cleared up soon – surely." Pip spoke to Maggie's turned back.

Maggie turned and sat back on her cot. Finally talking about this after so long lessened the almost-constant knot in her stomach. Without a twin to talk to in order to ease her fears, fighting her swirling thoughts alone had made her feel frantic. Pip was a good mate.

"Yes, of course you're right," she said with a watery smile. "And thanks. That ache in my heart is a bit lighter for sharing with you."

Pip patted her hand.

"Right. Let's not borrow trouble. It will all be a misunderstanding, you'll see. Your Micah will soon be home and I'll get to meet this man who has captured the heart of Lance Bombardier Margaret Kingston."

Maggie smiled back but inside, she felt bleak.

***

By December 1942, the British people were well worn out with war and it's struggles. Although the Blitz was a distant memory, the war didn't seem to be ending anytime soon. Three years in, and with Japan now in the fray, the Allies were fighting on multiple fronts.

Earlier in the year, the alleged impregnable fortress of Singapore surrendered to Japan in just seven days. In what Winston Churchill describes as the 'worst disaster' and 'largest capitulation' in British history, around 80,000 Commonwealth troops were taken prisoners of war.

By mid-year, Germany's forces had invaded deep into Russia. In North Africa, the British Eighth Army had been forced all the way back to Egypt. Massive Canadian casualties had been sustained during a failed attempt to land by sea in Dieppe, France.

A massive win at El Alamein in November turned the tides for the Allies. After fierce fighting on both sides, General Montgomery ordered the final blows against Rommel's forces. The Axis army of Italy and Germany suffered a decisive defeat by the British Eighth Army.

In Britain, the church bells were rung for the first time since May 1940 to celebrate 'a glorious and decisive victory' as hailed by Churchill.

The landscape at home was changing. With mandatory conscription for women since December 1941, all unmarried women and all childless widows between the ages of 20 and 30 were eligible for the call-up. Serving in all branches of the military, and in vital munitions factory, nursing, and land army jobs, every available woman was needed to do her part.

Eyeing the Christmas season, Londoners felt hopeful about an eventual Allied victory, whilst living in grim day-to-day conditions. The shops were empty, and neither goose nor turkey could be found to bring joy to a Christmas table. Some families had joined together to form pig clubs and eagerly awaited their share for a roast pork dinner. Rationing was endured, but endlessly bemoaned. And it was foggy and cold.

***

"Should we even bother making a list for the shops? There's nothing to be had, in the event." Shirley sniffled with a cold and pulled her cardigan closer round her body.

Alice eyed her sister. She'd not regained any weight since Geoffrey's death and the long-term effects of rationing. Her red nose and dull eyes gave her a decided gloomy impression.

"We must, darling. It's only once a year, and it's important to try to make it special." Alice worried for her sister. "More tea?"

Shirley pushed her teacup towards her sister and nodded.

"What for? There's no wine or drink to be had, and we've had our names down at the butchers for weeks now. No sign of a turkey or goose, or even a chicken. There's naught to bake with – even if we knew how to properly make a pie or plum pudding."

"Don't be such a grump, luv. Something will turn up for Christmas dinner, and Isla has already offered to bake something. At least most of the family will be here – albeit Katie won't be here and Maggie only has a twenty-four- hour pass. Pull yourself together. If we don't lead the charge, everyone else will be glum."

"I suppose you're right. Pull out the list then. Where shall we start?" Shirley forced a tight smile.

"That's better, luv. Alright – so perhaps we forego a Christmas Eve do this year and focus on the twenty-fifth?" Alice held her pencil up.

"I like that. I don't think I'm up for hosting a drinks party."

"Right. On Christmas Day, Maggie won't be here till late morning at the earliest." Alice's voice caught. Neither Maggie or Katie would be here for Christmas morning. *When will life return to normal? Will it ever?*

"Sorry, luv," Shirley rallied a reassuring smile.

Alice shook her head. No sense being low-spirited.

"For dinner, it will be us, the men, Tillie, Hannah, and Isla. My, what a small number," she couldn't help herself, counting on her fingers. "Only eight." She sat back in her chair.

"Don't forget Kenny," Shirley added.

"My goodness, of course," Alice burst out. "How could I forget? We must make it lively for him – his first one back since his ordeal."

"How is he getting on? He seems to have put on some weight." Shirley slurped the last of her tea.

"Going from strength to strength. His nightmares are lessening, and he is getting back to his cheery self. But not quite the same." Alice sighed.

"He's not your little boy any longer, luv. He's a young man. That bouncy chap is growing up." Shirley rose to stick on the kettle for a fresh pot.

"I suppose you're right. He doesn't confide the way he used to – at least not in me. I expect I must get used to it. This war has driven young people into being adults far too soon." Alice shook her head.

"At least he's safe at home," Shirley said softly.

Alice immediately felt guilty. *What's wrong with me? My dear sister lost her only child, and here I am whingeing about my son not sharing confidences with me anymore.*

"Does it get any easier?" Alice placed her hand on her sister's.

"Some days, yes." Shirley shrugged. "Other days, it feels like I just heard the dreadful news. Christmas is especially hard. You know I still expect to see Geoffrey bounding in the door, asking for cocoa and biscuits." She sniffled.

Alice didn't know what to say. Damn that Hitler.

"He was a fine young man. I miss him too."

The whistling kettle pierced the silence. Shirley jumped up to take it off the hob.

"Thank you, luv. Now – about the tick list. I'm going to have a word with Charlie. He's always had a soft spot for me, and maybe I can coax a turkey or chicken out of him." Shirley forced a smile.

"That's the spirit." Alice brought the teapot to the counter.

It felt hollow to them both.

***

"What a long day. I didn't think I'd ever get off." Katie tossed her cap on her cot and fluffed her hair in front of the tiny communal mirror. "Am I late?"

Cecily straightened her uniform.

"Not at all. We've still got loads of time before the dance." She nudged Katie. "I need the mirror for my lipstick. How was watch?"

"At times fascinating, others tedious. The usual." Katie shrugged, rummaging in her small dresser drawer for a comb.

"Too right," Cecily pursed to apply her lippie. "But always exhausting."

Katie's WREN journey had been rather a whirlwind. After basic training, she'd been assigned as a postal censor up north. She loved the freedom of being away from home and the shadow of her sisters. However, the bloom had gone off the rose after weeks of reading letters and blacking out anything that could reveal the sender's location or any Allied movements.

At first, she'd enjoyed reading the letters from husbands, fathers, sons and boyfriends overseas. Some were cheery, others poignant, and only a few expressed the fear and terror they must have all been experiencing. She was more than a little uncomfortable reading vivid declarations of love and longing, even blushing at the occasional long-distance proposal.

It hurt her heart to have to scrutinize and rather spoil the letters with heavy black marks that sometimes made the meaning confusing. She could imagine a young wife eager for word of her husband trying to muddle through a marked-up letter to find words of comfort.

She did her best, and found she could get through a pile of post in no time, even deciphering the odd French or German word for amusement. Her superiors picked up on this, and when she remembered she'd learned rudimentary Morse code as a Girl Guide, she was swiftly removed from her position, vigorously tested, and declared fit for Special Forces as a wireless telegraphist – decoding incoming German messages. She'd taken pause signing the Official Secrets Act, knowing she could never speak of her work to anyone – not even a future husband.

Having passed through the grueling training, she was now stationed at Southwold Y Station in Sussex. The work was exacting and required intense concentration, but she felt much more fulfilled than she had as a censor. And she was meeting ever so many people at the busy station which held frequent dances, sporting events, and all manner of social activities.

"Right. I'm for a quick washup and change out of these lisle stockings into something a little prettier. I hope I have stockings that haven't laddered." Katie made for the wash basin.

"You can borrow a pair of mine," offered Cecily. "The Americans seem to have an endless supply."

"Where you're concerned." Katie laughed.

Cecily was tall, long-legged with curly red hair and dimples. She never lacked dance partners or sailors asking her out – albeit she only accepted officers' advances nowadays.

In no time, they'd freshened up, donned navy-blue greatcoats, and made their way onto packed lorries to the dance being put on by the Americans.

"What a squash." Katie surveyed the hall. Couples in blue and khaki swarmed the dance floor to Glenn Miller's *In the Mood*. The few tables on the perimeter were crowded with WRENs waiting to be asked to dance. "We'll never get a seat."

"Oh, yes we will."

Cecily spied a couple leaving a corner table, grabbed Katie's hand and snatched it before anyone else could.

"Smashing." Katie smiled at her chum. "Now let's see what – or should I say – who is on offer tonight." Before she could look around, a tall American with a big smile had asked Cecily to dance. Katie was soon on the floor herself, with a series of friendly seamen.

The girls lost their table, but as they were constantly being whirled around the floor, it didn't seem to matter.

"May I have this dance?"

Katie was trying to catch her breath when an officer came up and bowed to her. He was of average height with dark blond hair, blue eyes, and a dashing moustache.

She nodded and took his hand. Unlike many of the young servicemen, he was an excellent dancer, and didn't once tread on her toes. He held her close, and smelled of a lovely soap. She closed her eyes. This was much nicer than the sweaty men she'd been dancing with.

"I'm Major Ralph Buckley. You are light on your feet, Petty Officer...?"

Her eyes flew open.

"Acting Petty Officer Katie Kingston, sir." She fought the urge to salute. "And thank you."

After the dance, he brought her a welcome orange squash. She'd worked up quite a thirst. He looked so clean and elegant. She was sure she was a damp mess, her hair curled and matted.

"How long have you been on base, Acting Petty Officer? I don't think I've seen you around."

"Just a few weeks. I was a postal censor, but now I'm...here." She hoped that wasn't giving away anything.

"I'm glad of it. You are the loveliest WREN here tonight."

Doubting it, Katie basked in the compliment nonetheless.

They danced together a few more times before the evening ended. They even did the jitterbug, albeit Katie thought she was hopeless at the intricate steps.

"Can I see you again?" Ralph asked as Katie fetched her coat for the ride back to base. "It's been splendid meeting you."

"I expect so," she replied quickly. "There's a dance pretty much every Saturday night. When we're not on watch, of course."

"Brilliant. Barring a wartime emergency, I'll see you next Saturday night, then. Goodnight, Katie."

Katie floated on air, thrilled with her handsome officer. Even Cecily was impressed.

"You've snagged a gorgeous one. I lold on to him."

Katie nodded, glad of the dark lorry where she could collect her thoughts. Perhaps this was the start of something special.

***

"Have you heard from Katie, lately? She's not the best at writing."

"You're being kind, Mum. She's rubbish at it. And no, the last post was weeks ago. Something about being transferred to a base with new duties. Maddeningly vague, as always." Tillie rose from the kitchen table. "Shall we get on with it? I'm keen to rummage through the baby boxes to see what we might find for junior here." She rubbed her tummy which was getting rounder by the day.

"May I join you?" Hannah looked up from her porridge.

"Sure, luv. You can help us carry down the boxes. I don't want Tillie exerting herself too much." Alice tidied the table and removed her apron.

"Mum, I drive ambulance and tend to wounded patients all the time. I can manage a few cartons." Tillie laughed.

"You can't be too careful," Alice replied.

"Whatever you say, Mum." Tillie hurried them up the stairs. "I'm hoping for some lovely knitted things for his or her layette."

"There's that and more, luv. You know I never throw anything away. Mind your step." Mum sprang forward to protect Tillie's back on the wooden attic stairs.

Once all three were safely up, Mum pulled the ropes on two hanging bulbs. They threw little light, mostly illuminating dusty sheets covering shapeless objects.

"I expect it's scary up here at night," Hannah said, gazing round the mysterious items.

"Kenny loved playing hide and seek up here, but we girls didn't fancy it near as much," Tillie replied. "Except Katie – she loved it." She peeked under a few covers.

"Not there, dear. Over in the corner." Mum pointed.

Tillie and Hannah took the sheets off a few square-looking piles.

"These look promising." Tillie pulled open the top box, labelled Children's Toys.

"I expect those are blocks and dolls and such for older children. We need the infant boxes." Mum uncovered a large brown box. "Aha, this is it."

As Mum carefully unwrapped tissue-bound packages, the trio oohed and aahed over tiny booties, hats, and jumpers in pink, blue, and yellow.

"Mum, these are beautiful. Did you knit them?"

"Not by half. My mother – your grandmother did. She taught me but I wasn't near as good as her. Oh, this brings back such memories." She sniffed a tiny pink hat. "You and Maggie had so many matching outfits. I hope it's a girl – there's so many pink and frilly dresses."

"I see lots of blue too," Hannah said, picking up an exquisite baby blanket.

"Well, Kenny was the only boy and spoiled," Tillie said matter-of-factly. As the youngest and only boy, this was natural. Tillie didn't resent it. It's just the way it was.

"No, he wasn't," Mum objected, handing Tillie a tiny red cardigan. "How about this for next Christmas?"

"That's darling, Mum. Is it alright if I borrow some of these things? I promise I'll take care of them and pass them along when it's Maggie and Katie's turns." *How amazing are all these things? I can't wait to sort through them all. With clothing on the ration, this lot is a godsend.*

"Of course, luv. That's why I saved them." A house full of grandchildren. Wouldn't that be wonderful? War over, the children settled, and more babies on the way. Heaven.

"Mum, is this our old rocking horse?" Tillie had uncovered some larger objects. "Look at old Cinnamon. Remember Katie could never pronounce it right?" Tillie dusted off his brown neck and promptly sneezed.

Mum clapped her hands.

"Of course, I do. Dear old Cimamum. He looks a little worse for wear. We'll get Pops to give him another coat of paint."

Tillie had started a pile near the stairs, and was rapidly adding to it.

"This cradle is lovely, too." She gently rocked it.

"I found some rattles," Hannah cried from the back corner.

"I think that's rather enough for now. I'm freezing up here. Leave the bigger things for the boys to bring down. We'll carry the clothes so we can give them a proper wash when your time is nearer. Time for a cup of tea."

"Ta, Mum. This has been brilliant. And I still have an hour before I need to catch my train to Cambridge." Tillie beamed. *I'm going to be a mother. I hope I'm as loving as Mum. She is bloody marvellous.*

"I'll help. Tillie, you just get safely down the ladder." Hannah held it fast whilst Tillie climbed down with a grunt.

Alice switched off the lights. What a delightful afternoon. It almost made her forget the war. Almost.

***

All that Tillie could see out of the window was a grey fog. She must be getting close to Trevor's station. With all the signage taken down for the duration, it was guesswork to identify how far you were from your destination – by time and landscape. Imperfect at best.

At last, the train slowed, and a train platform appeared out of the mist. Tillie stood up, straightened her skirt, and reached overhead for her carryall. A kindly soldier lifted it down for her. Peering out the window, she saw shapes and shadows – none of which were recognizable as her husband. Screeching to a halt, the train stopped. Tillie rushed to the door and down the stairs as soon as the station master opened it.

She stood, scanning the faces for her beloved Trev. A deep voice came from behind.

"Looking for me, ma'am?"

She turned, colliding into a muscled chest as Trev's arms wrapped tightly around her. Wasting no time, he dipped his head to kiss her until she was breathless.

"Nice to see you, sir, but I think my husband might have an objection."

"Let him get his own girl." Trevor kissed her again.

Tillie shivered – from excitement and the cold.

"Darling, how are you doing? Let's get you out of this icy weather. I have your billet sorted, but first supper." He hoisted her carryall with one arm, and tucked her arm into the crick of his other one. "The restaurant is nothing special but the food is plentiful and it's warm. Mama takes care of us. It's just a short walk. Can you manage it?"

"Trev, I'm expecting, not sick. And who is Mama?" She snuggled up to him, glad of his warm bulk.

"She owns the Italian restaurant. I don't even know her real name, but her husband Marco was killed in the Great War, so she opened the restaurant to make ends meet. She has two boys – both in the RAF. One is a mechanic and the other is a rear gunner."

After a bracing ten-minute walk, they reached the café. Warm smells greeted them as Trev opened the door. Tillie hadn't realized how hungry she was. The cheese and pickle sarnie and flask of tea that Mum had packed for the train was long gone.

"Mister Trevor. Finally, you have brought me your beautiful bride." A petite, roundish woman with grey hair down to her waist greeted them with a wide smile. "Come in, come in."

"Mama, this is Tillie, all the way from London. Tillie, Mama – the owner of this fine establishment."

After being seated at a cozy corner table, Mama brought a warm pint for Trev, and hot tea for Tillie.

"Why did she call you Mister Trevor?" Tillie whispered, leaning forward.

"She can't keep track of the ranks of the different services, so she calls everyone Mister."

"Ah. She seems warm-hearted." Tillie looked up to see Mama juggling two steaming plates of spaghetti and a small salad.

"House speciality," Mama puffed as she put the salad between them, and presented the hot dishes with a flourish. "Pasta with meatballs."

"Thank you. It looks delicious." Tillie's stomach rumbled. It smelled divine.

"Mama, you're the best. Tuck in, Tils."

Coffee and Italian biscuits later, the couple were fit to bursting. Tillie sat back, patting her tummy.

"Little Drummond is proper happy at the moment. Thanks, luv."

"You're welcome. I'm that glad to see you, darling. But I see you are drooping, so let's get you to your billet."

After thanking and paying Mama, Trevor and Tillie walked to the nearby billet – a room over a café.

"The landlady knows we are married, so has given special permission for me to see you to your room." Trev raised an eyebrow, giving her his most wicked smile.

"Marvellous, darling. What are we waiting for?"

In the event, Trevor overstayed his welcome by about an hour, but the landlady didn't disturb them. It was bliss to be together again. Tillie clung to Trev, begging him not to go.

"The bed is too large without you. Please stay," she cajoled, nibbling his ear.

"Darling, I must go." He disentangled himself from the golden beauty lying next to him and stood to dress. "Most regretfully." He put on his trousers and the rest of his uniform. "I'll be back early tomorrow morning. I've managed to borrow a mate's car for the day. I'll show you 'round the base, meet the rest of the chaps, maybe a walk if it's not too bloody cold. We'll make the best of our time together." He put his cap on as Tillie snuggled under the coverlet.

"Brilliant, Trev. What time will be you be back?" Tillie was already feeling sleepy. It had been a long day.

"Early. Eight o'clock. Be ready, darling."

He bent to kiss her. She wound her arms round his neck and kissed him back.

"Tillie, you are making this extremely hard," he groaned. "Please, you and the baby need to rest. I'll see you in the morning. I love you." He placed her arms under the covers, and kissed her one more time. "Sleep well."

She turned over and closed her eyes. She wanted to stay awake, but just couldn't.

"I love you, too," she murmured.

Trevor smiled and closed the door quietly behind him.

He was true to his word and arrived promptly at eight a.m. the next day. Tillie was up and dressed, eager for the day. Trevor was as excited as a schoolboy, showing her the base, his digs, the most recent planes he'd worked on, the NAAFI and pretty much every square inch of the airfield. They lunched with a couple of his mates, and Trev proudly introduced her to his commanding officer.

After a brisk afternoon walk, they found a quiet corner to exchange Christmas gifts. Tillie loved the small bottle of perfume Trev had somehow obtained. He'd carved several wooden animals for the baby, promising to make an ark before he or she was born.

Trevor was touched that Tillie had knit him a dark green scarf and hat. He didn't need to know that Mum had helped a good bit. She'd also managed to find a shaving kit to replace his worn and battered one.

Too soon, it was time to drive to the station for Tillie's train back to London.

Tillie hadn't felt nauseous for a while, but her tummy was queasy, dreading their parting.

"Darling, where has the time gone? It seems I just arrived, and now I'm leaving again." She clutched his hand with both of hers.

He looked over at her.

"It's wretched, Tils. But I'm over the moon you came. We had our own special Christmas – just the two of us."

Tears sprung from…where? *Hold it together, girl. Be brave for him, for both of us.*

"Can you ring me on Christmas Day, darling? Just write me when you're available, and I'll dash to the post office to take your call."

"Of course, sweetheart. And we'll keep writing. As soon as I get another forty-eight-hour pass, I'll be on the next train to London."

He parked the car and turned to face her.

"I'll do whatever it takes to be home when this little one is born." He kissed her. "Whatever notice you can give me will help me get there faster." His eyes crinkled as he smiled.

"I'll do my best, darling. I can't do it without you – you know that." *I sound weak, but I need you Trev. I'm scared. I don't know how to do this.*

"Yes, you can, Tillie Drummond. And it's still months away. With the Americans fighting alongside us now, we just have to hang on a little longer. Where's my smile?" He stroked her cheek.

"Perhaps you're right. But you will ring and keep writing?" *Oh dear, I sound so desperate.*

"I will." He checked his watch. "We can't miss your train. Let's get a move on. And you won't forget what we talked about? You'll consider leaving the ambulance soon? I don't want our baby in any more danger than this bloody war serves us every day."

She nodded.

"Happy Christmas, my love."

He kissed her one last time.

"Happy Christmas, darling."

***

The annual ladies' Christmas Claridge's tea the next afternoon was a subdued affair. Tillie's eyes were red-rimmed from crying. She desperately missed both Trev and Maggie. The absence of Katie's cheerful presence was only slightly diminished by the addition of Isla and Hannah. They enjoyed the rare delicacies, but it didn't feel Christmassy. Alice consoled herself by fervently hoping next year would be different. Would all her girls be home? The new baby would surely bring joy to the Kingston household.

***

"You don't mind coming with me? I'm not quite sure how to manage this." Hannah sat on Tillie's bed, patting a contented Robbie.

"Not at all, luv. Goodness knows I've sent enough bombed-out families to refugee centers. If anyone can get answers from officials, it's me." She pinned back her hair into Kirby grips and took one last look in the mirror. "Or if stern questions don't work, I can always pretend I'm faint to gain some sympathy."

Hannah smiled, saying nothing. She'd turned sixteen in November, and was becoming a young lady – albeit a serious one. The loss of her grandfather, and the news that her parents and Micah had been taken to an exportation camp near Paris had snuffed the light in her eyes. She was her usual studious and helpful self, but ever-watchful and edgy at times.

Poor girl, Tillie thought for the hundredth time. *Through so much in*

116

her young life. And all this waiting and uncertainty was surely taking a toll. I'm doing my best to help her, but it seems cold comfort.

"Right, let's get on, Hannah. It looks to be another cold day. Bundle up proper and let's hope for a seat on the train.

The fog had lifted slightly, but it was bitterly cold. Arriving at the Jewish refugee center, they were dismayed to see a long queue.

"We Londoners have gotten rather good at queuing, haven't we, Hannah? I should think after the war we won't know what to do when the shops are wide open and we can walk right up to the counter."

"Are you alright, Tillie? I hate for you to be standing out in the cold."

"I'm fine." Tillie stamped her feet. "At least there's no snow. Let's mind how fast the queue moves. If we don't make progress in the next quarter of an hour, I expect I'll need to ask for a glass of water." She winked at Hannah.

And that's exactly what they did. Shameless, Tillie put on an outstanding performance as an expectant woman in discomfort. It did the trick, and they were soon at the front of the queue, facing a kindly-looking woman at a large desk.

"The name is Goldbach. Samuel, Ruth, and Micah. They were taken in a roundup in Toulouse and the last we heard they were sent by train to Drancy, near Paris."

Whilst Tillie gave the particulars of the situation, Hannah looked around. On every wall were notes and posters with names and pictures of lost ones, asking for any information as to their whereabouts. Begging for news, truth be told – in bold letters. So many were missing – it was overwhelming.

There were two queues – one for Jewish refugees looking for asylum, the other like her and Tillie – desperately hoping to find the names of their loved ones on a list safely rescued or somehow safe.

The refugees waiting for homes, clothing, and ration books all wore the same look – haunted but hopeful. Most were thin with meagre belongings. Hannah ached to help them or to ask if any of them had come from the Vichy region in France.

"I'm sorry for the wait, dear. We are so short-staffed and the need is great." The woman behind the desk scanned various lists looking for the

Goldbach name. She looked up, sadness clouding her eyes. "I'm sorry but I don't see their names anywhere. I don't believe they've made it to British shores."

Hannah let out a small gasp and edged closer to Tillie.

"So, what has happened to them? Can you tell us anything?" Tillie pressed.

"It's difficult to say. The news is sketchy and rumors are rife but unreliable. They may still be at Drancy, but more probably they have been sent to a work camp – in Germany or Poland. We've been hearing that fairly consistently over the last few months." Her voice was low.

"To do what?" Tillie asked. "Work for the Germans?" *What? Micah and his parents in Germany put to hard labor? No, it can't be.*

"Again, I can't confirm anything, dear. But it's believed that Germany needs workers to make munitions and for manual labor. They've sent all their young men to fight, and need replacement workers."

"But how? Against their will?" Tillie had turned white. Hannah was still.

"France is occupied by the Germans. It's war and they are playing dirty, very dirty indeed. Hitler seems to have an unexplained aversion to the Jewish people, and is rounding them up for an unpaid work force. I can't confirm anything, you understand? This is all speculation. I'm sorry. You can check back here again in a fortnight's time."

Tillie realized they were holding up the queue. She nodded.

"I understand, and we thank you for your time and the information. We'll come back again, won't we, Hannah? Next time it will be good news."

"I'd like to help." Hannah stepped forward, standing a little taller. "I volunteer for the WVS, but this is just as important. I need to help other families, just like mine." She bit her lip.

"Thank you, dear. We need all the help we can get." The woman pointed Hannah to an office to complete some paperwork. "And bless you."

Leaving a short while later, Tillie turned to the young girl.

"You are brave, indeed. Your parents would be proud of you."

Hannah nodded.

"Now, shall we sort a cup of tea? I think we need a little restoring warmth."

"This is a turn up – me waking *you* for a change on Christmas morning." Tillie plopped Robbie onto Kenny's chest.

"Happy Christmas, Tils. It hardly seems worth getting up early when it's just you and me." He sat up and pushed Robbie away.

"Shh. Don't say that. There's Hannah. We need to make the day merry for her. And Mum."

"You're right. But before we go down, I want to talk to you alone about something."

"Sounds serious." *Uh oh, please no more bad news. Especially today of all days.*

"I suppose it rather is, Tils. I'm going back to the navy. I had my medical a fortnight ago and was declared A1 – fit for service. I'm feeling well enough, and gosh – it's not right for me to sit at home when I'm needed to fight the Nazis."

Tillie sat back. Kenny leaving again, back to sea. Mum won't be able to bear it.

"Isn't that rather sudden, luv? Are you sure you're ready?" Tillie thought of all the nightmares, disrupted sleeps, and Kenny's filled-out but still slender frame.

"Not at all. It was down to the navy, in the event. I didn't show anyone the letter because – well I didn't want to upset Mum or ruin Christmas. So, it's not even my choice. I'll go where I'm sent." He smiled lopsidedly. "I haven't even told Pops yet."

Tillie swallowed before speaking.

"Of course, it's the right thing to do. But Mum will be gutted. We all will. This ghastly war."

Kenny shrugged.

"I'm not keen to get back on a ship after what happened aboard *HMS Dainty*, if I'm honest. But what can I do?"

"Stop it. The chances of you being in that type of explosion again are slim. You've had your bad luck. It's clear sailing from here on out." *I hope I'm right. I can't bear to lose you or have you injured again.*

"Too funny, Tils. I suppose I'll just make the best of it. Now – please don't say anything. I'll tell Pops in a day or two, and he can break it to Mum. Alright?"

"It's a deal. Now, let's go wake Hannah. She'll be right cross that Robbie abandoned her for my bed last night."

Christmas gifts were modest that morning. Due to paper rationing, books were in scarce supply, as was anything new in the shops. Wrapping paper was reused from years gone by, and carefully preserved. Pops gave everyone war bonds to help the cause, and Mum had unpicked old jumpers to knit hats and mittens for everyone. She'd knitted an entire white layette for the baby, including an exquisite blanket. The girls exchanged soaps which were in short supply everywhere. Hannah had worked magic with Isla and given everyone small packages of decorated shortbread biscuits. Kenny hand-wrote IOU slips promising chores and errands as his gifts.

"I can't wait to see you sweep the kitchen," laughed Mum.

"And hoover the morning room," Hannah joked.

"I don't have a job or any money. It's the best I could do," Kenny objected, throwing his hands up.

"I think it's a wonderful idea. I will definitely take advantage of your offer to run errands for me. Thanks, luv," Tillie reassured him.

"And how about our Katie? Coming in at the last minute with a telegram?" Pops waved it in the air.

"Read it again, Pops," Tillie urged, as she carefully tidied up the wrappings.

"Happy christmas dear family stop miss you stop package with american chocolates on the way stop that's all stop katie stop"

Friendly laughter filled the room.

"That's our Katie," Mum said. "I miss the little scamp."

"We all do, Mum. But she has leave in a few weeks. We'll see her soon. And our Maggie should be here in no time." Tillie didn't want Mum to be sad on Christmas Day.

"Righto. Thank you everyone for the lovely gifts. Now, we'd best make a start on dinner. Shirley and Thomas will be here soon. Tillie, why don't you put your feet up and wait for them and Maggie? Hannah, will you help me, dear?"

The family scattered for a short while, eager for whatever Christmas dinner the women could produce.

"How ever did you manage a turkey, Aunt Shirley?" Tillie asked over a table that, despite everything, still managed to groan with food.

Shirley held up her hands, looking wide-eyed.

"I couldn't say, dear. Just enjoy it. There's just a bit for each of us, but it's something."

"It's more than something. It's splendid." Alice smiled at her sister.

"Everything melts in your mouth. So much better than mess food," Maggie said between mouthfuls of sprouts. She'd arrived just before dinner, bearing gifts of small drawings, chocolate, and homemade jam, courtesy of her ack-ack mate Lou's farm.

"How are you getting on, Maggie?" Thomas asked, helping himself to more spuds and a tiny speck of gravy. "Many callouts?"

"Not too many lately, thank goodness. We drill every day to improve our speeds, but it's been quiet overhead. Sometimes dead boring, but when the air raid signal blares – it is terrifying. And strangely satisfying. I'm glad to do my bit to fend off German invasion."

"We're proper proud of you, luv," Tillie said, patting her sister's hand.

"We all are, dear," Mum echoed.

Food was passed and consumed in the silence that followed.

Pops cleared his throat.

"I know we are missing our loved ones today. It's impossible not to count the empty chairs. But we also have plenty to be thankful for. I for one, am grateful that the Allies are winning at every turn – American troops landed in North Africa, the Soviets trapped the German army in Stalingrad, the Japanese were taken down in Guadalcanal and New Guinea, and we have defeated the Germans in Egypt. A brilliant start to 1943."

"Hear hear," said Thomas, raising his glass.

"I'm happy to make whatever small contributions I can on the gun site. And proud to have shown off our battery squad to Princess Mary this past summer."

Alice turned to her.

"That was lovely, dear."

"I will forever thank all the Kingstons for helping me escape France and welcoming me into your home," Hannah said in small voice.

"You are part of the family now," Pops said for all of them. No one mentioned Micah or his parents.

"I'm thankful to be included in your family gatherings. You are so kind to have me. And that my son married your daughter in a beautiful wedding this year." Isla fought a catch in her throat, missing her son dreadfully. "And for this new baby coming – a joy for us all." She smiled at her daughter-in-law.

"A new baby – at last something to look forward to," Shirley said, eyes down.

It was Tillie's turn.

"I'm happy to have married the man of my dreams, and that despite the dangers out there – we are all alive and safe. And for the baby. Albeit right now, he or she is giving me horrid indigestion."

They all laughed.

"I'm grateful for all of that. A beautiful wedding, a new infant coming, and most of all – that our darling Kenny is recovered and home safe with us," Mum added.

"I'm happy for this turkey and all the smashing food. I'm hoping for plum pudding." Kenny rubbed his hands together.

It broke the somber mood, for which they were all grateful.

"Isla, will you do the honours? You prepared the pudding. You should light it for us." It was a fitting end to a splendid meal.

After the clear away, the family gathered around the wireless, eager to hear what HM King George VI had to say to his subjects:

"It is at Christmas more than at any other time that we are conscious of the dark shadow of war. Our Christmas festival today must lack many of the happy, familiar features that it has had from our childhood. We miss the actual presence of some of those nearest and dearest, without whom our family gatherings cannot be complete...

In this spirit I wish all of you a happy Christmas. This year it adds to our happiness that we are sharing it with so many of our comrades-in-arms from the United States of America. We welcome them in our homes, and their sojourn here will not only be a happy memory for us, but, I hope, a basis of enduring understanding between our two peoples…

Many of you to whom I am speaking are far away overseas. You realize at first hand the importance and meaning of those outposts… which your faithfulness will defend…

The Queen and I feel most deeply for all of you who have lost or been parted from your dear ones, and our hearts go out to you with sorrow, with comfort, but also with pride…

The lessons learned during the past forty tremendous months have taught us how to work together after the war to build a worthier future…

So let us brace and prepare ourselves for the days which lie ahead…

On the sea, on land, and in the air, and in civil life at home, a pattern of effort and mutual service is being traced, which may guide those who design the picture of our future society…

So let us welcome the future in a spirit of brotherhood, and thus make a world in which, please God, all may dwell together in justice and peace."

They stood for the national anthem. Kenny turned off the wireless.

"A sturdy message. The Allies are well-named – a collection of nations with a single-minded purpose to restore freedom," Pops declared with satisfaction.

"Proper moving," Alice agreed over the clacking of knitting needles.

"Who is for charades? We need to have some fun whilst Maggie is still here. I'm too sluggish for a walk, and it's cold, in the event." Tillie said from the couch, enjoying the Christmas Day fire.

"Brilliant. I'll sort the teams." Kenny jumped up.

And for a short while, it was laughter and happiness at the Kingston townhouse.

Chapter Six

WHERE IS THE SUN?

1943 – Maggie

"*Dear Mum and Pops,*

I know it's been some time since I've written. I'm hopeless and I'm sorry. I'm fine – fit and working hard. I've met some good chums, and we have a laugh when not on duty.

How are you getting on? The house must be frantic with a new baby commanding all the attention. How old is Master James now? He must be coming onto six months. Give my love to him and my big sis.

I haven't heard from Mags in a while. Is she alright? I'm afraid to ask – any word from Micah or his parents? The winds of war are blowing in our direction now, so it's just a matter of time till we are victorious. Perhaps that will signal the release of the Goldbachs.

As usual, I never hear from Katie but trust that she's tearing up the Women's Royal Navy in her own little corner of the war.

I can't say more, but I think there will be big news in 1944. Perhaps I'll even be home for Christmas next year.

Wishing you all a Happy Christmas.

Kenny xx"

Alice dropped the letter into her lap and sighed.

"He doesn't know, poor love," said Tillie, burping Jamie over her shoulder.

"I suppose Maggie hasn't had the heart to write him. She's grieving her mate, and still hasn't heard a word from Micah." Mum tsked.

One of Maggie's team-mates on the ack-ack site had been killed in an air-raid attack just last month, and Maggie had taken it hard. Little Lou had been hit by a shrapnel shard and died instantly. The entire squad had been devastated. It was one more harsh blow that poor Maggie didn't need.

"I'll write to him later," Tillie offered. "I'm behind on my correspondence. I owe Katie a letter too. Perhaps at nap-time. If Prince James here goes down."

Alice studied her daughter. Shadows under her eyes gave away too many sleepless nights. Her eyes lacked their usual shine, and she slumped in her chair.

"He's not sleeping well, the little lamb. Do you still reckon he's teething?" Mum took Jamie and put him in the high chair. "Shall we try some pablum, young man?"

"Ta, Mum. He'll likely spit it up but it's worth a try. And to answer your question, I don't know when he'll finally get some teeth. It's been weeks now that he's fussy at night. I'm sure you've heard him waking over and over. I'm so sorry for the noise. He puts his fists in his mouth, but nothing yet."

"That's what babies do, dear. No need to be sorry. Open up, darling. Let Granny have a look." Mum peered into Jamie's mouth. "His gums are a bit red, but nothing's poking through yet. All in good time, I suppose." She busied herself with the cereal, attempting to spoon it into her grandson's mouth.

Jamie was the spitting image of his father – from tufts of black hair to his cobalt-blue eyes. He even had a matching dimple.

"Why don't you have a lie-down, luv? You look all in. I can mind Jamie. He's no trouble."

Tillie laughed.

"Spoken like a loving granny. You know, maybe I will. Just for a bit. I'm meant to go to the shops with Aunt Shirley later – albeit there's nothing to buy. I think it's going to be handmade gifts again this Christmas – more's the pity."

"You don't sound like your usual chipper self, luv. Babies can be hard, can't they?"

"I shouldn't moan, Mum. You and Trevor's mum give me loads of help. So does Hannah when she's around. It's just tough going some days. I'm always so tired."

Mum stood up and gave her daughter a kiss on the cheek.

"It will get better, luv. You are still recovering from the birth and teething is a wearisome time. And you don't have a husband to lean on. Go and lie down. Every task seems insurmountable when you're knackered."

"Thank you, Mum. I shouldn't be too long." Tillie kissed her messy-faced son and slowly climbed the stairs.

"Take your time. I'll pop Jamie into the pram, and we'll have a walk around the block, shall we?" He smiled toothlessly, waving his arms.

***

Tillie smiled as she heard her mum nattering to Jamie. *I'm lucky to have her. I don't know what I'd do without her.* Climbing to the third floor seemed like scaling a mountain. She dragged herself to the bed and sank down gratefully. *I should really write some letters, or fold some of Jamie's wash. I'll just close my eyes for a few minutes to regain some pep.*

Glancing at the wedding snap on her bedside table, she felt a wave of longing for her husband. *Trevor, I need you. When will you be in my arms again? I hate this uncertainty and apprehension. Jamie needs you, too.* Clutching a pillow for comfort, she drifted off.

***

Maggie, Pip and the rest of Mixed Battery 677 dragged themselves through their shifts, each dealing with the loss of Louise Greenwood in their own way. Pip and Addy snapped at each other, and the men just carried on grimly. Maggie withdrew further into herself, finding comfort in her natural shyness. She worked, wrote letters to her family and Micah, drew pictures on precious scraps of paper, and took long, solitary walks.

126

As 1943 drew to a close, the war toiled on. The year marked major progress for the Allies. The British and Americans pushed the Germans out of North Africa and were in Italy. Mussolini had been forced out of power, and Italy was out of the war. The Soviets halted German advances into Russia. The Japanese lost key battles at Midway and Guadalcanal, and were swiftly falling from their position as a force to be reckoned with. And the strength that the Americans brought to the Allied effort showed not only in the military might, but in industrial power as they churned out ships, planes, combat vehicles, rifles, and bullets to supply all the Allied forces.

Bombing over London had virtually ceased, so a sense of wary normality prevailed in Britain. War-normality, that is. Intense rationing, daily blackouts, long queues, and the over-fatigued public continued without respite. The fifth wartime Christmas filled almost no one with joy. Loved ones were still far away, missing, or forever lost. It was hard to muster much enthusiasm for the festive season.

No word from Micah or his parents after such a long time was near-impossible for Maggie to bear. She wanted to retain hope – at least no word of their deaths had come forward, so that was something. Were they still at Drancy, the exportation camp after all this time? If not, where had they been sent? Reports of the Nazi plan to kill all of Europe's Jews had been coming since early in the war, although downplayed by the British press to protect morale. As far back as 1941, Prime Minister Churchill said in a public broadcast:

"As [Hitler's] armies advance, whole districts are being exterminated. Scores of thousands, literally scores of thousands of executions in cold blood, are being perpetrated by the German police troops upon the Russian patriots who defend their native soil. . . . And this is but the beginning. Famine and pestilence have yet to follow in the bloody ruts of Hitler's tanks.

We are in the presence of a crime without a name."

Maggie was smart enough to realize that the Goldbachs had almost certainly been sent to a German work or extermination camp where word of harsh conditions trickled back over the continent.

It drove her to frenzied shifts on the ack-ack guns, determined to do whatever she could to hasten an Allied victory so that Micah, his parents, and thousands of Jews could be liberated and come home.

***

"How many days in a row is this with no sun?" Pip asked, straightening her cap. "It's bloody dismal."

"Ten or twelve, I suppose. I don't know," Maggie said, nose in a book.

"Better than snow, I expect. Or rain. Easier to man the equipment," Pip added.

"Hmmm," Maggie replied.

"We've got two hours before duty. Fancy a walk to clear your head?" Pip suggested. "Full moon tonight, so it's bound to be busy."

"I don't think so. I'm going to stay warm whilst I can. I'll meet you at the mess for supper before we head over to the gun site." Maggie hadn't even looked up from her book.

Pip hesitated, staring at Maggie's bowed blonde head.

"Suit yourself. I'll meet you at the usual time."

She left. Maggie peeked up to ensure she was alone, put down her book, and pulled out her worn sweets tin with the carefully preserved stack of letters. Well-read, she still found comfort in Micah's words of almost two years ago; *'My little one, I long to share more words of love and hope for you and us... Believe that you are in my heart and mind each day.'* She couldn't give up hope for a future together. She wouldn't.

After a supper of corned beef, veg, and yet another prune custard, the squad made their way to the command center for evening duty. Cold and clear, the full moon was rising into a cloudless sky.

Waiting in the ops room for a potential air raid signal, the group was tense. Would it be another quiet night? Or would they be called out again and again to divert or shoot German planes out of the sky?

With the advent of radar and several years' experience, the battery teams had gained efficiency and accuracy against German fighters and bombers. Few now even got through from the French coast, and those that did, were swiftly pinpointed and either jolted into retreat, confronted by RAF fighters, or shot down by the ack-ack guns themselves.

For the soldiers on the guns, this didn't make the job any easier. Danger was real and present, and each air attack was different. Added to that was the shadow of Lou's recent tragic death – right here on the site. Her presence was everywhere and it unnerved more than a few of them.

"Who 'as Christmas leave?" Addy asked. "I've put in fer it, but 'avent' 'eard yet."

"I have a forty-eight-hour pass but I have to be back Christmas Eve. At least I can see the family this year," Morris said.

"Ditto," said Pip. "How about you, Mags?" She turned to her mate.

"I've got five days leave owing, so I'm going home for Christmas. I can't wait."

"That's brilliant. You always come back in a better frame of mind," teased Pip. "And loaded with goodies to share."

"Give over," Maggie punched her in the arm. "I'm always in a good mood."

The air raid signal pierced the night. As one, the team donned their tin hats, and rushed up the stairs and outside to the gun site within seconds.

The searchlight operators were first to action, flashing high-powered beams across the sky, seeking first sight of enemy aircraft. Pip worked the tripod-mounted binoculars to get eyes on the aircraft. After identifying the type and angles, she shouted it to the squad – a pair of Heinkels. Then it was over to Maggie and Addy on the predictor machines. They monitorred the gauges to track the height and speed of incoming aircraft, factoring in atmospheric conditions. Compiling the figures, they calibrated the plane's position as it flew toward a target location. Then the shooting crew set the length of fuse required on the anti-aircraft gun before firing.

The first plane scuttled away at the first cannon shots, darting back over the channel to safety. The second one swooped and ducked as RAF fighters came in, ready to pick him off.

"Three spits approaching," shouted Pip.

"Stand down," cried the Sergeant on duty.

The crew stepped back – no anti-aircraft fire could be launched with RAF planes on the attack. All eyes were on the dogfight above them.

"Come on, come on," muttered Pip.

Maggie's eyes were glued to the remaining Heinkel as it dipped and swayed to avoid the Spitfire barrage. One more plane down, one step to closer to Micah coming home.

The drones and buzz from above blended with shots firing from both sides.

"It's three against one. We've got him, I know we have. Come on, boys," urged Morris, the unofficial team lead.

With the full moon and intertwining searchlights illuminating the sky, the dance was clear to the crowd below.

After what seemed like an hour but was sheer minutes, a loud explosion and flash of light confirmed that one of the planes had been hit.

"Did we get 'em?" called Addy over the noise.

"I think so," one of the men answered. "I still see the spits in the air."

Another burst of light and fire revealed that the German plane had been hit. A cheer erupted from the squad and ops personnel.

Maggie and Pip clutched each other and danced around.

"We got the bugger." Pip's face shone.

"Our boys can't be beat," Maggie said with a huge smile.

"Do yer see any white comin' down? Is ter pilot bailin' out?" Addy peered through the binoculars, trying to spot the parachute and pilot.

"I see him." The Sergeant pointed west. "Likely a mile or two from base. The military police should be able to track him down if he doesn't crash into a barn."

"Or be killed by a civilian mob," added Morris.

Although it was against the law to shoot German prisoners of war, as the years went on, many locals took the law into their own hands when faced with enemy pilots on British soil. Deeming it only fair given all the death and destruction wrought by the Germans, a good number had been shot and killed on sight.

"You lot can have your tea break. Be back at half-past," Sarge shouted.

"Too right," Addy cheered, as she removed her tin hat and wiped the sweat from her brow. "Me nerves are shot. Come on, girls."

"I'm gasping for a cuppa." Pip put an arm around Addy. "Maggie, you coming?"

"I'll be right along. I just want to clear my head." Maggie turned away. Her head throbbed and her thoughts were muddled. She needed a short walk to reconcile her intense feelings of satisfaction and retribution with her abhorrence of all things violent. It never got any easier.

Her thoughts jumbled as she wandered towards a clump of trees. Naturally seeking cover on a moon-lit night, she just needed the cold air to free her mind so she could continue with her shift. There could yet be more German planes that had slipped through British radar and were on their way to drop their bomb loads on innocent civilians. *Not on my watch.* She walked with purpose.

A flash of white caught her attention. *Is that...? Could it be a downed parachute?* No. The German pilot couldn't be this close. She needed to warn her C.O. Her heart raced.

Turning back, she felt a presence and something hard pressing into the middle of her back. She gasped.

"*Ruhig sein. Ruhig sein,*" a grating voice growled in her ear.

Not understanding, Maggie froze. She didn't dare move or even try to look at him.

"Quiet." His breathing was raspy. *Was he injured? What should I do now?* Her mind scrambled to think of her training. "*Hande hoch.*"

He pressed the gun harder into her back, and she smothered a cry as she raised her arms in surrender. Pushing her towards the trees, she noticed he was limping on his right side. Had he been shot? No, he wouldn't be able to walk if he'd broken a leg in his fall. What was he planning to do? Kill her? Use her as a hostage to somehow escape? Maggie's thoughts darted frantically about as she surveyed the landscape. Damn, why had she been so stupid? She knew better than to walk by herself. Hadn't this been drilled into them a hundred times?

"*Schnell, schnell.*"

He must know the military police would be searching for him. He was in a hurry. But what was he going to do? Use her as a human shield to dodge a bullet meant to kill him? Bargain with her? But for what? There was no path to freedom for a German bomber pilot in England.

Maggie slowed her steps. Once in the trees, any sound would be muffled. Who would hear anything? How could she stop him before he got her out of the light?

She formed a crude plan. If she startled him somehow so that he fell

– on his bad leg? – could she wrangle the gun? It was outrageous. And highly dangerous. He was bigger than her and trained in gun combat. His instincts were probably razor-sharp.

She only had a few seconds to think. What had she learned in her training? An elbow or a knee in the right place could immobilize him – at least momentarily. But it would have to surprise him, and she would have to hit just the right spot. Would it work? She had to act. Her life depended on it.

Mid-stride, she let out an enormous scream, and turned to elbow him in the stomach, whilst pushing him off-balance so that he crashed down on his right leg, yelping with pain. As he fell, he grabbed her ankle and pulled her down to the ground, knocking the wind out of her. Dazed, she sucked in air, struggling to breathe. She felt him move around, swearing in German. He'd dropped the gun. Rolling away from him, she thought she heard a rustle or whistle off to her left. Getting to her hands and knees, she crawled in that direction, not daring to get to her feet to make herself an easy target.

A gunshot pierced the night. Maggie held her breath. And heard nothing. No voice, no movement, nothing.

"I got him," a man's voice said quietly.

A torch flashed to her right, landing on the pilot.

The man knelt and felt for a pulse.

"Yep. He's dead. I got him," he repeated rather proudly.

"Maggie, are you alright?" Pip rushed forward, flashing her torch on Maggie who was slowly rising to her feet.

"Yes. I... I think so." Why was her voice quavering? And why did she suddenly feel sick?

"Luv, you're shaking. Are you hurt? Let's get you back to the base and let the medics give you a once over." Pip removed her greatcoat and placed it around Maggie's shoulders.

"I'm fine, Pip. Really. He twisted my ankle but it just throbs a bit. That's all." Why was she feeling so close to tears? Shock, most likely.

"Yer daft cow. What were yer doin fightin' a German in ter dark by yerself?" Addy gave her mate a hug.

"I was foolish to walk by myself. I know that. I'm sorry I've made such

132

a fuss. I didn't know what else to do. I thought he was going to kill me." Her voice choked.

Within minutes, she was sitting in her GPO's office with MPs taking down her statement. She clutched a warm cup of tea for dear life, grateful for the dash of brandy someone had added to it.

"Stop apologizing, Lance Bombardier Kingston. You were exceedingly brave under dire conditions. Your level head most certainly saved your life." The GPO removed his glasses. "But please don't go walking off on your own again. There's a war on, you know."

Maggie managed a tired smile.

"So I've heard."

Pip and Addy were waiting outside to escort her back to the hut.

"I'd say we're done for the night, girls. We were relieved by B squad. Let's try to get some sleep." Pip wasn't going to let Maggie out of her sight. Mates made during war were mates for life.

***

Katie rubbed her eyes, looked around the room and was momentarily bewildered. Oh yes, Capel Le Ferne. She smiled happily. It was wonderful to be here.

Ruby sat up at the alarm ring, took one look at Katie's face, and buried her head under the coverlet.

"What are you smirking about? Another chilly day on watch?" Her mumble was barely audible.

"Go back to sleep, Rubes. You're not on duty for four hours. Sorry to wake you." Her tone couldn't have been more cheerful.

"Mmmmm," Ruby said with an unintelligible curse word thrown in.

Katie stretched and bounced out of bed. She was due on watch in just under thirty minutes. Taking her sponge bag to the bathroom, she was chuffed to find it free. There were never fewer than ten Wrens stationed in the requisitioned Edwardian house on the edge of the cliff about 100 feet up from the sea. On a clear day, you could see the church tower in Calais, France. It was dreadfully close to the Germans across the English Channel.

But Katie couldn't be happier. As much as she'd enjoyed her time at Southwold "Y" Station, she was relieved to be transferred to this base where she knew no one – and even more important – no one knew her. After the wretched affair with Ralph, she'd been mortified. When her travel orders came through, she couldn't wait to be transferred – she hadn't cared where. But Capel Le Ferne had turned out to be a treat. It was a bustling station near the white cliffs of Dover. The walks were spectacular, even in the cold weather. What an unexpected bonus. What's more, she'd found a trusted friend in dear Ruby. They'd been assigned as room-mates, and had gotten on like a house on fire. She didn't need a man in her life. She was doing just fine. The past was in the past. Just where it would stay.

Donning her navy-blue Wren uniform, she collected her tricorn hat, fluffed her short dark curls in the mirror, and headed to the kitchen for a bite to eat before watch.

The girls from night duty were dribbling in, yawning. Night watches were the worst – the work itself was grueling – tuning into individual HRO radios for Very High Frequency communications from German u-boats. These were extremely short-range transmissions that required transcription precision. The wireless telegraphists turned the radio dials infinitesimally, straining to catch the slightest signals, taking them down verbatim, and passing them to a senior officer. The work required an above-average IQ score, intense concentration, the ability to work under pressure and stay alert while waiting for hours, and coping with erratic sleep and meal patterns.

Katie loved the work, and her enthusiasm, attention to detail and patience made her an exemplary Y-interceptor.

"Hallo, girls. Are you alright? How was watch?" Katie poured a full kettle onto the tea leaves in the brown teapot.

"Quiet," Jinx replied, throwing her hat onto a chair. "Watch seems twice as long. Any toast with that tea?"

"Too right," agreed Edith. "Nothing for me. I'm going to sleep my eight hours off before reporting back. Ta ra, girls."

Katie chatted with the sleepy Wrens, as she munched toast with a scrape of margarine and jam.

"I'm off," she said as she took her dish and cup to the sink. "Come on chicks," she called to her other watch-mates. "Let's go turn in some Germans."

Whistling as she bundled up against the cold, Katie felt bright as a penny. All was well at *HMS Lynx* here on the coast, and she had a forty-eight-hour pass to go home for Christmas. Marvellous.

***

"They'll all be home Christmas? Brilliant." Shirley smiled.

"Yes, all but Kenny. Maggie has a five-day pass, Katie and Trevor each have forty-eights. All overlapping so it will be a jigsaw puzzle sorting all the trains. And meals. But I couldn't be more delighted." Alice pulled an old envelope towards her and flipped it over. Pencil in hand, she turned to her sister.

"I have my trusty tick list, luv. Let's get a start on. Katie arrives sometime on the day of Christmas Eve, so we'll have to do our ladies tea as soon as she gets here. I've already rung for a reservation for seven of us – our largest tea ever."

"That's splendid, but what about Jamie? Who will mind him if Tillie comes along?"

"His father, of course. With a little help from Pops. They'll manage just fine."

Shirley laughed.

"I expect they will – somehow. I'd volunteer Thomas to lend a hand, but he's hopeless with babies."

"Trevor and Walter can look after him for a few hours. Heaven knows Tillie needs a break. But I think we should forego a Christmas Eve get-together. We'll all be full from Claridge's and won't need to put on another do. We just need to sort something for the men. Woolton Pie or maybe we can procure some sausage?"

"Leave that to me, luv. I'll take care of that. What I'm more concerned about is Christmas dinner itself. What in the world are we going to serve?" Shirley helped herself to a biscuit.

Alice chewed the end of her pencil.

"I've been giving that some thought, luv. Aggie from the WVS is in a pig club with some of her neighbours. I sounded her out about buying any parts that aren't spoken for. Obviously, the shoulder, ribs, and loin are set aside for the other members. But she did say they might be able to spare a few chops or pork belly."

Shirley clapped her hands.

"That would do us a treat."

Alice held up a hand.

"But there's a catch. She doesn't want any money. She's looking to barter. I promised her any veg from our allotment that she fancies. She's already sorted there. She's after two things – spectacular baked goods and some muscle. Her mother was just bombed out of her home and is moving in with her. Aggie needs help with the move, and shifting furniture around to accommodate her ailing mum."

"That shouldn't be too hard. There's Trev, Walter, and Thomas for the heavy lifting," Shirley suggested.

"The girls are strong too, don't forget. As for the pudding, I'm certain we can convince Isla to pull something together – even if it means sacrificing our own sweets for Christmas Day. Am I right?" Alice's eyebrows knitted. She so wanted this holiday to be perfect.

"I should think we can muster that and more. We've all been saving up our sweets rations. And I'll scour the shops for any bits and bobs to add to the feast. For some fresh pork chops, we'll all make the sacrifice. My mouth is already watering."

"Righto, that's sorted. I'll speak to her tonight at the clothing drive. You're planning on coming?" Alice was all smiles. "There is a new batch of donations that need to be sorted, folded, and stacked for the homeless and refugees."

Shirley gathered the teacups and saucers for the sink.

"Of course. I'm always up for a good natter with the girls while we sort and fold."

"That and knitting. It may not be much, but we're doing our bit." Alice rose. "I'd best get on with my ironing. I've got masses to get through."

"And I need to get to the shops or there will be nothing for Walter's tea. Ta ra, darling."

Ta ra.

***

"Another pint?" Thomas held up his empty mug. "It's my round."

"Just a half. Alice is expecting me home." Walter lit his pipe whilst Thomas went to the bar with their orders.

The brothers-in-law met from time to time for a pint after work. They'd become friends of their own accord, and sought conversation and advice from each other. Walter's senior position gave him insider war information, most of which he was obliged to keep to himself. But the men loved to get together and speculate on the status of the war and possible future strategies.

"What do you make of this Teheran Conference, Thomas? Is this really the start of the big push?" Walter drank deeply from his mug.

Thomas paused.

"It's significant that Churchill, Roosevelt and Stalin met for the first time. I never thought I'd see the day when Allied leaders would meet with the Russian head."

"Considering where Soviet sympathies lay at the outset of war, it seemed improbable. But now they have turned to our side, he is a wily but valuable ally."

"So, the second front is inevitable, then?" Walter stated more than asked.

"It seems highly likely," Thomas said. "It's common knowledge that we've needed to band together to attack the Germans in a coordinated manner. Preparations have been underway for many months now. I think 1944 is going to be a pivotal year. You've seen the German losses this year. They are crumbling before our eyes. With a Soviet, American, and British alliance, we will take back France, which will lead to the ultimate fall of the Nazis – albeit likely not as soon as we would all like."

1943 had ravaged the German forces. Earlier in the year, they had lost an estimated 250,000 soldiers in Stalingrad. In May, Hitler's last foothold in North Africa had been lost with the occupation of Tunisia by Anglo-American forces. During July and August, German forces took further blows in the Kursk, Orel, and Kharkov battles. Allied assaults on Sicily in July and on the Italian mainland in September led to the collapse of Mussolini's Fascist regime.

With this decisive turn of the tide of war in the Allies' favor, the 'Big Three' leaders convened to draw up the plan for the final victory.

"Indeed," Walter said, sitting back in his chair. "And not before it's time. "This is definitely the most optimistic I've been in a long time. It gives me great cause for celebrating this Christmas."

Thomas nodded.

"Our wives deserve nothing less. They've been through so much." He sipped his bitters.

Each thought of his own wife and the trials and tribulations of the last five years.

"Just so." Walter agreed.

They gulped the last of their pints, and donned their overcoats to go home for tea.

***

"Mum, he's asleep, so hopefully he'll be no trouble. Thanks ever so much for minding him. I must run. I'm meant to meet Maggie's train and she wants to pop round the shops to see if she can find any Christmas gifts. Chance is a fine thing. I could bring Jamie but it will be so cold, and heaven knows how long I'll have to wait." Tillie put on her hat and overcoat and paused to look at her mother.

"You'd better get off, luv. We'll be fine. Isla may pop by. With two grannies to dote over him, he won't even miss you."

"Ta ra, Mum. We'll be back in a few hours."

Alice put on the kettle. Isla was sure to be here straightaway.

***

Bloody hell, the station is freezing. When is that train going to arrive? Tillie stamped her feet and blew on her fingers. She considered nipping to a café for a restorative cup of tea, but sure as chips are chips – that's when

138

Maggie's train would whistle in. After all this wait, Tillie couldn't risk missing her. It was a little strange that Mags had written to ask her to meet the train alone. She usually didn't like a fuss. *I suppose I'll find out soon enough. Hopefully Mum is alright with the baby.*

The station was busy with Christmas arrivals. Not too many tearful departures, it seemed. *It's going to be a lovely Christmas. Us girls all home, Jamie's first Christmas, and Trev due day after tomorrow.* Tillie was starting to feel that holiday excitement.

She saw Maggie before her twin spotted her. She looked exhausted.

"Darling," Tillie called as she ran towards her.

"Tillie." Maggie dropped her bag and gave her sister a tight squeeze. "I'm that glad to see you."

Were those tears in Maggie's eyes?

"You're so pale, luv. Are you alright?" Tillie held her sister's arms, looking at her with concern.

Maggie's lower lip quivered.

"I really need you. I've had the most wretched time."

"Right. A cup of tea and a twin talk." Tillie took charge, picking up Maggie's bag and hustling her out of the station to a nearby café.

"It was a dreadful train journey. The car was filled with soldiers and smoke. And we stopped three times for no reason."

"Enough about the train. What's happened?"

For the next three quarters of an hour, Maggie explained, words tripping over each other, what happened on the ack-ack site. How terrified she'd been when the German pilot held her at gunpoint, how she thought she was going to die when she turned to elbow him and he grabbed her ankle. And what a huge relief it was to be rescued. All of it. She choked up at times, and wiped the odd tear, but managed to keep from letting it all out.

"You poor darling. What a horrible time you've had. And you were so brave. If you hadn't turned on him, goodness knows what might have happened. I'm so proud of you."

"Thanks for listening, Tils. I didn't think I could keep it in for another minute. I feel so much better for having told you. My heart feels lighter." Maggie gave her a limp smile. "But you must keep this to yourself. Mum and Pops have enough to worry about, and it's Christmas. We'll all be home save Kenny, so we must make it fun and a holiday to remember."

"Are you sure? Mum is a terrific listener, and even Katie has her good moments as a sister."

A bigger smile from Maggie.

"I'm certain. Now that I've confided in you, I feel a load lifted. Now, I want to hear all about young Jamie. I'm that eager to see my little nephew. Any sign of teeth yet?"

Tillie had her misgivings about keeping Maggie's secret, but she had to honour her twin's wishes. As always.

"Finally, two broke through the other day, the little love. I've actually had a couple of good night's sleep and it's made all the difference."

"Brilliant. Shall we get on with the shopping then? Let's just do a quick pop-by. I want to get home."

"Of course, darling. Anything you want."

***

The reunion of the Drummond family was just as poignant.

"He's grown so much, Tils. Look at his chubby cheeks. And two teeth. Aren't you the clever little chap."

Trevor lifted him in the air, waving him from side to side. Jamie giggled.

"Be careful, darling. I don't want him to spit up his feed."

"He's just fine. Aren't you, Jamie-boy?" Trev snuggled his warm neck and threw him in the air again.

Secretly, Tillie was relieved. She had been afraid that Jamie would play strange or not recognize his daddy. But he'd known him straightaway.

"And he's just the image of you, Trev. Look at that black hair. And big blue eyes. Those don't come from the Kingstons."

"He's going to be a rough and tumble Drummond, aren't you? After the war is over, I'm going to buy you a ball and bat and teach you to throw. We'll have a grand time."

Tillie beamed. After the war. What a marvellous thought.

Trev looked at her sideways.

"Any chance of your Mum or Maggie watching him for a bit? I need to get reacquainted with my wife." He pulled her towards the bed, and the three collapsed onto it into a jumbled pile of Drummonds.

"Maggie has offered to take him for a walk in the pram. Shall I fetch her?" Tillie kissed her husband.

"What are you waiting for?" He kissed her back hungrily. "I've missed you, Tils."

She jumped from the bed, taking Jamie from her husband.

"I'll be back in two ticks," she promised.

Trev was already unbuttoning his shirt.

"Happy Christmas, Tillie."

"Of course, darling," she beamed.

**

"Can you tell us anything more about what you do, Katie? Your letters are exasperatingly vague." Tillie sipped her tea.

Suddenly it was Christmas Eve. Katie had arrived late this morning and met the women at Claridge's just as the enormous tea trays landed on the table.

"I've told you. It's dead boring. Administrative duties. Typing, filing, running errands for important-looking officers. But I've made some great mates, and my billet is atop a beautiful cliff. We even have an indoor bathroom – heaven. The walks are lovely." There. She'd nimbly changed the subject. Tillie raised an eyebrow but said nothing.

"The views must be splendid. But aren't you fearful being so close to the French coast?" Isla asked.

"We do see loads of overhead action. The German bombers often fly right over the house on the way to their targets."

Hannah was glued to Katie's every word.

"Aren't you afraid they'll drop bombs on you?"

"No, luv. We're just a house on a hill. Their aim is farther north. But they rarely get through these days, thanks to you lot." She nodded to Maggie. "Between the radar, anti-aircraft and our RAF fighters, most never reach their destination. And you get used to the noise. We're so dead tired after our duty watches, we can fall asleep anywhere."

"Us too," echoed Maggie. "Who knew we'd all be so whacked all the time that sleep comes in an instant."

The women nodded. They all knew about interrupted sleep and getting by on little over the last years.

"Can you see France from your house?" Hannah pressed.

Maggie knew she was thinking of her parents and brother. She placed a hand on the younger girls.

"On a clear day, we can see the clock tower at Calais. And we can hear the German guns booming across the water," Katie continued.

"I think that's enough gun and bomber talk," Mum said crisply. "We're meant to be enjoying our Christmas tea."

"Sorry, Mum." Katie helped herself to another ham sandwich and scone. "This food is smashing. I haven't tasted anything like it – since our last tea, I suppose. Two years ago."

"Much better than the slop they dish out in the mess," Maggie agreed. "Thanks for keeping this tradition alive, Mum."

"And look how we've grown. We've got the biggest table in the room." Mum looked around the table – Shirley, Isla, Hannah, and her three girls. Perfect. She couldn't be happier.

"Maybe it will be our last Christmas in uniform," Katie said. "Wouldn't that be splendid?"

"Brilliant," said Tillie, thinking of Trev home at last. They could really be a family then.

"Marvellous." Maggie pictured Micah returning to her arms for the reunion she longed for, at last.

"Lovely," Hannah said in a small voice. *Please come home, Mama and Papa. I need you.*

"And then Faye will be back to cook us a proper Christmas dinner," Katie sighed.

This broke the mood.

"I doubt it, dear. Many women aren't going to be satisfied coming back from the war to the old ways. Faye is an independent woman now. She may stay on nursing." Mum called to the waiter for more tea. "And what's wrong with my cooking?"

The women all looked from one to the other, trying to keep from laughing.

"Your cooking has really come on," Shirley said loyally.

"Right, let's enjoy these fancy pastries whilst we can," Tillie said. "And I wonder how the boys are getting on without us. Do you reckon between Trev, Pops, and Uncle Thomas they can manage one tiny boy?"

"They'll be knackered when we get home. So, let's enjoy this quiet feast while we can," Isla said with a smile.

***

There was no need for the girls to wake each other on Christmas morning. Young Jamie woke the entire household at six a.m. – as usual.

"How can one baby be so loud?" Katie rubbed her eyes, looking at the clock. "What an absurd hour to wake up."

"Come on. You're up earlier than this on night watch. Happy Christmas, you humbug." Maggie pulled the coverlet off her sister. They were bunking together a floor above the Drummonds who had taken over Tillie and Maggie's old room.

"Alright. Happy Christmas to you, too." Katie scampered out of bed, pulling on her dressing gown. "It will be a treat to see Jamie opening his gifts."

The family gathered in the drawing room, with a special fire lit for the day. They missed Kenny's spirited presence, but the baby more than made up for it – or at least, almost.

The gifts were even sparser than the year before, but no one minded. They had mostly put their hearts into making it special for Jamie.

"Mum, these knitted animals are darling." Tillie held up a knitted giraffe and elephant. "Thank you."

"You're welcome, luv. When this war is over, I promise I won't be knitting any more Christmas gifts. We're going to be as extravagant as we can." Mum made a face.

"We appreciate all the lovely warm things you've knitted for us," objected Maggie. "I use the scarves and hats on base – usually in bed where it's freezing."

"Me too," said Trev.

"Glad to hear it," Mum chuckled. "Because you're getting more this year."

Trev had carved a beautiful wooden Noah's ark for Jamie's collection of animals.

"He doesn't seem too impressed," Katie said as Jamie put one of the animals in his mouth.

"He'll get loads of play from it when he's older." Tillie opened yet more gifts for him. "Blocks. These are smashing. Thanks, Katie."

Albeit new clothes and toys were out of the question, many of the Kingston children's old ones were re-fashioned into new garments or refurbished playthings.

"Tillie, I'm sorry I've nothing new for the lad, but I hoped he would get some use out of Geoffrey's old books and things." Aunt Shirley offered her packages, her face composed into a smile.

Tillie paused.

"Are you quite certain? These things are special, indeed."

"I've no use for them anymore," Aunt Shirley sniffed. "I'd rather see Jamie play with them – really."

Tillie rose to kiss her aunt on the cheek.

"We'll take good care of them."

Aunt Shirley nodded as Tillie and Trevor opened up the storybooks, blocks and playsuits.

"Are you alright, luv?" Alice quietly asked her sister.

"I am. Don't worry about me," Shirley replied. "Happy Christmas, everyone."

Echoes of Happy Christmas called back to her as more gifts piled up around young Jamie, who was more content to chew on the brown paper they were wrapped in.

***

"Mum, how did you manage these pork chops? They are divine." Katie closed her eyes in rapture.

"A little arrangement that your Aunt Shirley made with Aggie from the WVS. It's no turkey or goose – but certainly respectable for a Christmas dinner." Mum looked around the table, comforted to see so much of her family surrounding her. By tomorrow, it would be train schedules,

144

goodbyes, and more separation. For now, every moment was precious.

"More than respectable, dear. You ladies have outdone yourselves," Walter said through a mouthful of pork and gravy.

Somehow, the ladies had pulled together a veritable feast. Loads of veg, some of Isla's home-made fluffy scones, and stuffing. But the star was the pork chops.

"I'm afraid it's at the expense of afters. We had to barter Isla's plum pudding."

"Well worth it," Thomas proclaimed. "I'm not sure I'd have room for it, in the event."

"I still have something for the sweet tooth. It is Christmas, after all," Isla confessed.

"And I've some chocolate. Don't ask me how I got it." Maggie put a finger to her lips.

"I may have a treat or two myself." Trevor grinned.

"Goo da," said Jamie as he banged his spoon on the tray, his green paper hat lopsided on his head.

"Did you just say Dada?" Trevor almost jumped out of his chair. "Say it again. Dada, Dada."

"Trev, he's just babbling. He doesn't know what he said." Tillie shook her head.

"Give over, the lad has just said his first word. And brilliant it is!" Trev chucked him under the chin.

"I'm not quite sure about that, Trev." Katie laughed. "Maybe he said Happy Christmas."

"I stand by it," Trevor said stubbornly. "He's been waiting for me to return. He saved it."

"With that, I think it's time for the sweets." Isla rose, and swiftly returned with a carrot cake and a few biscuits.

They all agreed it had been a marvellous dinner.

"Almost time for the King's speech," Maggie announced. "Let's clear away so we don't miss it."

"I'll put Jamie down," Tillie said.

A short while later, they gathered once again around the wireless, all eager to hear what the King promised for 1944:

145

"And once again, from our home in England, the Queen and I send our Christmas greetings and good wishes to each one of you all the world over. Some of you may hear me on board your ships, in your aircraft, or where you wait for battle...

To many of you, my words will come as you sit in the quiet of your homes. But wherever you may be today of all days in the year, your thoughts will be in distant places and your hearts with those you love. I hope that my words spoken to them, and to you, may be the bond that joins us all in one company for a few moments on this Christmas Day...

I wish to all who are on service good luck and a stout heart. To those who wait for them to return, proud memories and high hopes to keep you strong. And to all the children here and in the lands beyond the seas, a day of real happiness...

I know you would wish me to send a message of hope to our gallant allies who fight with us, and to all with the loneliness of exile of a hammer of invasion, look forward to our coming victory.

In this year almost passed, many things have happened under God's providence to make us thankful for his mercies. The generous strength of the United States of America, the tremendous deed of Russia, the endurance of China under her long ordeal, for the fighting spirit of France reborn... All these have played their part in the brightening of our fortunes on sea, on land, and in the air...

We know there's much hard working and hard fighting, and perhaps harder working and harder fighting than ever before are necessary for a victory. We shall not rest from our task until it is nobly ended...

Wherever their duty has called our men and women, they have gained new friends and come to know old friends better. They have learnt to share the burdens and to read the hearts of their neighbours. They have laid the foundations of new friendships between nations and strengthened old ones formed long ago...

So, as we see the cloud breaking on this Christmas Day, we should take comfort from our faith that out of desolation so lies a new hope, and out of strife be born a new brotherhood..."

"He didn't come right out and say it, but that was the most uplifting speech yet. 'Bright visions of the future,'" Trev said.

"Can you tell us any more about the big push, Trev?" asked Aunt Shirley. "Surely your RAF boys are preparing for it."

"I'm sorry, I can't. But I think we all know something is brewing," he replied.

"Loads of soldiers and airmen at Paddington station. Plenty of Yanks, too," Katie put in.

"I like his message of brotherhood and helping your neighbours," Mum said. "We've all learned about that in the last four years. We couldn't have gotten by without helping each other."

"Too right, Mum." Maggie smiled.

"I don't know about you lot, but I need to work off that delicious dinner. Anyone interested in a little skating party before Master James awakes?"

"I'll listen for him," Isla offered.

"Ta, Mum," Trev said.

"I'm in," Katie said, rising. Let's put Dad's old gift of ice skates to good use." That had been a splendid Christmas before the war. She could still see Kenny whipping round the ice, laughing and pulling her along.

"We'll come too, right, Mags?" Tillie said. "Hannah, I'm sure we can scrounge up a pair of skates that will fit you."

The young people dashed off for their party, whilst Alice, Shirley, and Isla sipped sherry and put up their tired feet. Walter and Thomas disappeared to the library for a wee tot of brandy and war talk.

Chapter Seven

FOGGY AND DENSE

1944 – Katie

"Are you sure you are up to it, Queenie? You've only just gotten over a serious case of the measles." Ruby paused from combing her hair.

"I'm back to full strength – pretty much. Being pampered by Mum at home was just the tonic." Katie grinned.

"And the help of a certain Irish paratrooper," teased Ruby.

Katie responded by chucking her tricorn hat at her mate, who easily ducked it.

"Ciaran was so sweet, collecting me from the hospital here and taking me back to London. I felt so safe and protected."

"Sounds like you are besotted by the lad." Ruby smoothed her uniform and whistled. "Katie's in love, Katie's in love," she sang off key.

"Sod off, Rubes. I'm not sure how I feel. I care about him loads, and he's been ever so kind to me but…"

"But what? He obviously fancies you. He wrote to you from France after the Allies took it back, he comes to see you here in Portsmouth any chance he gets leave. What's the problem?"

Katie sank to the narrow bed.

"I don't know what's wrong with me, and that's the truth. I do care for him. When he went missing after his jump blew off course, I worried about him every day. Finally hearing he was safe, I almost collapsed with relief."

Ruby sat next to her.

"I remember."

"I don't know if I can trust him. I haven't had the best luck with men."

She gave a harsh laugh. "As you well know."

Ruby's jaw dropped.

"This isn't still about that rotter from Southwold, is it?"

"Ralph? No – not the way you think. I'm over that married man. I don't have any feelings for him whatsoever. But since it happened, I'm just better off alone. I don't want to be hurt like that again." A lump formed in her throat. *Bloody hell, I swore I would never let that man cause me to shed another tear.*

"But don't you see luv? If you let that moment – and it was just a moment – put you off men for the rest of your life, who suffers because of it? Certainly not that cheat. *You'll* be the one without love in your life." Ruby's blue eyes bore into her chum's brown ones.

"I do see that. And Ciaran is slowly thawing my icy heart. I'm just not quite there yet. Maybe it's a matter of time." She looked away.

"Katie, is there something else? You're not putting me into the whole picture."

"The obvious, I suppose. Ciaran is an Irish farmer with ailing parents. He's been honest since I met him in Dover that he plans to go back there after the war. Longs for it, in fact. Do you see me as a farmer's wife?" Katie wrinkled her nose.

"Now, you are getting ahead of yourself. I don't know what to do with you, luv. Either stuck in the past or worrying about things that may or may not happen in the future. Why not just enjoy the way things are now? The war will most certainly be over next year. Plenty of time to plan. And I do think you'd be a smashing farmer's wife. You could do a lot worse."

"I suppose so." Katie wasn't so sure.

"Look, has he even spoken about love or the future?"

"He told me he loved me in London." Katie sounded miserable.

"You daft cow. You never said." Ruby jumped up. "Did you say it back?"

"No. I was taken aback and it was so sudden and…no. I've probably put him off now."

Ruby laughed.

"I don't think so. Isn't he coming to fetch you for Christmas at your house in London? Maybe he'll bring you a lovely present."

"Bloody hell. You don't think it will be an engagement ring, do you?" Katie felt her heart clutch. "I'm not ready for that yet, by half."

"Doubtful if you didn't tell him you loved him. Just remember what I said. Enjoy your time with him, and see where it goes. Now, are we off to the dance or not? Our transport won't wait forever." Ruby took a last look in the mirror and nodded. "With Australian, Canadian, American and our own lads on offer, I plan to do just that – enjoy myself."

Katie smoothed the coverlet, nudged Ruby away from the mirror and gave herself the once-over.

"Let's get on, then. And Rubes – thanks for the talk." *Mum's right – a trouble shared is a troubled halved.*

***

"I'll warm up the teapot, shall I? This is stone cold." Tillie juggled Jamie on one hip whilst lifting the teapot with the other.

"If you like." Mum didn't even look up from the kitchen table.

Tillie filled up the kettle, put it on the hob, turned on the gas, and looked out the window.

"More fog. It doesn't feel Christmassy at all, does it?"

"No," Mum said.

Tillie put Jamie on the floor with his pile of blocks.

"I've got a brilliant idea. Why don't I help you make your famous tick list for Christmas? It's getting near time and we must decide what to serve on Christmas Day. I can pop to the shops later."

Mum shrugged.

"If you like. It hardly seems worth the bother."

"Mum, I know you are desperately missing Aunt Shirley. We all are. But you must make an effort. Maggie and Katie will both be home – albeit for short leaves. And Trev, too. I think even Katie's beau Ciaran will be here for a short while. We can't just hope for the best – there will be rather a mass of us."

"But not my sister." Mum looked up with a somber expression.

After months of planning and cooperation between not only the combined Allied forces, but all branches of the military, Operation Overlord had been a resounding success. On June 6th, the first Allied troop ships left England's south coast ports for multiple landing points across France's west coast.

Shortly thereafter, British and American airborne troops began taking off from British bases. They were the first Allied soldiers to land in Normandy, by glider and parachute, in the early hours of the following morning. Then, the Allied fleet crossed the English Channel, led by minesweepers, who cleared a safe route for the other ships.

Landing on five different beaches, the Germans were taken by surprise, expecting an attack at Calais, not Normandy. Although thousands of Allied forces were killed, the German defence suffered far greater losses, and France was recaptured, signalling a major victory for the Allies. But it was just the beginning. The Battle of Normandy lasted for twelve more weeks as the Allies captured key locations to expand the area under their control.

Although Britons rejoiced, they knew it was far from over. They held a collective breath, waiting for a Nazi retaliation. It came in the form of the V-1, *Vergeltungswaffe Eins* or Vengeance Weapon One, commonly called a doodlebug or buzzbomb. Pilotless, they were frightening in number and damage. Thousands launched over London, killing and injuring thousands more…so far. Buzzing overheard, Londoners quickly learned to run for cover at the moment when the motor cut out. Otherwise, they would fall victim to its deadly explosion.

Shirley Fowler had been one of the V-1's casualties. She and Alice had been on a bus headed for a summer WVS shift when the dreaded sound buzzed overhead. With no time to escape to a shelter, they were trapped on the bus. Huddling under the seats, the passengers were prime targets. Shirley and many others were killed instantly. Alice had been seriously injured, breaking a leg, and sustaining cuts and bruises to most of her body.

Her recovery had been slow, not the least because of her overwhelming grief at losing her sister, somehow feeling responsible for not protecting her. Her body was now healed, but her heart and mind were far behind. The entire family worried about her, hoping that time would ease the pain and anguish that she carried like a hundred-pound sack.

Tillie sighed, pouring the tea.

"No, Aunt Shirley won't be here. And we all miss her dreadfully. Do you think she would want us being miserable, and skipping the Christmas festivities? She'd be scolding you something proper."

A ghost of a smile.

"I suppose you're right, luv. Alright, let's make the list, but I'll need your help. I'm not up to much this year. Shirley always did the Christmas Eve celebration – well before the war, that is." Her hand shook as she lifted the teacup to her lips.

"I think we should give that a miss again this year," Tillie said briskly. "With all the comings and goings 'round here, it might as well be Victoria Station. I'm not quite sure who will be here when, but I'll sort it."

"That sounds nice, dear."

"Mama, bikkie," a baby voice came from the floor.

"You smart boy. You said a whole sentence. Mum, did you hear that?" She picked him up, and spun him around.

Mum roused.

"Lovely," she said.

Tillie deposited the little boy on her mother's lap. Young Jamie was about the only person that could stir up happy emotions in her mother.

Mum bounced him, cooing.

"You are a little love, aren't you?" She kissed his cheek and hugged him to her. "Such a comfort."

"He adores you, Mum. We all do."

Mum straightened her back, giving Tillie a reassuring smile.

"I'm working on it, luv. I miss her so much. I'm trying to find a bit of joy in life again. My heart hurts all the time. This little lamb helps more than you know."

Tillie nodded.

"I know it's tradition, but I don't think I can manage the annual Claridges tea this year. I just can't face it."

Tillie's heart plummeted. She gulped.

"Mum, I understand, and the girls will, too. It meant so much to Aunt Shirley that it doesn't feel right doing it without her. Let's put our energies into the day itself. I'll talk it over with Trev's mum. You don't need to worry about a thing. We'll sort it so that's it's simple but still a proper Christmas – especially for everyone who is longing to come home."

"Thank you, dear. It's for the best."

The fact that she agreed so quickly alarmed Tillie no end. She didn't recognize the mum she'd known for twenty-seven years. The pain ran even deeper than she'd thought. She couldn't wait for Trev to come home. She needed his quiet strength and broad shoulders to lean on. In the meantime, she would do her best to make this as joyful a Christmas as possible for everyone, especially Mum.

* * *

"Maggie, we need to get on. It's not like you to dilly dally." Pip shook her awake. "You are usually the one hurrying me along."

"Keep your hair on. I need five more minutes," Maggie mumbled, pulling a pillow over her head.

"We don't have it. We're meant to be on duty in thirty minutes. And I don't intend to miss breakfast."

"Breakfast?" The thought of manky porridge, watery tea, and powdered eggs made Maggie's stomach lurch.

"You go on ahead. I'll meet you straightaway." Maggie ran for the bathroom, barely making it in time before chucking up what little was in her stomach. Wiping her mouth, she caught a movement behind her.

"When were you going to tell me, Maggie?" Pip stood with her hands on hips.

"Tell you what?" Maggie turned, face white.

"That you are expecting a baby, you daft mare." Pip grinned from ear to ear.

"Hmm, well soon, I suppose. I thought I was hiding it rather well."

"You are. But I see you sick in the morning, and flagging as the day wears on. Does Micah know?"

"Yes. And my family. But no one else. And I want to keep it that way. I want to keep working – at least for a few months."

Pip hugged her.

"I'm that chuffed for you, luv. You and Micah deserve all the happiness in the world after what you've been through. It's been such a year for you."

And it had. Early in the year had come the terrible news that Micah's parents had died in Auschwitz concentration camp. They'd been sent almost straightway from the Jewish roundup that had brought them and Micah to Drancy transit camp years earlier. The news had come much later that they'd both died there – from typhus, starvation, or any number of other privation diseases. Micah stayed on in Drancy, making himself indispensable as a translator, administrator, and most horribly – the man responsible for maintaining the lists of prisoners coming in and out of the camp. He had made endless inquiries as to his parents' whereabouts and wellbeing, but found nothing but ghastly reports and rumors about the conditions at the camps, and how innocent men, women, and children were being treated. Eventually, it was confirmed that his parents died there, but he never discovered how or when.

After two long years of appalling living conditions and suffering from near-starvation himself, Micah had been released as the Germans realized they were losing the war, and started to cover their tracks. Being a British citizen, Uncle Thomas had been able to pull some strings – after many months of failed attempts – to secure the young man's release.

The reunion between Maggie and Micah had been poignant. Micah was painfully thin, and bore deep scars from his experiences, but their quiet and long-blooming love blossomed and deepened at first sight of each other. All of Maggie's doubts disappeared.

They had married quietly a few weeks later at the registry office – a muted affair that suited them and a contented Hannah to the ground. The Goldbachs were sorely missed, but the trio were now a firm family, planning for the future.

Maggie had been dazed but pleased to discover she was expecting a baby almost straightaway. Glorious news in a year that had brought enormous joy and dreadful heartache in equal measure. She hoped that new life would restore Mum's spirit. She was sure to be delighted.

"I'm not sure how much longer you will be able to hide it," Pip continued. "You're already looking a bit chubby, and your bosoms are – well – quite something."

Maggie looked down at her blooming body in dismay. Pulling Pip into the bathroom, she shut the door.

"I have something to tell you, but you must keep it to yourself. Only

Micah knows. I'm going to tell the family at Christmas. Promise?"

Pip put her hand over her heart.

"I swear on the life of His Majesty, King George VI that I won't tell a soul. What is it?"

A smile swept across Maggie's face.

"I'm having twins."

Pip shrieked.

"You're not?"

Maggie cradled her growing belly, and nodded.

"I am, indeed."

"Well, I never. I suppose they run in the family, don't they. Congratulations, luv. What a turn-up for the books. And your secret is safe with me. Although I don't imagine you'll be able to keep it for long. You're expanding at an alarming rate."

The girls giggled, hugged once more, and dashed off for another day on the ack-ack site.

***

"My dear mavourneen,

Duties are certainly slowing down here at Bletchley. It's just a matter of time now until utter triumph is ours. The fog has been keeping the lads from our hockey games on the pond and it's lucky that we work and live on the same grounds, otherwise we'd get lost on our way to and fro.

I trust you are not too hard at it, my love. You are just now recovered from that dodgy case of the measles. Your time at home put the roses back in your cheeks, and it warmed my heart to see a bit of life coming back into your mum as she cared so lovingly for you.

Please don't be angry at me for expressing my true feelings for you that day in the park. It was too soon, I know – but it just came out without a thought. I suppose that shows my feelings are true, but I hope and pray I haven't scared you off. You need more time, and I will give it to you. But not too much time, please?

Thank you for your kind invitation to join you and your family for Christmas in London. I've sorted a five-day pass and travel warrant, but I need *most of that time to get over to Ireland and back. My folks are dead keen to see me, and I miss them, too, come to that. I will be able to stop on the 23rd overnight, but must catch the train and ferry on Christmas Eve to my parents, or they'll be terribly let down. I hope that's alright. It will be grand to see you and them again, and to meet everyone that I've heard so much but haven't met as yet.*

Send me a telegram if these arrangements don't suit. Christmas is fast approaching and I can't wait to see you and hold you in my arms again. Till then...a thousand kisses.

Love,
Ciaran xx"

Katie crushed the letter to her chest. Heart beating fast, she re-read it again. Bloody hell – Christmas with Ciaran at home. What could be merrier than that?

***

"Come to Nana, Jamie," Isla swept the little boy into her arms and smothered him with kisses. "You're such a pet, and growing all the time. Oh, come in, luv," she added, nodding to the mother of her grandchild.

Tillie inwardly groaned. She knew her place now. Jamie was the star of every conversation – especially with Nana or Granny. She was just an afterthought.

"Hello, Nana. Are you alright?" She kissed her mother-in-law on the cheek.

"I'm fine. Come through. I've got the kettle on." She led them into the small sitting room. "How are you getting on? Any letters from Trevor?" Isla held Jamie in her lap but gazed over at Tillie. Tall and willowy, she shared her son's piercing blue eyes, but no dimple. The small flat was graciously decorated with some of her own water colour paintings.

Jamie squirmed in her arms, demanding to be put down. Toddling over to his favorite corner, he immediately climbed onto his rocking horse, swinging furiously back and forth.

Tillie shook her head. At nineteen months, he kept her on her toes morning till night. Having mastered walking, he now ran everywhere, and had even taken a tumble or two down the stairs. His little hands were exploring everything, and Tillie despaired of Mum's lovely bits and bobs being smashed to smithereens. But she couldn't keep him cooped up in their bedroom all day, so she tried to find him safe corners to play with his animals, blocks, and toy soldiers.

"Yes, I heard from him last week. It's brilliant that he's stationed back here in London again. Especially now that the V-1's and V-2 rockets seem to have slowed down."

Isla nodded as she prepared the tea things.

"Too right, luv. Poor Trevor was in in the thick of it with the Baby Blitz, and then almost on top of that – the revenge rockets. How is a mother supposed to cope with all this strain? On one hand, my son is closer to home and can pop by when he has leave. Yet, he's fighting fires night and day. You never know when a stray bomb will have his name on it." She passed Tillie a cup, eyebrows furrowed.

"You mustn't dwell on that. The worst is over – surely it is. We can't think on what might have been."

"You're right, darling. But he's my only son. I can't help worrying about him."

"Me too." Tillie sipped, keeping one eye on her son. He could get into mischief in no time. "You've heard that he has three-day's leave for Christmas. That's smashing news."

Isla brightened.

"It is, and you're right. We've gotten through so much. We just have to hang on a little longer. How is your dear mother doing? I'm meant to pop by later. She's invited me to supper."

"About the same. Good days and bad days. We're proper thankful for all your help around the house. We couldn't manage without you," Tillie said quietly. That was true. With Mum so listless, Isla had been a god-send to keep the household going.

Isla waved away the compliment.

"If we learned anything from this war, it's that we have to help each other. I'm obliged to you for your support. Without your family, I would

157

have been wretched – just sitting here in this flat, waiting for my son to come home."

The quiet morning was disturbed only by Jamie's babbling. A sudden sunbeam glimmered through the window.

"There's a good sign, Nana. After all this fog, a ray of sunshine boding good times ahead."

Isla passed her the plate of biscuits. "Help yourself. Can Jamie have one?"

Hearing one of his favorite words, he waddled over, hands outstretched. "Bikkie, bikkie."

"What can I say now? Yes, he can have one," Tillie replied with a shrug. She put down her teacup and turned to Isla.

"I've come to talk to you about several things. Besides bringing this little minx for a visit," she amended. "It is about Mum. We had a chat about Christmas. She's not up to much this year. She doesn't even want to have our annual Claridge's tea. I'm that worried about her." Dammit, her voice was quavering.

"Oh dear, that is serious. She treasures those traditions. Her grief is overpowering. We must do everything possible to make it easy for her. How can I help?"

Tillie smiled. She knew her mother-in-law would come up trumps.

"I was hoping you'd ask that. Everyone is expected home save Kenny, so it will be a full house, and the schedules are hectic. Even Ciaran will be stopping by on his way to Ireland."

"Do you have room for him at yours? He can stay here in Trev's old room."

"Right. We might need that, ta. I'll make a note." She scrambled in her bag for a scrap piece of paper and pencil. Meanwhile, young Jamie was screaming for another bikkie. Nana distracted him with some of Trevor's old toys.

"With Aunt Shirley gone, we've decided to forego any Christmas Eve celebration. But what shall we do instead?" Tillie chewed her lip.

"We could go out for supper, but no. That's pretty much the same as going for tea," Isla considered. "I could prepare some appetizers. If the family is arriving higgly piggly, maybe we could just set up a table for people to nibble at."

"That sounds brilliant."

"It's unlikely there will be any air raids. Maybe we could go to the local church for Christmas Eve service and carols?" Isla asked.

"Even better. Jamie would love that, and maybe it would give Mum a little peace."

"And I'll come by early on the twenty-fifth if that's alright to help make breakfast and prepare the dinner. Hannah will be home by then, right? She's always a huge help in the kitchen," Isla continued.

"Come as early as you like. I'd have you stay over, but we'll be full to bursting. You must come and see Jamie opening his gifts from Father Christmas."

"Santa?" Jamie perked up. "Santa coming?"

"Oh dear. What have I started? Santa coming soon, Jamie. Not yet."

Tillie could see that he was working himself up to a right tantrum.

"Shall we do some colouring, darling? You can make a picture for Father Christmas." Isla picked him up and produced some discarded paper and crayons.

"Pitcher for Santa?" He was momentarily distracted.

"You mentioned several things. Is there something else?" Isla asked gently.

Tillie took a deep breath.

"This next is good news. At least I think it is. But I'm not sure how to tell Mum. I rang Trev yesterday at the RAF base to tell him, and he's more than excited. We are expecting another baby."

Isla jumped up, causing Jamie to startle. Tillie snatched him for a cuddle before he started to cry.

"How marvellous, Tillie! What a perfect Christmas gift. Another baby. Congratulations." Isla hugged her and Jamie, causing him to squirm. "You've brought a tear to my eye. How are you feeling this time?"

"Not as sick in the mornings, but deathly tired. Some days I can hardly get through – especially with this little monkey. So you can see why the upcoming days are rather – overwhelming." Tillie pushed back a stray hair from her forehead.

"Yes, of course, and I'll do everything I can to ease the load. My, you and Maggie both expecting at Christmastime. What next, I wonder?"

Twins are what's happening next, but that's Maggie's news to share, not mine. Tillie smiled to herself.

"That brings me to the subject of living arrangements. We'll all double up for the holidays, but Trev and I are outgrowing the Kingston house. In fact, it's already too small for us – having Jamie in our room. He's too little to move upstairs on his own. Where are we going to put another baby?" Tillie rocked Jamie who was slowly stilling.

"My offer still stands for you to come here, but there's even less room."

"Ta, Nana, but you're right. Trev and I have been talking about getting one of those pre-fabricated houses the government are promoting. After the war, of course. They have all the modern conveniences, and we'd finally have our own home. Don't get me wrong – I'm happy to have a roof over our heads and the help and company. But I'd like my own kitchen, and places for my own things where I don't have to worry about Jamie crashing Mum's precious knick-knacks." Peeking down at her son, she was glad to see his eyes closed. She slowly stopped rocking.

"That sounds like a lovely plan. Would you be likely to qualify for one?"

"I think so. Trevor's service in the RAF will put him on the list. Mum will take it hard, though. I don't know how I'll put her through that."

Isla put on a hand on Tillie's arm.

"Don't borrow trouble, dear. The end of the war is still a way off, and your mum is getting stronger every day. By the time you're ready to move out, Maggie and Katie will be home. Everything will change. It will all work out. You'll see."

"You always make me feel better. Thanks ever so much."

"More tea, luv?" Isla held up the teapot.

"No, but could I ask one more thing?" Tillie's voice turned sweeter.

"You want me to mind him? I'd love to. Just lay him on my bed. I adore having him all to myself."

"Ta. I need to nip out to the shops. With the queues and in this cold, it will be much faster without him," Tillie almost whispered as she gingerly tip-toed with him to the bedroom.

Isla collected the cups and brought them to the kitchen.

Tillie left and the flat fell silent. This suited Isla just fine. She had loads to think about, and young Jamie would be up and a going concern in no time. She was going to be a Nana again. She must ask Tillie when the baby was due. She'd totally forgotten in all the excitement.

***

Hannah arrived two days before Christmas, and Katie almost on top of her. Hannah's light blue WAAF colours blended with Katie's navy-blue Wren uniform as they hugged.

"How was your train journey? Lots of stoppages?" Katie asked as they came through the townhouse door. She'd come from the south, and Hannah the north.

"Not too horrid. The train was jammed, but everyone was friendly and festive. You?"

Katie's answer was muffled by the sound of a nineteen-month-old wailing. Tillie dashed up the kitchen stairs, stopping at the site of Katie and Hannah in the hallway.

"Darlings, you're here. Splendid." She hugged them both. "I'm being summoned by the young prince. I'd best collect him from his nap." Tillie disappeared up the stairs.

"Right, let's drop our kit. I suppose Mum is in the kitchen. I hope she's feeling better." Katie raised an eyebrow.

The pair clattered down, feeling the warmth seep towards them.

Sure enough, Mum sat at the worn kitchen table with the ever-present teacup at her elbow.

"Katie, Hannah, you're here. Are you alright?" Mum rose slowly as the girls each kissed her on the cheek.

"Cold, and could hardly see our way home in this bloo – blasted fog," Katie corrected herself. "We're home now. That's all that matters. How are you getting on?" Katie sat as Hannah put the kettle back on the hob.

Mum is still looking frail, Katie thought.

"A bit better, I suppose. I'm off the crutches, and all the bruises have healed."

"Brilliant, Mum. Excited for Christmas? When is Maggie expected?"

Ignoring the first question, Mum answered the second.

"I'm not quite sure. I can't keep everyone straight."

Katie stole a glance at Hannah. This was not good. Mum was always on top of everything.

"Ciaran is coming later today. I'm not sure about Maggie or Trevor," Katie said.

"They're both due to arrive tomorrow about mid-day." Tillie was back, Jamie in arms.

"Darling," Katie cried, taking her nephew from her sister. "You've gotten so big. Do you have a kiss for your Auntie Katie?"

"No," Jamie shouted. "No," he repeated as if no one had heard him.

"I see," Katie said, putting him on the floor. "That's me told."

"Don't take it personally, luv. It's his favorite word these days," Tillie apologized.

"Not at all. I've heard worse – much worse on watch," Katie joked. "Any biscuits on offer with this tea?"

"Uh oh, that's the magic word," Mum said. "Now you'll have to give him one." Jamie was already reaching for the tin. "We've started to spell it since he hears and understands everything."

"I suppose I'll need to watch my language then." Katie chewed a ginger biscuit.

"As you should, dear," Mum said, as expected. They all chuckled.

"How's Portsmouth? Quietening down?" Tillie asked.

"Rather. It's nowhere near as busy as Dover. But then, it wouldn't be, would it? The castle was crawling with servicemen of every nationality and uniform before June. Now, they've gone to France, and are keeping the country safeguarded for all of us." Katie smiled thinking of Ruby, dating soldiers and flyers from every Allied country.

"How's your billet?" asked Hannah. "We're in a requisitioned Victorian estate. Lovely rooms and high ceilings, but freezing, with temperamental water flow."

"Tough luck," Katie sympathized, discreetly handing Jamie another biscuit. "Ruby and I are on our own in a room overtop a pub. Toasty warm, and we can always get a hot meal and something to drink. It's a hefty walk to the ship, though."

The Women's Royal Navy motto was *"Never at Sea,"* but the working quarters were always called ships, even though they were typically buildings on dry land. It had taken a little getting used to, but Katie now handled all the Navy terminology with ease.

"And the weather forecasting? Keeping you busy?" Tillie asked, as Jamie pulled a tea towel off the rack. She shrugged. It could be worse.

"Up and down," Hannah said, removing her jacket. "It's definitely less hectic, so some shifts are slow. We've been hearing rumors that our station may be shutting down, and we'll be scattered to other RAF sites."

"That's the way of the military. Shunting us here, there and everywhere." Katie also took off her navy greatcoat.

"We've certainly mastered the art of packing and unpacking in a hurry." Hannah smiled.

"Ho, ho, ho," called a voice from the hall upstairs. "Can someone give me a hand?"

"What in the world?" Mum said, looking at the girls.

Tillie scooped up Jamie and made for the stairs, but Katie was already ahead of her. Mum and Hannah followed.

"Uncle Thomas, is that a Christmas tree?" squeaked Tillie.

"Indeed, it is." Thomas pulled the large fir tree in by the trunk. Katie rushed to help him.

"How on earth did you manage to find the only Christmas tree in London?" Mum asked with a gasp.

"Someone in the office brought it from his house in the country. We've had it up for a few days, but now that the office is closed for the holidays, he offered it round to anyone who wanted it. I was the lucky bloke who got it. Now, who is going to help me drag it in? I'm sure young Jamie will want a hand in dressing it."

Katie clapped her hands.

"What a brilliant start to Christmas. Let's drag it into the drawing room, and we can fetch down the cartons with all our ornaments."

Tillie put on the wireless to add Christmas carols to the mood.

"Mustn't touch." Tillie kept Jamie's little fingers out of the more breakable items. "Why don't we throw the tinsel on the tree? Listen, folks, we'll have to leave the lower branches clear. The tree may look a little strange, but otherwise Master Drummond here will have at it and these precious bits will be smashed to smithereens." Tillie was exhausted keeping up with her exuberant toddler. *When would Trev arrive to share the load?*

Micah arrived home to find the family sprawled around the drawing room, drinking cocoa and admiring their handiwork. First to spot him was Hannah, who ran across the room to throw herself in his arms. She still wasn't used to him being home and within arm's reach. It had been a wrench being so far away on base when he was finally released, but they had kept up a steady correspondence. She had been thrilled to be included in their small wedding, and was beyond excited about becoming a proper aunt.

Katie lurked around the door, listening for the knock that would bring Ciaran. Finally, she heard a loud bang and ran down to answer it.

"Ciaran," she greeted him breathlessly.

"Mavourneen." He pulled her into his arms, heedless of the cold he brought in with him. He kissed her long and passionately. She felt warm despite the cold air blowing in. Closing her eyes, she swayed into him, wanting to be as near as she could.

"Who is this wild stranger freezing us out?" Tillie called from the doorway.

Ciaran and Katie broke apart reluctantly, and Katie closed the heavy door.

"Tillie, how are you?" Ciaran strode forward and kissed her on the cheek. "And where is the young lad?" He made a show of looking around the hall until he peeked around Tillie to see Jamie hiding behind her. "There you are, Jamie. Me wee mate."

Ciaran and Jamie had become fast friends several weeks ago during Katie's measles convalescence. Ciaran loved to play horsey with him on the floor or chase him around as the Big Bad Wolf. Jamie adored him and had followed him everywhere.

"Keekee," Jamie shouted, throwing himself into Ciaran's arms.

The rest of the adults drifted in, greeting Ciaran as "Happy Christmas" was heard all around.

"Come through. You must be wanting some hot tea. Those trains are frigid," Tillie said.

"It's a short ride from Bletchley, so it wasn't bad, and all. But I do have a few gifts for you from Ireland. From me Ma and Da."

Walter walked in as the string and brown paper came off, revealing undreamed-of luxuries.

The Kingstons were nothing short of astounded to unwrap two small chickens, a dozen real eggs, rashers of bacon, an Irish Christmas cake, and a small bottle of Irish whiskey.

"What in the world?" cried Mum.

"At Christmastime, all the farmers trade goods between them, so there is plenty for all. And we're not on the ration in Ireland. Me parents don't have a lot, but it's a time for sharing, isn't it? They sent me the parcel to bring to London."

"We're overwhelmed with their generosity. We'll send them a telegram straightaway, and thank you so much, Ciaran." Walter spoke for them all.

"A letter will be grand. If they see the telegram boy bicycling down the lane, they'll be frightened to death thinking the worst has happened to me."

"Indeed. We certainly don't want that. We'll write a letter instead."

"There's our Christmas breakfast and dinner sorted," Tillie said, eyes wide. "We are ever so grateful, Ciaran."

"'Tis nothing. You've been so kind and welcoming to me. Now, how about that tea?"

"Right. I'll go," Hannah offered.

Katie ushered Ciaran into the drawing room where he was properly impressed with the Christmas tree.

After a simple supper of offal, turnips, cabbage, and apple custard, Tillie pried a sleepy Jamie from Ciaran's lap and took him to bed. Micah and Hannah drifted down the kitchen for tea and a chat. Dad took Mum up to bed, planning on an early night with his book. That left Ciaran and Katie in the drawing room, snuggling, whispering and getting reacquainted as only reunited lovers do. They stayed up until way past midnight, enjoying every second together whilst they planned for the future.

Frost and ice shards coated the windows on Christmas Eve morning. The fog had temporarily lifted, and a weak winter sun filtered through the cloudy windows. The house was abuzz with excitement, awaiting the arrival of the final two family members – Trevor and Maggie. Tillie left

Jamie with Mum and Hannah so she could wait for her husband's train. Maggie was expected a few hours later, and Micah would welcome her home for a five-day leave.

Only Katie was filled with despair as she waved off Ciaran at Euston Station.

"You've such a long journey ahead, darling. A train, a ferry, and then a bus." Katie pulled her collar closer. She was that frozen; her breath wafted in the cold air.

"And then a walk to the farm. But I don't mind. They'll be that glad to see me. And Ma will have put on a feast fit for a King."

Katie punched him gently in the arm.

"Go on then, Irish. Aren't you going to miss me at all?"

"I will miss you dreadfully. I just don't want to think about it. Give us a kiss."

Katie happily obliged.

"Not to rush you, luv, but me ma and da will be asking when you're coming for a visit. They are dead keen to meet you, and all."

"And I want to meet them, too. As soon I feel up to my old vigor and I can wangle a respectable leave, you can take me there. I used so much sick leave that I don't dare ask for even a smidge."

"I understand. They'll be over the moon to hear you want to come. We've plenty to show you, mavourneen."

The whistle blew and the pair froze.

Ciaran picked up his bags, which included gifts from the Kingstons along with a letter of thanks. He leaned down to kiss Katie one more time.

"Happy Christmas. Next year will be even better. We'll be together, and perhaps it will be a grand day in Ireland with me folks."

"I'm not sure about that, Irish. I can't imagine not being home for Christmas. But I'm sure we can sort something – together."

The whistle blew again.

"Go, go," she urged as he turned to climb the stairs to the railway car.

He disappeared from view, but then a window opened and his head popped out. *I love you*, he mouthed.

She waved and waved, wiping a tear as he vanished into the distance.

She felt slightly sick to her stomach. Was this love? She ached for him, and he had just left.

Turning, she walked slowly through the busy station, re-living every moment of the last twenty-four hours. *Pull yourself together, girl. You'll see him soon. And he's safe at Bletchley. It's Christmas Eve, the family is gathering, and 1945 is going to be a remarkable year.* Her step quickened.

***

By six p.m., all the travellers had arrived, and Isla had put out a surprising array of delicious foods. Both Tillie and Maggie were happily reunited with their husbands – each held a secret she was keeping until Christmas Day.

"Darling, I'm that relieved your journey was short. You look done in," Mum said to Maggie, who was looking decidedly peaky.

"I'm fine, Mum, just tired. Expecting a baby will do that to you. But I'm happy to be home." She gazed at her husband.

"You two look blissfully happy." Katie sighed. "And well deserved, too." *I hope I'm as happy someday – with Ciaran. I finally think I might be.*

Trevor and Tillie stayed behind with Jamie while the rest of the family went to Christmas Eve service. Alice felt peace for a time, listening to the familiar songs, especially Silent Night. The hole in her heart would never go away, and she missed her sister desperately. But the ache subsided for a little while, and she was comforted.

Christmas morning was almost as chaotic as when the children were small. Like last year, most of the attention was fixed on young Jamie, who didn't disappoint. Husbands and wives, sister to sister, and parents with children exchanged simple but heartfelt gifts. Isla joined them for the first time, and was happy to spend the morning with her son, grandson, and adopted family. Micah, Maggie, and Hannah spent their first Christmas together in almost five years. Only Kenny was missing.

"I think you should keep this Ciaran. We haven't had such a Christmas breakfast since before the war." Tillie spooned eggs into Jamie's mouth. He was so surprised at the taste, he kept saying "mo, mo."

"He's never tasted real eggs, the little lamb." Tillie smiled.

167

"Wait till he gets a bite of that bacon. There'll be none left for the rest of us." Trevor broke off a piece and fed it to his son.

"Oh no, you don't," Katie snatched the plate, helped herself and passed it to Hannah. "How can the smell of bacon and eggs frying suddenly feel Christmassy?"

"Because we haven't had it for so long." Isla sighed. "It brings back memories."

"None for me, thanks," Maggie passed. "My stomach is still a bit wobbly. I'll stick with toast and tea."

"Goody. More for me." Katie took an extra piece of bacon.

"Don't get too full. We have a splendid dinner coming in just a few hours," Mum warned.

Laughter filled the warm room. No one had felt completely full since before the war. They were luckier than most – there was always food on the table, but like all Britons, they were heartily sick of the same old dishes and rationed portions.

Katie and Hannah helped Mum and Isla prepare the Christmas feast. Isla hadn't known about the bounty from Ciaran's folks, and had outdone herself with a small ham, masses of the usual veg and stuffings, and a hoarded jar of cranberry sauce.

Tillie put her hand on her Mum's.

"Remember when we started planning and we thought we'd have a barren holiday table? Just look at this abundance. It all worked out, Mum."

For a moment, the worry crease on her face softened. "It did, luv. Thank for you for all your help. I just couldn't manage this year."

"And that's why we all pitched in. Happy Christmas, Mum."

"Happy Christmas, luv."

Talk turned inevitably to when the war would be over. Everyone agreed it was just a matter of time now.

"And then our work will really begin," Micah said quietly. "There are so many families to be found, repatriated, and re-homed."

Micah had begun working at the Jewish Refugee Center. It was heartrending work as so many wives, children, parents, brothers and sisters had been lost. Both Micah and Maggie were determined to help as many families as they could. Mostly, the news was appalling as so few people could find anyone who had survived. But once Hitler's grasp had been permanently severed, they held out hope of eventual reunions. If it took his lifetime, Micah was dedicated to this cause.

"And this young lady is bound for university," Micah changed the subject, giving his sister a bright smile.

"That's smashing, Hannah. What will you study?" Tillie asked.

"I'm not sure yet, but perhaps some type of international studies. I want to help Micah with his work. Maybe even the law." Hannah was smart and hard-working. Tillie had no doubt she'd succeed in anything she turned her hand to.

"And we'd like to help any way we can," Walter said.

"Thank you," Hannah turned a little red. She hated having attention on her.

"We have a little announcement to make." Micah sat back in his chair. "Don't we, little one?" He turned to his wife.

"What in the world?" Mum halted the fork halfway to her mouth.

"Not so little, it seems. Mum, Pops, everyone – we're having twins," Maggie twinkled.

"Marvellous!"

"Congratulations, you two."

"How wonderful."

"You don't look too surprised," Katie accused Tillie.

"Twins can't keep secrets," Tillie said, a trifle smugly.

Trevor cleared his throat and took Tillie's hand.

"Our turn, I suppose. Tillie and I would like to say that come next June, young Jamie here will have a little brother or sister."

"Oh, my heavens," cried Mum. "My girls both having babies. Splendid, indeed."

"I believe this calls for a toast. Katie, may we serve the Irish whisky your young man graciously donated?"

It was on the tip of Katie's tongue to say he wasn't her young man, but she stopped. He *was* her beau.

"Be my guest, Uncle Thomas. That will go down a treat with the Irish cake," she added.

"And my small but mighty Christmas pudding." Isla rose to serve the afters.

As always, they gathered for the King's Christmas Message:

"Once more, on Christmas Day, I speak to millions of you scattered far and near across the world… where the Queen and I and our daughters are fortunate enough to be spending a Christmas at home.

At this Christmas time, we think proudly and gratefully of our fighting men wherever they may be. May God bless them and protect them and bring them victory…

Our message goes to all who are wounded or sick in hospital and to the doctors and nurses in their labor of mercy. And our thoughts and prayers are also with our men who are prisoners of war, and with their relatives in their loneliness and anxiety. To children everywhere, we wish all the happiness that Christmas can bring…

We have rejoiced in the victories of this year, not least because they have broken down some of the barriers between us and our friends, and brought us nearer to the time when we can all be together again with those we love…

We do not know what awaits us when we open the door of 1945, but if we look back to those earlier Christmas days of the war, we can surely say that the darkness daily grows less and less. The lamps which the Germans put out all over Europe, first in 1914 and then in 1939, are being slowly rekindled…

Anxiety is giving way to confidence, and let us hope that before next Christmas Day, God willing, the story of liberation and triumph will be complete…

The defeat of Germany and Japan is only the first half of our task. The second is to create a world of free men, untouched by tyranny…

I wish you from my heart a Happy Christmas and for the coming year a full measure of that courage and faith in God… until the day when the Christmas message – Peace on earth and goodwill toward men—finally comes true."

As Alice readied for bed, she couldn't help thinking that despite everything Hitler had thrown at them since 1939, he couldn't break the spirit and morale of the British people. For the first time in a long while, she felt everything really would be alright.

On Boxing Day, the fog returned and with it an icy cold. Katie, Trevor and Hannah all had trains to catch, so it was a whirlwind of thanks and goodbyes. Only Maggie could stay on for two more days.

Mum and Tillie put away the lovely crystal and special Christmas crockery, feeling a trifle sad that it was all over.

"We'll leave the tree up till New Year's, Mum. It's too soon to take it down."

Mum nodded.

"Care for a cuppa?"

Pops strode into the kitchen.

"That will have to wait, dear. We need to take a short walk."

Tillie and Mum exchanged confused looks. *What in the world?*

"Come on, dear, there's a parcel at the post office we need to collect at the corner. Come and put on your coat."

The women were baffled, but Alice meekly agreed. It was rare that her husband bossed her about.

Ten minutes later, they entered the shop.

"Hallo, Arthur. Thank you for opening up today for us. Did you have a good Christmas?" Walter greeted him.

"Brilliant. Our Martin made it home so we had a jolly time. If you want to wait over there, your call should be coming through any minute."

Alice followed her husband to the phone box, completely bemused.

The telephone rang five minutes later, and Walter motioned for his wife to pick it up.

"Hello," she said tentatively.

Loud crackles and beeps greeted her.

"Mum, is that you? It's Kenny. Happy Christmas, Mum."

Alice burst into tears, and didn't even care.

"Kenny, is that you, son? Are you alright? Where are you?" *My son. He's alive and ringing me from across the world at Christmas.*

More buzzing and crackling.

"I'm fine, Mum. I have shore leave so Pops and I cooked up this plan to ring you. Are you alright?"

Alice clutched the receiver.

"I'm doing better all the time. Oh, it's so good to hear your voice. How are you getting on? I miss you dreadfully." Alice could barely speak through her tears.

"I only have a few minutes. There's a queue behind me. But I'm fine. Healthy and…" The telephone cut out.

"Kenny, Kenny, are you there?" Alice clutched the telephone. But the line went dead. She turned to her husband.

"Oh, Walter, he's gone. Can we get him back?"

He shook his head.

"I don't think so, dear. This was a miracle itself in trying to get this call put through. How did he sound?" Walter wished he'd had the chance to talk to his son.

"He sounded lovely. Alive. Oh, what a marvellous Christmas gift. Thank you, Walter." Inside the tiny telephone box, she hugged him tight. "Let's go tell the girls."

Chapter Eight

WINDY AND WONDERFUL

1945 –Alice

Alice sat at the table, gazing around the kitchen. A lone teacup and saucer sat in front of her. Her knitting bag was untouched next to her chair – unimaginable after so many years of constant industry. A lone gas mask sat in the corner – Tillie's? A harsh wind howled and whistled, triggering half-forgotten memories of icy nights in the Anderson shelter. It had been disused now for many months save as a makeshift garden shed after it was dug out and repositioned with new doors fitted to it

The war is over, and I still don't believe it. And all my children will be home for Christmas. Can it be true?

Alice took a sip of tea, a quiet smile playing around her lips. *And I'm alone in the house. How strange is this?*

Taking the rare opportunity to reflect, Alice considered what the year had meant to each of her now-adult offspring.

Tillie. Older than Maggie by mere minutes, she was ever the oldest of the family. Looking after everyone, a little bossy at times, she was the first to offer a helping hand or loving ear for other's problems. Now a devoted mum to two beautiful children: darling Jamie, almost three, and sweet baby Victoria, born just a few days after VE-Day in May.

It had been rough going for Tillie and Trevor, Alice tsked to herself. Poor Trevor had been temporarily blinded by a V-2 explosion at the RAF airfield. For months, he'd struggled to live life as normal, always certain that he would regain his eyesight. Which he had after a near-accident with Jamie at the London Zoo had hurtled him into action to save his son from drowning. His sight had returned – spotty at first, but now almost back to full strength. What joy that had brought the entire family – and just before his daughter was born.

It had been a wrench when the little family had moved out, but Alice knew it was time. The rooms they had at home were just not enough for a growing family. And it had worked out so splendidly. It had been a shock to the family, but not to Alice when Thomas and Isla had quietly announced they were getting married. Dear Shirley was gone almost eighteen months now, and wouldn't have wanted her Thomas to be alone and sad. It was rather fitting that these two quiet souls had found each other. As it was just the two of them, they'd moved into Isla's flat, leaving the way clear for the young Drummonds to take over Shirley and Thomas's old house down the street. Near enough for cuddles and child-minding, but Tillie finally had her own front door, and some room to spread out. Alice still saw her most every day. Marvellous.

Maggie. The quieter twin, she had grown into a confident young woman. In some ways, the war had been good for her. Being on her own as an ack-ack gunner, she had made new friends and grown independent of her sister. Steadfast to her love, Micah, she had shown undaunted fortitude and courage – waiting for years with no word, fearing the worst for him and his parents, and dealing with the horrific news that his parents had been killed in Auschwitz.

Now, she too was a young mum with twin girls of her own – Ruth, named for her Baba, and Rachel – both adorable, but naturally a handful. They were a bit older than baby Victoria but Alice was sure they'd all be dear chums growing up.

Katie. How her bouncy younger daughter had come into her own this year. She astonished everyone – especially herself – when she rescued a number of seriously ill hospital patients during a V-2 air raid. She'd been volunteering, and, caught during a raid, her innate bravery overcame her fear as she helped injured men to the hospital shelter. She hadn't given it a second thought, and was gobsmacked when she received a letter from Buckingham Palace advising she'd been awarded the George Cross for courage. The ceremony at the palace had been top drawer from start to finish. She and Walter had almost burst with pride seeing their daughter handed the award by His Majesty himself.

And hadn't the little darling gone and gotten herself engaged to her Irishman at the McElroy farm. They'd come home smiling like the cat who swallowed the cream and had been floating on air ever since. And now they were knee-deep in planning for a Christmas wedding. Alice couldn't be happier.

Kenny – her baby. Like many mothers of adult sons, he was rather a mystery to her. His war letters had been bright and breezy, saying almost nothing except he was fine. She longed to know his hopes and dreams, but he kept his feelings close. And hadn't he shown up home with a new bride – from Norway, mind? Astrid was a beautiful young woman, and the couple were obviously in love, but she and Walter had been knocked for six when they arrived from a long overseas journey. *My son, married, of all things.*

And finally, Hannah. Albeit not her blood daughter, Micah's sister was fully entrenched in the family, and she and Walter saw her as a cherished fourth daughter. Still serving in the Women's Auxiliary Air Force, she wasn't due for demobilization for some months. But she had moved her things to Micah and Maggie's, who insisted Hannah's home was with them. Micah had discovered the couple renting his family home in London had decided to move to the country, so the little Goldbach family had quickly settled into Micah's childhood home, also in Earl's Court. Still close, but able to set up their own household and bring up the twins where they felt most comfortable. They'd even taken Maggie's cat, Robbie.

So, it was just Walter and Alice, and Kenny and Astrid at #40. And Katie – but not for long. No crying babies or fretful toddlers.

The wind howled again, and she hugged her arms to herself, fending off a sudden chill. A wisp of wind lifted the hair at the back of her neck. She froze, feeling a presence in the room.

"Stop your woolgathering, luv. Isn't it time to get on with your Christmas tick list? Can't you do anything properly without me?"

Alice stood, looking around the room in a panic.

"Shirley, is that you?"

She could have sworn she'd heard her sister's voice, but there was no one in the kitchen. She sat back down, shaking her head, listening. Nothing. *Get a hold of yourself, woman. You're hearing ghosts.*

"Alright, sis. I'll get on with it." Feeling foolish for talking to herself, she resolutely pulled a scrap of paper and pencil towards her. That was spooky.

This year was going to be the busiest since before the war. All the children, their respective spouses and children, plus Ciaran's parents coming all the way from Ireland for Christmas dinner. Even Katie's best chum Ruby and her new husband Dan were expected before they left for America. Tillie had invited everyone to hers for drinks and appetizers on Christmas Eve. The wedding was just a couple of days after that, so there was plenty to sort.

Best get on with it. She wrote busily.

***

"Come through, darling. And how is baby Victoria?"

Maggie greeted her sister at the door.

"About ready for her morning nap, thank goodness. We almost blew over on the way here. It's gale forces today. Where are your two?" Tillie handed the baby to her sister as she removed her winter things.

"Shhh. Asleep. For now. Both teething but Rachel is suffering the most, so not sure how long she'll stay down."

The twins sat on opposite sofas in the drawing room.

"It feels good to sit. I've been walking this young miss in hopes she'd fall asleep in the pram, but no luck. I'm hoping after this feed, it will be lights out. How are you, luv?" She took the baby back, and began nursing her.

"Tired, but alright. I'll fetch us some tea, shall I? Then we can have a proper natter."

Tillie nodded, and the sisters busied themselves.

Victoria fell asleep at the breast, and Tillie carefully took her off. She accepted a warm cup of tea, and tried not to slurp it.

"This is marvellous. Just what I needed. Can I put her down on your bed?"

"It's rather a mess in there, but yes, of course. The twins are in the nursery. I can't say for how long. One usually wakes up the other." Maggie sipped her own tea, sitting back into the cushions.

Within a few minutes, Tillie returned.

"She went down a dream. Let's hope it stays that way. So, how are you getting on?" She studied her sister's face – scant lipstick, limp hair stuffed into a turban, and a little tired around the eyes.

Maggie shrugged.

"As well as can be expected, juggling these two. They are in a respectable routine these days, but teething throws a wrench into things, doesn't it? I expect Jamie is with Mum?"

"No, he's at Nana Drummond's today. She wanted to take him to the park. Who was I to say no?" Tillie wiggled her eyebrows.

"You're lucky to have two grandmothers who dote on the children. Mum has been smashing, but I can't help wishing Micah's mum could be here to enjoy these darlings." Maggie bit her lip.

"That must be so hard, luv. And for Micah, as well."

"He thinks of them every day. It's getting a bit easier, but that ache will never go away. He misses his parents so much."

"And he always will. I suppose it helps keeping busy. Babies certainly take up a lot of time, don't they?"

"That's a fact. I consider it a good day if I can pass a flannel over my face and get Micah's tea ready before he gets home from work. The rest of the time it's feeding, nappies, rocking, soothing, and endless washing. I can't believe how many nappies these girls go through in a day. And in this weather, there's no putting the wash out on the line. It will either freeze or blow away. So don't peek in my kitchen – it's a disaster of lines strung with baby clothes and nappies everywhere." Maggie shook her head.

"Mine is the same. I'm thankful to have my own house. Now Mum can't see the mess." She rolled her eyes at her sister.

Maggie chuckled.

"She'd have a fit to see how we live. That's why I always take the babies there when she minds them. I don't want to have to clear everything away to have her here."

"Me too." Tillie drank more tea. "But I will have to get it all in hand before Christmas Eve when everyone comes to mine. I expect Katie's mate Ruby and her new husband are kipping down with us." She paused. "Any chance of a biscuit, luv?"

Maggie jumped up.

"Goodness. Sorry, I forgot them in the kitchen." She scurried away to bring the dish.

"Store-bought, sorry. No baking 'round here. Would you like me to come over the day before to help you clean and set up?" Maggie offered.

"Ta, luv. This is brilliant. And yes, that would be grand, as Ciaran would say. We've rather a crowd coming."

"Are you making a tick list?" Maggie teased.

"Perhaps I should. Keeping anything straight these days is hard going. It's so hard with two babies – especially with one as active as Jamie. I can't keep my eyes off him for a minute, and he's forever waking up his sister or trying to feed her blocks."

"That does sound trying. But just imagine me juggling two babies who want attention at the same time, one setting the other off, crying at every turn," Maggie countered.

This was a common debate amongst the sisters. Which was harder – having a toddler and a baby, or twin babies with the work all at once? Neither had the answer.

"Well, I wouldn't trade my babies for anything." Tillie smiled. "Despite all the work, sleepless nights, and never feeling like my body is my own. But I am looking forward to weaning. Victoria is well onto Pablum now, and maybe she'll sleep better at night with a bottle."

"Mine were doing well at night, but teething throws our well-planned schedule into the air. But I love them to bits," sighed Maggie. "Life certainly has taken a turn since the war ended, hasn't it? I miss my mates at the ack-ack site. But not the terror of it all, or the freezing Nissen hut, or the wretched nights out in the freezing cold or blasting heat. Do you miss the ambulance?" She held the teapot aloft, and Tillie nodded.

"Rather the same. I miss Ernie and the crews. But fighting the London streets during air raids, scared stiff all the time, no. And Mags, I've seen far too many dead people. Coming to a call, and finding dust and debris-covered corpses buried under rubble, and laid out on the street for identification – it's gut-wrenching every time. Especially the little ones." Tillie gazed off, seeing so many lost souls in her mind – mothers, fathers, children – too many. "I'm rather happy with peacetime," she finished softly.

"Hear, hear." Maggie was thinking of little Lou, the tiny but mighty gunner girl who had been killed during an air-raid. Just a young girl, life snuffed out in an instant.

"Why are we dwelling on the past?" Tillie sat up. "It's almost Christmas, we are all home and healthy, and 1946 is looking brighter than ever."

"You're right, luv. Let's leave the past in the past. What do you make of our Kenny, then? Bringing home a bride, of all things. You could have knocked me over with a feather."

"I think Mum was right put out not to have a wedding, but it was too late. Astrid seems nice, but has war wounds, like all of us, I suppose. It won't be easy for her – moving to a new country with no family but Kenny." Tillie tilted her head, thinking she head a baby cry.

Maggie stilled, unconsciously mimicking her sister, then shook her head slightly.

"I think it's just the wind. Isn't it strange how we hear phantom baby cries even when it's not them?"

"Yes," Tillie cried. "It happens to me all the time – in the kitchen, the loo, or even when Mum is minding them. All part of motherhood, I suppose."

Maggie nodded.

"I can see that Kenny and Astrid are in love." She picked up the thread. "I expect she went through so much during the war, living in an occupied country. Perhaps, over time, she'll come to trust us and tell us more about it."

"Perhaps, but let's not push her. Just welcome her into this big, noisy, family. I'm glad that she'll be there with Mum for a little while. She must be missing us living there."

Maggie fairly sputtered her tea.

"Not likely. She was probably more than happy to see the back of us – crying babies, more mouths to feed, extra cleaning and never-ending wash."

"Maybe," Tillie said. "Still, I rather suspect she's missing having us to fuss over, and she loves her grandbabies so."

"Right, well we'll all be together for the holidays, and she'll adore that. Albeit there are still no gifts in the shops, and rationing is worse than ever."

With the declaration of peace, Londoners, and in fact all British people believed that food would become plentiful again after six hard years of sacrifice. However, importing was more difficult than ever, and the British government was fundamentally bankrupt, causing more hardship. And, all eyes were on Europe where whole communities were starving. Many in England wanted to send food to the inhabitants of war-torn countries, but it was proving difficult to make happen.

"Make do and mend again, I suppose," sighed Tillie. A slow smile spread across her face. "Although I expect we'll be alright – what with Ciaran's parents bringing lamb and other farm extravagances."

"And Isla's tremendous baking. She's a marvel."

"Good thing, too," laughed Tillie. "You and I are both hopeless at cookery, and we've rather our hands full at the moment."

"And then, our little Katie getting married. It will be splendid. I rather like her young man."

"Me too. Although I don't fancy her moving to Ireland. It's going to be awful not seeing her all the time."

"I suppose we've gotten rather used to the separation with the last few years." Maggie was philosophical. "Does she have all the preparations in hand?"

Tillie laughed.

"Not by half, I imagine. She's not one for a load of planning." She sipped the last of her tea.

"We'll all help her," Maggie said loyally. "No one expects much from a war wedding. Although I suppose it's a post-war wedding, now, isn't it? She'll be a lovely bride."

Just then, a soft wail came from upstairs.

"Mine or yours?" asked Tillie, already beginning to rise.

"Mine. It's Rachel. I'll go." Maggie was up on her feet.

"Well, that was nice while it lasted. I reckon it's three girls awake in no time." Tillie sat back down, keeping half-an ear cocked for young Victoria.

***

"Are you sure we shouldn't wait for Mrs. McElroy to come across from Ireland for our ladies Christmas tea?" Mum asked with a worried frown. "I hate not to invite her."

Katie shook her head.

"It's fine, Mum. They are coming so close to Christmas itself, and the trip will be tiring for her – for them both, really. I asked her, and she said she didn't think she was up to that much commotion. We will be quite a number as it is. Let's see – you, Tillie and Maggie, Hannah, Astrid, Aunt Isla, and me, of course. Goodness – that's seven. What about the babies?"

"I've asked Pops to help Trevor and Micah with them. The girls need a treat – they are up to their eyeballs with nappies and bottles these days."

Katie whistled.

"And Jamie too? They'll need a trip to the pub after that." Katie had minded young Jamie a time or two and knew how exhausting it could be. She was glad it wasn't her looking after four children.

"They'll manage," Mum said shortly. "We women need an extravagance after all the queues, rationing, and making suppers out of nothing these last years." Resolutely, she kept thoughts of Shirley from crowding into her head. She would be sorely missed at the Claridge's tea. No sense in fretting about that now.

"I miss her too, Mum. I wish she could be at my wedding." Katie had been close to her aunt, and her death had come as an awful shock. She'd lost herself in her Y-station work, but now that she was home in familiar surroundings, the grief overtook her at times. Aunt Shirley had been such a dear, listening to Katie's problems, and being in her corner when all the attention seemed to be on her dazzling twin sisters.

Alice looked over at her daughter, who had placed a hand on hers. She fought a lump in her throat.

"I know you do, dear. There's a big hole in our family the size of a bomb crater. We will never forget her."

"Never," Katie said with a slight quaver. "But we must look forward. There is a wedding coming up, in the event." She fluffed her brown curls, now grown longer since being released from the Royal Navy.

"An important wedding," Mum emphasized. "I want your day to be as special as you are. Shall I stick on the kettle?"

"No, ta, Mum. I'm meant to collect Hannah from the train. I'd best get my skates on."

"I expect the train will be late." She stopped. "But perhaps they will be getting on to a reliable schedule again."

Katie snorted.

"Not likely, Mum. But at least the station will be chock-full of happy reunions. No more tearful goodbyes." She stood. "Ta ra. Micah is meeting me on his dinner break. See you later." She made for the stairs.

"Ta ra, luv. Tell Hannah I can't wait to see her for tea tomorrow."

But Katie was already gone.

* * *

"How are you coping, Micah? You and Maggie certainly have your hands full with the twins." Katie rubbed her gloved hands together for warmth. So far, Hannah's train was three quarters of an hour late.

"We're managing," he replied. "Maggie bears the brunt of it, but I do my best to help after work. She's a wonder with them, truly."

"They are cute as buttons. But loud." Katie smiled, blowing out cold air.

"That they are. Particularly at three a.m. They were on a sketchy but somewhat predictable schedule, but that's out the window. Apparently, babies don't sleep when they are teething." He gave a rare smile. "Or not much."

"I can't say I understand, but I sympathize. If I'm honest, I'm rather put off the whole notion. But then again, I'm not even married yet."

"All in good time, Katie." Micah pulled his collar closer as he scanned the board again looking for arrival news of Hannah's train.

"Right. Arriving in five minutes on Track Twelve. Splendid. Let's go." He was already walking away.

Katie struggled to match his long strides.

"Micah, we're not likely to miss her, are we? No one else is expected to fetch her, are they?"

He slowed.

"Sorry. I've missed her, is all."

The train screeched into the station with the accompanying whistles, grinding, and smoke. As passengers alighted, they were greeted with tight embraces, broad smiles, and happy tears. Anyone in uniform was universally cheered. Despite the wind whistling in and around the station, the mood was celebratory as families were reunited – once and for all.

"There she is. Hannah!" Micah waved in the direction of a young, blonde woman in a WAAF uniform.

"Micah," she called back, quickening her step.

Within seconds, brother and sister almost collided, and hugged tightly, Hannah's kitbag dangling awkwardly in her hands.

"Here, I'll take that. Welcome home, Hannah. Lovely to see you," Katie hesitated to interrupt the quiet reunion, as she relieved Hannah of her case.

"Katie, it's smashing you were both able to meet me. Are you okay?" Hannah smiled and pecked her on the cheek.

"Brilliant, luv. It's Christmas, everyone is coming home, and my wedding is in the offing. And now you're here. How could I not be alright?"

The trio walked briskly towards an exit, mixing with the busy throng. Bunting and flags were strewn amongst well-worn yet cheerful Christmas decorations. From somewhere, a small band played *It Came Upon a Midnight Clear*.

"How was your journey?" Micah asked.

"Fine, really," Hannah answered. "Everyone is in a gleeful mood, even if we were packed in like sardines. But I'm here now, and I can't wait to see everyone. Especially the babies. How are they?"

They stopped outside a busy café.

"I'm sorry, but I can't stop for dinner. I've used up my break waiting, but I just have time for a quick cup of tea, and Katie will see you home. She can fill you in on all the news."

The smoke-filled café was crowded, but they managed to find an empty table and swiftly ordered tea and scones.

"You'll hardly recognize them; they've grown so much. Smiling all the time. Both are sitting up, albeit Ruth is a little sturdier than her sister, who still tends to topple once in a while." Micah took a bite of scone with jam.

"Are they crawling yet?" Hannah asked, cupping her mug for warmth.

"In their own unique ways – yes," Micah said. "Rachel rather rocks on all fours until she moves an inch, whilst Ruth scuttles like a crab, her tiny rear stuck in the air."

Both girls laughed.

"I'm longing to see them. And Maggie, too," she added.

Micah smiled.

"That's alright. We're well used to playing second fiddle to our twins. People see right through us to those adorable girls." Micah checked his watched and gulped his tea.

"I'm so sorry, but I must dash. I'm already past my time. There are so many families to help, and each story is more heart-stopping and dreadful than the last."

"I understand, and remember – I want to help out at the Jewish Refugee Center for a couple of afternoons while I'm home. Soon enough, I'll be demobbed and we can properly plan for the future." Hannah smiled up at her brother, who had risen and shrugged on his overcoat.

"Splendid. Right, I'll see you at home tonight. Thank you, Katie, for helping to collect our Hannah and deliver her safely."

"My pleasure." Katie waved away his thanks. "I'll see you on Christmas Eve with my gorgeous Irish fiancé."

"I can't wait. Goodbye." And he was gone.

"Any further news on your demobilization date, luv?" Katie asked. "It's too wretched that you are the last to be released."

Hannah shrugged.

"Only fair, I suppose. I was called up later than the rest of you. I'm eager, believe me, but I must wait my turn. I'm hoping it's within three or four months, but I have to hang on until the British Air Force is done with me. It's dead boring on administrative duties, now that there's no need for my weather forecasting skills."

"It will be anything but dull once you're at home, believe me. Your house is controlled chaos with those babies, emphasis on chaos. Are you certain you want to jump into the fray?"

"Absolutely," Hannah replied firmly. "After being separated from my brother all the war years, I intend on staying as close as possible. Besides, they need my help with the babies."

"True enough, but you're young. Don't get caught up in nappies and pram walks. You're still planning on going to university next autumn, right?" Katie asked. "You must. Your parents would want you to," she amended.

"Yes, that's still the plan. I promised Mama and Papa before I left France that I would keep to my studies. I want to do them proud." Hannah's face had turned serious. "Something good has to come out of this war."

"You shall do grand things." Katie patted her hand. "You are young and bright, and the war is over. Hooray."

"Shhh, Katie. People are looking at us." Hannah kept her eyes down.

"I don't care. Ciaran and his parents are soon arriving, and I'll be a married woman in a few short days. I want the whole world to know how euphoric I am." Katie was loving this.

"And I'm so happy for you, but please keep your voice down," Hannah pleaded. "Tell me about your dress." She changed the subject.

"It's exquisite. You know how brides are sharing wedding gowns due to the shortages and number of coupons needed for a new one? I'm doing the same. Ruby found an old evening frock in her grandmother's attic. She wore it for her wedding, and gave it to me. Aunt Isla has been busy with it since – shortening it, and hopefully adding a touch or two to make it mine. I'm proper chuffed about it."

"That sounds brilliant. I expect your mum has everything else in hand – food, flowers and such? She's so organized that I'm sure every detail is well looked after."

"I hope so. That's not my forte. I just want to appear looking impossibly beautiful and marry my beloved." Katie couldn't wait. She and Ciaran had grown so close these last months. Her doubts about trusting this man and becoming a farm wife in Ireland had fallen away. She was in love with him and couldn't wait to start their lives together – finally.

"You will be a stunning bride," Hannah agreed. "Hmmm, Katie," she fidgeted. "Would you mind if we skipped a meal together? I'm restored from this tea and scone, and I'm that wound up about seeing Maggie and the babies. I just want to get home to them. You understand, don't you?"

"Of course, darling. We can have a proper chat tomorrow at our ladies' tea. I want to hear about the men at your airfield. Surely there is one or two that you fancy." Katie motioned for the bill, and the pair left, bound for the tube to take them home.

***

"What do you make of Claridge's, dear? It's quite a spectacle at this time of year, isn't it?" Alice turned to Astrid who was staring at the opulent surroundings, mouth wide open.

"Very good," she stumbled. "Please explain afternoon tea. We have nothing like this in Norway."

"It's a lovely extravagance," Tillie said. "A leisurely way to enjoy tea and fancy food. I'm not quite sure how it started, but it has developed into a late afternoon ritual that is delicious and much anticipated. We only come once a year – at Christmas."

"We each choose an elegant tea – I love Claridge's own brand. But there are loads to choose from. Then they bring us a three-tiered tray loaded with three courses of finger food, sweets, scones, and tea sandwiches. It's all quite elegant and refined."

"The men don't want any part of it – far too delicate for their sensibilities," Alice added. "So, it's a girls-only treat just before Christmas each year. We've been doing it since Maggie and Tillie were ten years old."

"Old enough not to break the fine china. Mum watched me like a hawk when it was finally my turn." Katie grinned.

"And you were good as gold," Alice said.

"Sadly, we haven't any new frocks. That was always part of the fun – shopping for lovely new Christmas dresses, hats, and shoes. Remember the white lace gloves, Tils?" Maggie poured tea through the strainer, setting aside the leaves.

"We loved those outfits." Tillie sighed, looking around the table at their worn and drab dresses. "Do we dare hope for any new finery in 1946?"

"Not utility." Katie rolled her eyes.

"What is utility?" Astrid asked, her gaze following the loaded tea trays approaching the table.

"Rubbish dresses meant to satisfy women's craving for something new, that's what," Tillie said. "Few sizes and styles, simple and ugly."

"Not so bad, luv," Mum objected. "The government was trying to give women a boost, since there's been nothing new in the shops for years."

Katie snorted.

"You're being too kind, Mum. Tillie is right. A dismal attempt."

"This food – all for us?" Astrid asked, staring at the array of dainty finger sandwiches, hot scones with real clotted creams and jams, and a display of pastries that she'd never imagined, let alone seen before her.

"It is, indeed," Hannah replied. "I couldn't believe it myself the first time I was invited. And everything melts in your mouth. Help yourself."

Astrid watched and mimicked the Kingston ladies as they each chose their favourites and placed them on individual plates.

"Is this real ham? And chicken? So delicious," Astrid mumbled with her mouth full. "I like this tradition."

Everyone laughed.

"We all do," Aunt Isla echoed as she lathered cream and blackberry jam on her raisin scone. "And you won't believe how full you'll become on such dainty food."

Astrid groaned as she crammed a chocolate custard tart into her mouth.

"*Nydelig*," she breathed.

"I assume that means some form of delicious?" Hannah asked, rather unnecessarily.

"Mmmm," Astrid replied, eyes closed.

"Help yourself, dear. There's plenty for everyone," Mum offered. The poor girl – what she must have suffered in occupied Norway over the course of the war. Tall, blonde, and thinner than she should be, she put on a smiling face, but undoubtedly the scars ran deep. *Thank heavens they've decided to make their home here in England. I couldn't bear it if she and Kenny had determined to live in Astrid's home country. I long to hear more about her life, family, and experiences, but the language barrier was an issue.* Kenny had taken her and Walter aside, begging them to let Astrid settle in and take her time sharing what she wanted when she felt comfortable. And not a moment before. Fair enough. They'll just keep feeding her and making her welcome.

"Mum, did you hear Katie?" Tillie prodded her. "Busy thinking about having the whole family home for Christmas at last?"

"Sorry, I was woolgathering. And yes, I'm over the moon about everyone being here. And more – four babies. I can't wait."

"You and Jamie both. He is chomping at the bit for Father Christmas to arrive. Excited doesn't even begin to describe him." Tillie chuckled.

"It's going to be splendid," Maggie said. "Albeit my girls won't take much notice. Playing with the paper, I expect. What I'm most looking forward to is our Katie's wedding. Darling, you've said nothing about it." Maggie turned to her younger sister.

"Once Ciaran and his ma and da arrive tomorrow, then it will seem real. I had a fitting with Aunt Isla this morning – eyes closed, and the gown seems to fit."

"Like a dream," echoed Isla. "And I may have a surprise or two on the day."

"Oh, goody. I love a surprise!" Katie clapped. "Mum says all the food is in hand. Tillie has promised to help with my hair – how you'll tame this mop into something elegant, I don't know." She fluffed her curls.

"I'll help, too. With your makeup and getting you dressed," Maggie rushed to add.

"I can mind the babies whilst you're at it," Hannah offered. "Tillie, maybe you can pop by with your two, and between Trevor and I – we can manage."

"Thanks everyone. That sounds smashing."

"How do you think the boys are doing with them all now? Bearing up?" Tillie giggled, knowing what a handful her young son could be.

"Between Trevor, Micah, Walter and Thomas – at least it's a fair fight. One child each." Maggie crossed her fingers.

"It's good for them," Tillie insisted. "Give them a taste of what our days are like."

"I don't think men ever truly understand everything we do around the house and for the family. They expect their socks to be washed, the house to be cleaned, children to be minded, and tea on the table promptly each evening." Mum sighed. "And you young lot have taken on so much more. You're all so brave. I don't know how you've done it." She gazed from one girl to the next. Tillie – driving the damaged streets of London in a beat-up ambulance, saving lives every shift. Maggie – who knew she had the pluck and the superior intellect to make the elite anti-aircraft forces, operating the predictor machine to pinpoint German aircraft targets, keeping Londoners safe from untold numbers of bombs? Katie – carefree and bouncy, she had surprised everyone with her dedication as a naval Wren, moving from base to base across England performing vital administrative duties. And then saving all those patients in a Portsmouth hospital. No mum could be prouder of a daughter presented with the George Cross by His Majesty himself. Young Hannah who had joined the family as a displaced waif. She had grown up before their eyes, coping with more pain and tragedy than any young girl should have to face. Joining the Women's Auxiliary Airforce and making her own mark as a weather forecaster, and now university-bound. And Astrid – the newest Kingston daughter. No one even knew she existed until Kenny brought her home as his new bride a few short weeks ago. Kenny hinted at terrible hardship when he'd found her in Norway. It would take time to get to know her, but it was obvious the couple was in love. That stood for loads. And she was proving to be indispensable around the house – a brilliant baker and cook, and offering a hand wherever it was needed. Welcome, indeed.

Isla caught her eye and they exchanged a smile. Seeing what these young women had done in the war was awe-inspiring. What would these post-war years bring for these capable girls?

"But we love it, don't we, Alice? Hearing the click of the front door and seeing Trevor come bounding through fills my heart with joy – every time. Even, when he brings a kitbag full of dirty wash."

"I agree. And now we don't have to lie awake at night, praying for their safe return. It's all over." Alice's heart was full.

"And it's Christmas," cried Tillie.

"And I'm getting married," Katie put in.

"And I love afternoon tea," Astrid said, wiping chocolate from the corner of her mouth.

The ladies erupted into laughter.

"I hate to break up this lovely party, Mum, but I must get home and see how Trev is getting on with the little ones. Thank you so much for a Christmas tea to remember. Mags, are you ready?"

The twins took their leave, and after one more cup of tea all around, with Astrid polishing off the last of the sweets, they said their goodbyes, each off to last-minute errands.

***

And then it was Christmas Eve. Katie had made a return trip to the rail station – this time Euston – to fetch Ciaran and his parents from the Liverpool train and was expected anytime.

Mum, Isla and Astrid prepared generously-named sausage rolls, Marmite and cheese rolls, and carrot cookies for the evening party at Tillie's.

"Should we also bring Faye's fruitcake?" Alice tilted her head to one side.

"Why not?" Isla said, pushing back a stray hair from her forehead. "Katie has assured us that Mr. and Mrs. McElroy will be bringing plenty of non-wartime foods for the day tomorrow. We want Tillie to have a full table – we're a substantial number of guests and her first Christmas party will be brilliant."

"Who is Faye?" asked Astrid.

"Sorry, luv. We forget you haven't been here all along. Faye was our treasured housekeeper before the war. She left to join up as a nurse. She's sent us the cake along with her regrets for not being able to rejoin us. She's found her calling nursing. It's disappointing but we wish her all the best. And we're thankful for the fruitcake." Alice made an effort to speak slowly, and used hand gestures to make herself understood.

Astrid nodded. Trying to sort out all the Kingstons was proving to be a trial, but she was determined to get them all straight – in time.

"Thank you for allowing me to make Pepperkake – ginger biscuits. Reminds me of home." Astrid's head was down, working her dough.

"We can't wait to try it, Astrid. A lovely new tradition for the Kingston family."

Astrid looked up and smiled.

The Christmas Eve party was a grand success – so said Ciaran many times over. Niall and Orla McElroy had come bearing many gifts – loads of food for Christmas dinner, including two large legs of lamb, a chicken, a massive ham, mince pies, Irish shortbread, and more. And homemade jams and jellies as Christmas gifts. The family was overwhelmed with their generosity.

Despite the long journey from Howth, Ireland, the McElroys were in fine form. Katie had been concerned the trip would be too much for them – Mrs. McElroy walked with a limp, and his da had to take it easy because of his weak heart. They had become parents a little later in life and doted on their only son.

"What a lovely party." Orla sipped her sherry, gazing around the drawing room, overflowing with people. "You must be that proud of your family."

"I am," Alice replied simply. "Isn't it marvelous that our children are finally home for good – safe? You must have been worried sick about Ciaran these past years – and with him a paratrooper before his injury."

"Aye, that we were. When we didn't hear from him for months after the D-Day drop, we hardly slept. When word finally came that he was safe, but with a serious hand injury, we were that relieved."

"He seems fine now." Alice and Orla scanned the room, landing on Katie and Ciaran laughing in a corner. "He's a good lad. Our Katie is smitten, and she's never even looked at another man."

"And we adore your Katie. She got mucked in on her farm visit, and gave it her all. They make a fine-looking couple." Orla paused and turned to Alice. "I'm sure it's a wrench and all – her moving to Ireland. I hope you're not too cross with us for taking her away."

Alice took a breath.

"It's hard, I won't deny it. But I've more than a quiver-ful 'round here, and it's what she wants. We'll miss her, but Ireland isn't that far away now, is it?" *I won't let her see how this cut runs deep. She and Niall only have Ciaran. I'm a lucky woman. I must let Katie follow her heart.*

Orla put a tiny hand on the other woman's arm.

"That's gracious of you, Alice. We need them both at the farm. Niall is not up to the hard graft like he was. And our Ciaran loves the land. It's where he belongs."

Alice nodded, fighting a lump in her throat.

A small hand tugged at her skirt. Alice looked down.

"Granny, Father Christmas is coming tonight. Is it time for bed yet?"

Alice gratefully swooped up young Jamie into her arms. *Thank you, luv. Perfect timing.*

"You are asking for bedtime?" Her voice was incredulous. Normally he fought it tooth and nail. "But look at our lovely party, darling. Don't you want to dance and have fun?"

Jamie shook his head seriously.

"No, Granny. I want bedtime. Then Father Christmas will come." He stuck out his lower lip.

"Let's find Mama," Alice said. The last thing they needed on Christmas Eve was a toddler fretting.

"You've done a smashing job, Tils." Maggie stood with Rachel in one arm, and a glass of punch in the other. "Well done you."

Tillie blew a blonde wisp of hair out of her eyes.

"Thanks, luv. It's been a load of work, but so worth it. Look how happy everyone is. And no one is stuck on a ship, airfield, or gunner site. It's going to be a wonderful Christmas."

Maggie nodded, eyes shining.

"It already is."

***

"Is it really half-past seven? And the girls are still asleep?" Maggie sat up in bed.

"I'll check on them. By the way – Happy Christmas, little one. A good night's sleep has done wonders for you." With a swift kiss, Micah threw back the coverlet, put on his slippers and dressing gown and tiptoed to the twins' nursery.

Maggie was close behind, stopping only for her own slippers and dressing gown.

Micah opened the door to the still-quiet nursery, Maggie peeking over his shoulder. Ruth was sitting up in her cot, staring at them both with a gap-toothed smile.

"Hello, darling." Maggie picked her up. "Are you ready for Christmas?"

Rachel rolled over and opened her eyes. Micah tried to rub her back. This usually resulted in her falling back to sleep – but not today. She rolled up and opened her mouth in protest.

"There, there, luv. We're all together. No need to cry. Let's start our Christmas." Micah picked her up for a snuggle. She settled into his shoulder and gurgled.

"Hey, is anyone coming down to open these gifts? It's Christmas morning, after all," Hannah's voice called from the staircase.

The little Goldbach family settled into the quiet Christmas morning they had all waited so long to share.

***

"Father Christmas came," cried Jamie as he spotted the gifts almost bursting from under the Christmas tree. "Look Daddy!" He pointed and started running.

"Whoa. Slow down, young man. We must wait for Mummy and Victoria. They'll be down directly. Did Father Christmas drink the milk and eat the biscuits you put out? We'd best check." Trevor led his son away from the tree, towards the low table.

"Daddy – he drunk the milk. And look – one bikkie is missing." Jamie almost shook with excitement.

"You're right, son." Trevor ran his hand through his tousled hair and whistled. "He loved what you left for him."

Tillie appeared at the bottom of the stairs, babe in arms.

"What's this about Father Christmas? He loved your milk and biscuits? He must have been so hungry leaving toys for boys and girls all over the world."

"Happy Christmas, darling." Trevor crossed the room to kiss his wife and daughter. "Shall I put on the kettle?"

"Happy Christmas, Trev, and yes, please. Isn't it a delight to have our first one in our own home?"

Trev nodded.

"The best. And Happy Christmas to you, Jamie."

"Open gifts, pwease?"

"Sure enough, son." Trevor chuckled. "We've waited long enough."

***

Down the road at #40, Christmas morning was a leisurely affair. With no little ones squealing with eyes like saucers, it was down to Kenny and Katie to bring the traditional Christmas spirit. Bounding the stairs, a bemused Astrid tagged along.

"Mum, the stockings look ace. I missed this when I was at sea."

"Mum, you didn't." Katie smothered a giggle. "We are all grown up. Kenny is married, and I'm all but. And here you are, putting out stockings as if we were children."

"Don't laugh at me, young lady. Under my roof, all the younger generation get Christmas stockings from Father Christmas."

"What's all this, then?" Ciaran entered the drawing room with a yawn. "Happy Christmas, everyone."

"And to you, Ciaran. Katie is having a go at me for putting out Christmas stockings. Here's yours, in the event."

Ciaran rushed forward, wide awake.

"I haven't had one of them in years. Ta, Mrs. K." He sat on the floor next to Kenny, pulling items out of the stocking.

"And good morning to you, too, Irish." Katie pouted. "No 'good morning, mavoureen?'"

"Sorry, luv. A most special Christmas greeting to my beautiful bride-to-be." He kissed her.

"Much better. Now, let's have at these stockings."

"That's it, mind. We're saving the main lot for when Tillie, Maggie and their broods turn up. Anyone for a cup of tea?"

"I'll go after I've gone through my stocking," Katie offered. "Ciaran, you can help me."

Ciaran's parents and Walter drifted down the stairs, joining the little group.

Sipping tea and ginger biscuits, the family chatted about the imminent wedding, if the weather would cooperate and debates over when to put the leg of lamb into the aga for Christmas dinner.

Maggie and her family arrived first to happy greetings.

"Where is Tillie?" Katie asked for the third time, peeking out the window.

"She's coming straightaway. What's the rush, squirt? Are you that eager for your gifts?" Kenny threw an orange at her.

Catching it, she shrugged.

"Lovely, another orange for me. After years of not seeing one, this will go down a treat." She neatly avoided his question.

She ran down the stairs to check on something in the kitchen, when the Drummonds arrived. Everyone settled, and Jamie raced towards another Christmas tree and stockings hanging from the fireplace mantel.

"You're finally here," Katie practically shouted.

"What in the world has gotten into that girl?" Kenny turned to his mother who shrugged.

"I'll fetch more tea." Katie winked at her mum. "Trev, can you give me a hand?"

"Certainly. Tils, are you alright here with the kiddos?"

She smiled and nodded.

"Lots of helping hands 'round here."

There was a strange air in the room. Maggie and Micah exchanged a questioning look, then got distracted with the twins who were both pulling on the same knitted whale.

Several minutes later, Katie and Trevor returned carrying a large carton that seemed to be – moving?

"I think Father Christmas has something special for Master Jamie." Mum clapped.

"For me?" Jamie jumped up.

Trevor placed the box in the middle of the floor and stepped back.

"Take a look, Jamie. Happy Christmas."

Tillie looked on fondly. She obviously knew what was going on. Everyone else looked confused.

Jamie almost dived head first into the box, shrieking.

Seconds later, two heads popped up – a beaming two and a half-year old and a wriggly, golden-brown puppy.

"Doggie…for me?" Jamie shouted with glee.

"Yes, he's for you, darling."

195

Katie couldn't contain herself. She ran over, and began stroking his head.

"Isn't he gorgeous? I've had such a hard time keeping this to myself, but Trev and Tillie wanted the whole family here."

"A cocker spaniel, if I'm not mistaken," Micah said.

"Ten weeks old, and full of energy," Trevor confirmed. "Now, we'll have to name him."

"Goldie," suggested Mum.

"How about Frisky?" Mr. McElroy put in.

"I like something Christmassy – like Noel or Jolly?" Katie had clearly given this some thought.

"Or a play on Kingston? Maybe Prince?" Walter said firmly.

"Sparky. Him name Sparky," Jamie proclaimed, nose to nose with the bundle of fur.

Trevor glanced at Tillie who shrugged, then nodded.

"Sparky, it is, then. Welcome to the Kington family. We are a noisy, crazy bunch," Trevor said.

Jamie was laughing, rolling around the floor with his puppy who licked him like mad.

The rest of the day was a happy mix of delicious food – most courtesy of the Irish guests – laughing, stories, babies, puppy, and family sharing. Thomas and Isla, and Katie's mate Ruby and her new husband Dan, added to the mayhem. The dining room table had never been so full. In fact, they'd had to lug in another one to fit everyone in.

"We haven't had meat like this in years," Tillie practically drooled. "Lamb, ham, and real bacon and eggs for breakfast this morning. We are spoiled rotten."

"You all deserve it. You've been through so much these past six years. You should all be proud of what you've done for victory." Mr. McElroy lifted his wineglass. "Congratulations for all your bravery, perseverance, and good cheer. Londoners, and all Britons have done a grand thing. Simply grand."

Alice looked at the young people around the table and felt her heart could burst with pride. All her children had served with courage. As had Micah, Hannah, Trevor, Ciaran, Ruby, and Dan. And everyone had been touched by loss and grief. Too much loss.

"Thank you, Niall. And welcome to the Kingston family. Shall we all drink to peace at last, and a bright future?" Walter stood, lifting his own glass from the table. One by one, they joined him, drinking to a sunny future for them all.

***

Crammed into the drawing room once more, with the children being put down for naps, it was time for the King's Christmas speech:

"For six years in the past, I have spoken at Christmas to an Empire at war. During all those years of sorrow and danger, of weariness and strife, you and I have been upheld by a vision of a world peace. And now that vision has become a reality.

By gigantic efforts and sacrifices, a great work has been done. A great evil has been cast from the earth…

This Christmas is a real home coming for us all – a return to a world in which the homely, friendly things of life can again be ours…

Most of all are we together as a one world-wide family in the joy of Christmas. I think of men and women of every race within the Empire returning from their long service to their own families, to their own homes and to the ways of peace. I think of the children freed from unnatural fears and the blacked-out world celebrating this Christmas in the light and happiness of the family circle once more reunited.

There will be the vacant places of those who will never return – brave souls who gave their all to win peace for us. We remember them with pride and with unfailing love, praying that a greater peace than ours may now be theirs…

There is not yet for us the abundance of peace. We all have to make a little go a long way, but Christmas comes with its message of hope and fellowship to all men of goodwill…

To the younger of you I would say a special word. You have grown up in a world at war in which your fine spirit of service has been devoted to a single purpose of the overthrow and destruction of our enemies. You have known the world only as a world of strife and fear. Bring now all that fine spirit to make it one of joyous adventure, a home where men and women can live in mutual trust and walk together as friends…

Let us have no fear of the future, but think of it as opportunity and adventure…

The light of joy can be most surely kindled by the fireside where most of you are listening. Home life as you all remember at Christmas is life at its best. There in the trust and love of parents and children, brothers, and sisters, we learn how men and nations too may live together in unity and peace.

So, to every one of you who gathered now in your homes or holding a thought of home in your hearts, I say – a Merry Christmas and may God bless you all."

The family stood for the playing of *God Save the King* yet again, tears in some eyes, but mostly smiles all around. Peace at last.

***

"Is it just me, or are you feeling a bit down after it's all done and dusted? Christmas, then a wedding. Naught to plan for now." Alice and Isla shared an afternoon cup of tea.

"There's always a bit of a lull feeling after all the run up to the day, the excitement, and all. And this year was something extra. Katie was a lovely bride. She couldn't have lit up more if she were a Christmas tree."

"You're right. I'm so happy she found such a splendid young man. She and Ciaran are perfect together. And it was lovely that Orla invited us to visit anytime. She insisted on setting a date for early in the new year. It made the leave-taking a little easier." Alice sighed.

"How long will they be able to honeymoon in Dover? It's so romantic they've gone back to the place where they met." Isla rose to bring some shortbread biscuits to the table. There was still loads of Christmas baking to be eaten.

"Just a few days. They are needed back at the farm. Ciaran has big plans to modernize. Luckily, they'll be stopping here in London before their journey across the sea."

"That will make it a trifle easier for you, luv." Isla patted Alice's hand.

"You did such a brilliant job of altering the wedding dress for our Katie. I had my doubts about a second-hand gown, but you made it look brand-new. She was breath-taking – especially the little cap and veil you made. She was proper surprised."

"Your girls were all so confident on their wedding days – no nerves in sight. Tillie was the same. A tribute to you and Walter. You've raised remarkable children – well, young people, I suppose."

"You're very kind, Isla. Your Trevor is a credit to you, too. It can't have been easy, raising him on your own. Then, him fighting fires all over London during the Blitz, and losing his sight. You've had to endure so much." Alice shook her head.

"No more than you or thousands of other mothers across England. We've all sacrificed. And we are luckier than most. Our children all came home. And look at us now – Tillie and Trevor have a home of their own, two beautiful children and…"

"And an adorable but rather destructive puppy," Isla finished for her.

"Our grandbabies will never remember the war, thank heavens. They'll grow up in a free world, with no bombs or shelters or air raid signals. What a miracle that is." Alice sighed. "More tea, luv?"

"I'll stick on the kettle. I'm not due at Trevor and Tillie's for another hour."

The pair of wives, mothers, grandmothers and now dear friends smiled together.

Epilogue

WARM DAYS AHEAD

1946

Hannah

"I've just finished my last examination. What a relief. I didn't realize how out of practice I've been at sitting tests." Hannah clutched the hall telephone. There was just one person in queue behind her, so she didn't feel too rushed.

"*That's smashing, luv. The worst for the last – how was Advanced Maths, then?*" Maggie's voice was a bit distracted. Likely one twin or the other grasping at her skirts. Hannah smiled.

"Not too bad. I kept up my brain working weather forecasts the last few years, so that has helped."

"*Lovely. Listen, sorry but I must run. I heard a crash in the drawing room. I think Rachel has knocked something over. See you for supper?*"

"Yes. I'll be home by five. I'm having coffee with friends – a little celebration," Hannah said.

"*Must go. Ta, ra.*" Click.

Hannah hung up, flipped her long blonde braid over her shoulder and left the telephone for the next student in queue.

Striding across the quadrangle towards the uni café, Hannah looked towards the sky. It was a grey day, but warm for December. She hoped it didn't rain. She'd left her umbrella at home.

She was truly coming into her own as an independent young woman. Always a bit shy, she'd found it hard to fit in with the boisterous Kingstons – albeit they'd always welcomed her warmly. She'd taken great comfort in Maggie's cat, Robbie, who had pretty much adopted her permanently. It was just too noisy for the feline with the twins toddling around. He much preferred sleeping with Hannah now, and she often found him snoozing on her bed when she got home from school.

She carried a sadness that would never disappear. Losing her beloved grandfather and parents had been a severe blow to the young girl. Particularly her mama and papa. The circumstances had been so cruel and violent. And she had no cemetery to visit, nowhere to pay her respects, bring flowers, and properly mourn the people who were closest to her. Micah had been a pillar of strength, and she'd taken solace in her relationship with Maggie and her two nieces. But the hole in her heart was deep. Would it ever repair? She had thought it impossible. Until Jacob.

As the image of him appeared in her mind, he came into view, waving. She couldn't help but smile.

She'd met him at the Jewish Refugee Center where she volunteered most weekends. He was almost twenty-nine, and when she'd first met him, he seemed even older. Recently liberated from Dachau concentration camp, he was emaciated, weak, and had barely survived the hospital before his release. He'd also grown up in England, near Kent, and had lost everyone in what was now being called the Holocaust – his brother, mother and father, and many aunts, uncles and cousins. It had created a bond between the pair, and a friendship developed. As he grew stronger, Jacob had shared his goal of finishing his university studies, and Hannah had been delighted and more than a little relieved, if she were honest. When he had chosen the same university as her – Queen Mary's – Hannah was reassured that she wouldn't be alone in a strange environment. He was studying engineering and had a small room on campus. Both serious students, they spent many hours with their books, sometimes alone and others together.

"Hullo, Hannah. How was your examination?" He kissed her and opened the door to the café.

"Pretty well, I expect. I'll find out in the new year. For now, I'm free as a bird until January."

He gave her a slow smile.

"Congratulations. I wish we had more than coffee and cake to celebrate."

"This is just fine."

They sat and ordered coffee and pastries, chatting about their days, Jacob's upcoming examination, and inconsequential things.

So far, Hannah had kept her blossoming relationship to herself – pretty much. She had confided in Micah, who had also met Jacob at the center. He had been to supper a few times. Micah and Maggie approved of the young man, but wanted Hannah to take things slow. No worries on that score – Hannah had no intention of rushing anything. She and Jacob both needed to heal. They could help each other, but it would take time.

So far, Hannah had kept him a secret from the rest of the Kingstons. Not a secret as much as an omission. She loved them dearly, but Aunt Alice and Tillie would pepper her with questions and want to know all about him. And thank goodness, Katie was far away in Ireland. She'd corner Hannah with questions and not rest till she had answers.

Jacob reached for her hand across the table. It felt warm and safe in her own. His hazel eyes gazed into hers with a look of understanding and love.

Christmas was fast approaching. Was it time to introduce Jacob to the Kingston clan?

Kenny

"Hello, little ones. It's Tante Astrid, bringing you sweets." She knelt a little awkwardly to hug the children. "And hello, Tillie. Are you alright?"

Jamie and Victoria eagerly greeted their aunt who always brought them boiled sweets.

"Come through, luv. And you mustn't spoil them. C-h-r-i-s-t-m-a-s is coming with masses of treats for them." Tillie smiled at her sister-in-law. "I'm just fine. But how are you?"

Astrid removed her things and sank into the nearest chair.

"Good. Just fine."

Tillie sat, keeping an eye on the children who were hovering near Astrid.

"You never whinge – about anything. Except for that growing baby bump, no one would know you were expecting."

Astrid grimaced.

"I am strong, and with just Kenny to look after, life is pretty easy."

"Your English is going from strength to strength, luv. And you are resilient, no doubt." She paused, carefully choosing her words. "It's also okay to grouse about morning sickness, swollen feet, and sleepless nights."

"In Norway, we take pride in our health. We don't give in to small pains."

Tillie gave her a reassuring smile, but didn't quite understand. Not that she was a big moaner, but Trev had certainly heard about her peaky mornings, backaches, and mood swings. Then again, her situation was much different than Astrid's. The family had been overjoyed to hear the couple were expecting a few months after their wedding. And equally as devastated when Astrid had lost the baby early on. She and Kenny had put on a good front, but they must have gone through loads of grief in private. And a few months later, they announced they were expecting again. Everyone was holding their breath that all would be well with this baby. With only three months to go, Astrid was thriving, and had the maternity glow that Tillie wished she'd had when she was expecting.

"You're proper brave, luv. And we are so excited for this baby. Whether it's a boy or girl – Maggie and I have plenty of clothes and toys and all sorts of bits and pieces for you. Shall I put on the kettle?"

"I thought we were going for a walk? It's warm today and the sun is trying to shine. It will be good for the children."

Tillie would have been just as happy to natter over some tea and toast. But she'd rally if that's what Astrid wanted. And it would be good for Jamie and Victoria. They'd been a bit fractious today, and some exercise would be just the thing.

"Righto, let's get you lot into your coats, hats, and mittens. Tante Astrid is coming for a walk with us."

With Victoria in the pram, and Jamie stopping to examine every stray leaf or rock, it probably wasn't the brisk exercise that Astrid wanted, but that was the way of little ones. Life sometimes slowed down – and that was just how it was supposed to be. They enjoyed a leisurely walk round the neighbourhood.

"Give my love to Kenny. Hopefully all the Christmas festivities won't be tiring for you. Please don't get stuck in doing all the cooking. Maggie and I will do all we can to help Mum." Tillie kissed Astrid on the cheek.

"I will, and don't worry. Many hands to be light work, right?"

Tillie laughed.

"Close enough. Ta ra. I have to get these monkeys down for a nap."

Astrid walked to the bus stop, then made her way home to their little flat. They'd moved out several months ago, and she loved having her own little place to care for, and a nest to build for their baby.

She prepared a simple supper of fish and vegetables, then tidied up an already clean kitchen. She couldn't wait for Kenny to come home.

"Hello, elskling. How is my sweetheart?" He was home a little early, and enfolded her in a lengthy embrace before planting a deep kiss on her lips.

"I'm good. I had a nice visit with Tillie and the children. She sends her love."

"How is my sister? Frazzled as usual?" He let her go, removed his things, and, taking her hand, sat down with her on the sofa.

"What is frazzled?" A frown appeared between her eyebrows. She worked so hard to understand new English words.

"Busy running after the children."

"Yes, she is. But she loves them. And they are …adorable?"

"Almost as adorable as you." He grinned.

"How was your day?" she asked.

"Aren't you the proper wife asking after my work? It was good. Still a lot to learn, but after all the uncertainty of the last six years, I'm enjoying being settled in one place. And Pops is taking good care of me. He introduces me to clients as 'my son who is taking over the business.' He couldn't be prouder. I'm often relieved that Katie doesn't work there any longer. She'd have a fit seeing Pops show such favoritism to me."

Pops and the entire Kingston family had been knocked for six when Kenny announced he wanted to enter the family accounting business. Loudly protesting his disinterest in numbers and working in an office for so long, he'd decided he wanted to give it a go. Having a wife and family to look after surely factored into his motives. He'd fit in right away – and much more smoothly than his summer jobs as a teenager. He was actually starting to mature. Who would have thought it?

"Let's eat, my love. Then we go to cinema, yes?"

"Sounds wonderful. It's good to be home."

Kenny was well aware that his wife was bored. She was used to an active life and found the flat confining. He hadn't wanted her to work after she lost their baby. Glad for his busy family to keep her occupied, he strived to spend as much time with her as possible. They both loved to hike, skate, and spend as much outdoors as they could. He trusted that once the baby arrived, she'd be so besotted that there wouldn't be any room for tedium and dull days. Besides, wouldn't life be just as frenzied for them as he'd seen with his older sisters? It would all sort itself out, he just knew it.

Katie

It was pitch black when the alarm wailed at half-past four.

"I'll never get used to that," Katie groaned into the icy room.

"You stay in bed a while longer, mavoureen. Ma will doubtless have already started breakfast." Ciaran kissed her, leapt out of bed, and pulled the coverlet up to her neck.

"Marvellous, darling." She pulled at his hand, coaxing him back to bed. "Why don't you stay, too? The animals won't mind if you're a few minutes late."

Damn, it was tempting. His beautiful young wife was lying in a warm bed, inviting him to share it with her.

"Come, my love. Keep me warm." She batted her eyelashes. The coverlet fell, displaying her sumptuous body and brown curls falling past her shoulders and down her back.

Groaning for a different reason, he gave in to her. How could he resist? He slid between the sheets, pulling her close. He covered her with kisses, starting with her lips, and moving to her cheeks, neck, and lower.

"Mmmm…" Katie fell into the exquisite sensations he was rousing all over her body. *I never dreamed I'd be making love to my husband at half-four in the morning and loving every minute of it.*

"Shhh," he mumbled from below. "We don't want Ma to hear us."

"I'll try," she whispered, as he flipped her over on top of him. Now it was her turn to rain kisses and caresses on his warm skin. He put his hands in her tangled hair, pulling her closer still.

After an ecstatic interlude, he kissed her one last time, as shards of light penetrated the window blinds.

"Bollocks. I'm going to catch it from Ma. And those pigs will be grunting at me in fury." He quickly donned a plaid shirt, jumper, and dungarees. Picking up his socks, he turned from the door. "I'll see you in the barn." He winked. "I love you, mavoureen."

"I love you, too, Irish. How am I going to face your Ma? She'll know what we've been up to." Katie rose and grabbed the first clothes she could find. It was bloody cold up here.

"Like you did Wednesday. And Friday, if I'm not mistaken." Grinning one last time, he ducked his head, knowing some random object would be flying towards him.

"Damn," Katie muttered as her slipper hit the wall and not her smirking husband's head. Then she smiled. Life on the farm wasn't half bad at times.

Ciaran had washed up and wolfed a plate of food whilst standing before Katie made it to the kitchen. As she rushed through, she stopped short. Her mother-in-law sat alone at the table, a cup of tea before her, as silent tears coursed down her cheeks. Katie didn't know whether to leave her alone in her grief, or rush to comfort her. Before tiptoeing away, Ma turned and saw her, wiping tears away, and pasting on a smile.

"Good morning. Your breakfast is ready. Ciaran is away to the barn. Come in."

Katie felt helpless. Her mother-in-law was a shadow of her vibrant self. Niall McElroy had died of a stroke whilst tending the spring lambs six months ago. Both Ciaran and Ma had said he would have been happiest to pass while working with the animals he loved, but they had been consumed with grief, nonetheless. He'd had a heart condition for years, and managing the farm pretty much on his own during the war had weakened him. Ciaran had many bleak days and nights torturing himself for having left his father to cope on his own. Nothing Katie could say touched his self-reproach and remorse. Only time had brought him an uneasy peace, knowing it had been out of his hands. It made him no less sad.

Katie tried to console them both – reminding them that she and Ciaran were here now and would carry on Niall's legacy. She feared her words meant nothing to the grieving mother and son.

They'd begun to brighten a little when the grain crops brought in a bountiful harvest. So, it was a setback to see Ma breaking down again.

"Good morning, Ma. Sorry I'm late." She tried not to blush. Sitting down, she pulled the plate of bacon, eggs, black bread toast, and mushrooms towards her. Ma's cooking was the best, and the hard work and long hours gave her a massive appetite.

"Are you looking forwad to Christmas? We'll miss Da, no mistake about it, but I'm longing to see my sisters, and well – everyone. Ciaran and I and are that chuffed that you're joining us again."

Ma mustered a smile.

"It won't be the same without Niall, but he wouldn't want us to wallow. He'd urge us to get on with it. Besides, I'm meant to bring along a leg of lamb, and some of our best jams and jellies, aren't I?"

"And your good self, too, Ma." Katie kissed her on the cheek. "It will be smashing, you'll see. We have our pick of where to stay – Mum and Pops, Tillie and Trev's or Maggie and Micah's. I think I fancy Mum's. Far less chaos. Too many babies at my sisters.'"

Ma gave her a sharp look. Katie resisted the urge to roll her eyes. No, she wasn't expecting yet. Ma gave her this once-over every morning. She and Ciaran hadn't wanted to start their family straightaway. It was enough of a wrench for her moving to Ireland and getting used to life on the farm. The homesickness had almost overwhelmed her at times, lessened only by frequent phone calls and a steady stream of British visitors. Mum and Pops had come over a few times, and were almost pathetically welcomed by Katie. She called on her navy training to steel herself to the absence of her beloved family. She still considered herself a city girl, but was learning country ways.

She and Ciaran had decided to try for a family in the autumn, but so far, no sign of a baby. She couldn't say she wasn't disappointed, but tried to be patient. Having Ma continually scanning her for signs she was expecting set her teeth on edge, but she tried to be sympathetic. A new baby would be just the thing to take Ma's mind off her sorrows. All in good time, I suppose.

"I agree. Your parents are always so lovely, and it will be a wee bit quieter there. It will be a grand Christmas, young Katie. Now, go away with you. Your husband is waiting. Something about mucking out some pens. Take him this soda bread. He'll be working up a hunger."

"Sure, Ma. I'll see you later."

Maggie

Maggie tiptoed out of Ruth's room, softly closed the door and almost ran into Micah in the dark hallway. Her shoulders sagged in relief to see him empty-handed. Putting her finger to her lips, she nodded towards the stairs where they both carefully tread them, taking care not step on the third step from the bottom. It squeaked. Bypassing the drawing room, they stole all the way to the basement kitchen before they took a steadying breath.

"We did it. And each in their own rooms. What do you reckon?" Maggie felt as if she'd just walked off a dreadful night on the ack-ack site. She was exhausted.

"I reckon this parenting business gets harder every day. And night." He sank into a kitchen chair and wiped his brow.

"Cup of tea, luv?" Maggie waved half-heartedly towards the kettle.

"No, I think we deserve something a little stronger. Sherry or wine?"

"A glass of sherry would be glorious." Maggie sat across the table from her husband. "Can you fetch it?"

"In just a minute." They sat in silence for a few moments until Micah dragged himself out of the chair and poured them each a generous glass.

"How did Mum do it? Tillie and I slept in the same room since we were small babies. How did she get us both to sleep at the same time?" Maggie shook her head and took a small sip.

Rachel and Ruth were eighteen months and a going concern. They'd shared a bedroom since the beginning but lately had taken to waking each other up – either by crying giggling, or simply making a racket. It had caused havoc with nap and bedtimes, making parents and children fractious and short-tempered. Something had to be done.

Micah and Maggie had made the tough decision to separate the girls – at least for now – until a predictable sleep pattern could be established.

It was night two, and putting them to bed without each other had been tough. Each cried for the other, wanting one more story, a glass of water, and lots of snuggles.

"I know it's hard, little one – but think of the sleep we got last night once they finally went down. Another night or two of adjustment, and we'll be in the clear."

"I hope you are right. It's killing me to hear them cry for each other." Maggie fought a lump. Stiff upper lip.

"We shall look back on this and laugh." Micah smiled kindly. "Let's take our drinks upstairs where we can relax and have a proper chat."

Hand in-hand, they walked up to the drawing room. Still quiet.

"How are you feeling about Christmas? I know you wanted to host the family this year, but I think your mum needs to have everyone over as usual. The house must be deathly quiet for her and your father now." Micah sat on the sofa next to his wife, putting his arm around her.

"I expect you're right. She's gone from years of us running in and out, never knowing who was going to be home when, and keeping it cozy amidst all the topsy turvy of war, that she deserves peace and quiet. But not too much quiet." Maggie snuggled into Micah's shoulder. "Between Tillie and I, there always seem to be grandchildren rushing around, making a mess. In fact, I'm taking the girls there tomorrow for a few hours so I can get to the shops. It's near impossible to stand in queue, and find anything reasonable with four little hands picking up everything in sight."

"Doubtless your mum will be delighted to mind them."

"Mmm," Maggie replied, feeling sleepy.

"Whilst we have this rare silence, and before Hannah gets home, I want to talk to you about our trip to Israel. I'm serious about going, and I'd like to go this summer, if possible. After meeting so many displaced Jews, the pull to finally go there is strong."

Maggie nodded.

"Trying to help these fractured families locate anyone who is still alive is almost unworkable. Records are so spotty coming from France, Poland, and Germany. So many were destroyed in the last months of the war. Wiping out evidence. Bloody Nazis. Trying to correspond with Jewish authorities in Tel Aviv by post is interminable. If I can meet with them in person – I'm bound to get more answers, and quickly. Even if they are not always the answers that our refugees want." He bowed his head.

"I know it's important to you, luv and it is too me, too. The work is vital. I just worry the girls are at an awkward age. The plane trip, managing them in strange surroundings and new routines – it all seems overwhelming."

"I understand. I just don't want to wait another year."

Maggie turned to face him. New furrows had appeared on his forehead, and more grey hair around his ears. The last few years had taken a severe toll on her dear husband. She raised a hand to smooth his forehead, kissed him, and nodded decisively.

"Then we must make it work. We'll plan it out, and it will be the trip of a lifetime. Besides, the girls will be six months older, and that much better able to cope." She kissed him again, trying not to think of the terrible twos that Tillie raged about.

"Thank you," he replied, a twinkle in his eye. "When is Hannah expected?" Micah raised an eyebrow, pulling her close for another embrace.

"At least an hour or two, I should think."

Micah stood and caught her hand.

"If we are as quiet as church mice, I have a grand idea."

A slow smile spread across Maggie's face, as her body began to tingle. Somehow, her fatigue was dropping away.

"I like the way you think, Mister Goldbach."

Tillie

"Can you pinch me, please? I must be dreaming. The two of us – together with no babies or toddlers in tow?" Tillie jammed on her hat, twirled and hooked her arm through her sister's.

"I won't pinch you, luv, but it's true. Two young and free Kingston twins on the loose." Maggie beamed.

"Not so young, but definitely free. Let's get on with the shopping."

"How did Jamie and Victoria do with Nana? Any tears when you left them?"

"No. Trev's mum knows all the tricks. They love going to her flat."

"Brilliant. And the sun is shining. Do you reckon we'll have a white

Christmas this year?" Maggie almost felt like skipping along the road to the tube station.

"With this warm weather, we're more likely to see primroses than snow."

"How is Trev getting on at the lumber yard?"

"He's loving it. He likes contributing to house rebuilding. He's that chuffed to be away from fires and coming home soaked and smelling of smoke and cordite every night."

After being demobbed from the RAF, Trevor applied at the lumber grounds. Having carpenter skills and enjoying building with his hands, it was a natural choice. With all the bomb damage, whole neighbourhoods been levelled, leaving hundreds of London families homeless. He got satisfaction from hammering, framing and seeing structures go up where destruction had lain. He came home bone tired each night, but more than fulfilled. He'd made the right post-war choice.

They nattered all the way to Oxford Street, ignoring the double takes and stares they always got when out together. Striking identical blondes, tall and willowy, they always garnered attention. Maggie had cut her hair shorter, but it was still difficult to tell them apart.

"My Christmas list is as long as my arm. I hope I can sort at least half of it today. The big day is around the corner."

Maggie sighed.

"Our family has gotten so enormous, it's masses to buy for. That's if I can think of what to buy. I'm drawing a blank when it comes to Mr. and Mrs. McElroy, Uncle Thomas and Aunt Isla, and even Pops if I'm honest."

"I don't suppose we could club together and buy joint gifts? Like a recipe book for Mum and Pops or new tea towels for Aunt Isla and Uncle Thomas?" Tillie joked.

Maggie chuckled.

"I don't suppose that would work, darling. What makes it harder is that everyone says not to bother, and don't buy me anything – so there's not even any ideas to latch onto."

"I say we just cross our fingers and hope that the shops are loaded with new lovely things for us to choose from."

"Alright," Maggie said doubtfully.

Two hours later, the young women entered a local pub, arms full of packages.

"We did a bit of alright, didn't we, luv?" Tillie sat in relief, bags surrounding her legs.

"I think I've checked off about half my tick list. It's a start," Maggie replied. She didn't have nearly as many packages as her sister, but this was far from unusual. Tillie was more of an impulsive shopper. Maggie liked to take her time and consider each purchase carefully. "And I don't know how you can say you've sorted so many gifts. Three-quarters of those bundles are for your own children." Maggie shook her head.

"So, what if they are?" Tillie argued. "Jamie has big expectations for Father Christmas."

"You're too much." Maggie ordered a shandy for them both as they scanned the menu. "Fish and chips for me."

"I fancy shepherd's pie." Tillie put down the menu and scrutinized her sister. "How are you getting on with the twins? I won't say you look tired, because I hate when Mum tells me that with sympathetic eyes and a pat on the hand, but – I know what it's like. You coping alright?"

"I can't whinge, Tils. Truly. Micah and I are team-mates in everything. He changes nappies, makes baby food, entertains them – all of it, really. And I couldn't manage without Hannah, or Mum, or you, for that matter. I'm luckier than many."

"That sounds brave, but it's me, Mags. You can be honest."

"I am, darling. Of course, I'm tired and I get down with all the wash and baby stuff strewn around, but I love being a mum. With Ruth and Rachel walking now, it's a whole new phase. A bit scary, really. Micah has more patience than I do." She laughed. "Although he kneels down and tries to reason with them – to no avail. He is that eager for them to talk and have real conversations."

"That's all well and good. Once they've gotten past the 'no' phase, they are less easily distracted. And Master Jamie is now mastering the art of negotiation. Do you think it just gets harder and harder? I figured the baby stage was the worst, but the problems just seem to get bigger as they do. And Victoria has now started grabbing his favorite toys, at the precise moment he wants to play with them. Not to mention a rambunctious one-year-old puppy. It never ends."

"You are a wonderful mum. I'm that grateful that you are ahead of me. I learn from you every day, and watch what you do. You have more patience than you think. And I still think you are a saint for agreeing to a puppy. I don't know how you do it."

"Trev is a huge help. He calms me down when it's been one of those days. He'll swing them into his arms and take them out for a walk with the dog so I can have a bath. Isn't it heaven not being restricted to three inches once a week?"

"I wish I knew. It was a monumental effort for me to get a proper wash-up before meeting you today. Who knew how hard it would be to get a comb through your hair and teeth brushed with two small children?"

"Mum never told us about that, did she?" Tillie giggled. "Who would have thought when we were green Nippies that we'd be mature ladies of twenty-nine with four children between us?"

"You know, we need to take the kids to see Alfie. I don't think we've ever brought them all together." Maggie giggled too.

"Smashing idea. And then, let's leave him to cope with all four whilst we go for a chat with the girls."

"I'm not sure that's fair on him. Or them. He was always good to us." Tillie snorted.

"Except for all his bad jokes and puns. Sometimes I could barely stand them – especially after a busy shift. But those were fun times, weren't they?"

"The best. Our biggest worries were making sure our uniforms were well-pressed and our stocking seams were straight. How innocent we were." Maggie looked thoughtful. "It's cheering to see London being rebuilt. But it's such slow going. Our poor city has taken a beating."

"She'll be back better than ever; you wait and see. She's as tough as we've all proven to be." Maggie was definite.

"I'll drink to that." Tillie held up her glass and the sisters clinked to the future, sleepless nights and all.

Alice

Alice paused to consider today's meals. Katie, Ciaran, and Mrs. McElroy arrived last yesterday. Tired from the long journey, they'd eaten a late supper and tumbled into bed.

Katie had bounced downstairs early and helped with the breakfasts. Now a steadfast early riser, she was cheerful and eager to meet up with the rest of the family and get on with the Christmas festivities. She was bound first for Tillie's, whilst Ciaran took his mum to the shops. This afternoon, Kenny and Astrid were meant to come by to fetch a Christmas tree with Katie and Ciaran.

Maggie, Tillie, and their families were eating on their own tonight. Tomorrow was the ladies Claridge's tea and then Christmas Eve the next day. Alice leaned against the counter, undoing her apron. Tonight, it would be the McElroys and Isla and Thomas, whom she'd invited as well. Hopefully she could convince Kenny and Astrid to stay.

Thank goodness for the McElroys and the bounty of their farm. The bloomin' rationing had droned on – even after the war had ended. In fact, this year was even worse than last. It had been painfully difficult trying to find anything to grace the table that was any different than the meagre foodstuffs of the barren years before.

Housewives across Britain were equally dismayed. Expecting food to be more plentiful this Christmas, they faced the same hardships as the previous six years. Even bread was on the ration now – for the first time ever. It lowered morale, just when Britons were more than ready for joy and abundance. Shop shelves were empty, but husbands, sons, brothers, and fathers were home. So, they were determined to grin and bear it, pulled out the worn Ministry of Food recipes to make pleasant and carefree holidays for their families.

Alice sat, pulled her tick list towards her, and picked up a pencil. What would she do without her trusty list?

Right, so that's today sorted. Tomorrow is our lovely tea, with the men minding the children. Isla offered to make Woolten pie and mash for them. Christmas Eve at Tillie's – she wrote *sausage rolls and wine.* Christmas morning would be quiet – until the family all arrived for dinner. *Orla's bacon, eggs, soda bread,* she wrote busily.

Walter sauntered in.

"Any tea going?" He felt the cold teapot.

Alice pushed her chair back.

"Sorry, luv. I was busy with my list. I'll put on the kettle, shall I? A nice cup of tea for the two of us before family Christmas takes over?" She smiled at her husband.

"I'll do it, dear. You sit. The next few days will be hectic, indeed. And you will have it all in hand, like you always do." He turned on the hob and put a hand on her shoulder.

"Thank you, Walter. May I be the first to wish you a Happy Christmas?"

ReadMore Press

Would you like a FREE WWII historical fiction audiobook?

This audiobook is valued at 14.99$ on Amazon and is exclusively free for **Readmore Press'** readers!

To get your free audiobook, and to sign up for our newsletter where we send you more exclusive bonus content every month,

Scan the QR code

Readmore Press is a publisher that focuses on high-end, quality historical fiction. We love giving the world moving stories, emotional accounts, and tear-filled happy endings.

We hope to see you again in our next book!

Never stop reading, **Readmore Press**

Appendix I

Traditional Christmas Dinner

After researching and writing about so many foods during wartime, and particularly at Christmas, I thought you might be interested in reading a menu for traditional Christmas dinners for our main characters.

England
The traditional Christmas hasn't changed much over the decades. During war, turkeys, chickens, and geese were difficult to find. Mock goose and lots of vegetables took their place.

Menu
Roast Turkey with Bread Sauce
Roast Potatoes
Cranberry Sauce
Brussel Sprouts
Cabbage
Parsnips
Carrots
Christmas Pudding with Brandy Butter
Also: Mince Pies

Ireland
Ciaran and his parents would have eaten a similar meal, although as Ireland was officially neutral in the war, they didn't suffer through the same rationing policies as the British. Also, being farmers, they could grow a lot of their vegetables, and had chickens and other animals.

Menu
Roast Goose or Goose with Potato Stuffing
Boiled Ham
Colcannon (mashed potatoes with kale)
Roasted Potatoes
Cranberry Sauce
Gravy
Brussel Sprouts
Cabbage and Winter Vegetables
Iced Christmas Cake

Norway
Astrid would have enjoyed a very different Christmas experience than her British husband, Kenny. The foods and how they were prepared were nothing like a traditional British Christmas.

Menu
Lutefisk (Dried cod)
Rack of Lamb or Lamb Ribs
Raspekake (Potato balls with butter)
Root Vegetables
Krumkrakers (Cloudberry jam and whipped cream pastry horns)

Appendix II

His Majesty King George VI's Christmas Messages

Finding the entire transcripts for the war speeches was a bit challenging. Eventually, I found (or transcribed) them all. There was no speech in 1938. It was really the outbreak of war that made the Christmas speeches an annual tradition. I thought you would enjoy seeing them in one place. It's a fascinating view of the highs and lows of the war years. Note that I've retained the UK spellings.

1939
"The festival which we all know as Christmas is, above all, the festival of peace and of the home. Among all free peoples, the love of peace is profound, for this alone gives security to the home. But true peace is in the hearts of men, and it is the tragedy of this time that there are powerful countries whose whole direction and policy are based on aggression and the suppression of all that we hold dear for mankind.

It is this that has stirred our peoples and given them a unity unknown in any previous way. We feel in our hearts that we are fighting against wickedness, and this conviction will give us strength from day to day to persevere until victory is assured.

At home, we are, as it were, taking the strain for what may lie ahead of us, resolved and confident. We look with pride and thankfulness on the never-failing courage and devotion of the Royal Navy, upon which, throughout the last four months, has burst the storm of ruthless and unceasing war.

And when I speak of our Navy today, I mean all the men of our Empire who go down to the sea in ships, the Mercantile Marine, the minesweepers, the trawlers, and drifters, from the senior officers to the last boy who has joined up. To everyone in this great Fleet, I send a message of gratitude and greeting from myself, as from all my peoples.

The same message I send to the gallant Air Force, which, in co-operation with the Navy, is our sure shield of defence. They are daily adding laurels to those that their fathers won.

I would send a special word of greeting to the armies of the Empire, to those who have come from afar, and in particular to the British Expeditionary Force. Their task is hard.

They are waiting, and waiting is a trial of nerve and discipline. But I know that when the moment comes for action, they will prove themselves worthy of the highest traditions of their great Service.

And to all who are preparing themselves to serve their country on sea, on land, or in the air, I send my greeting at this time. The men and women of our far-flung Empire, working in their several vocations with the one same purpose, all are members of the great family of nations which is prepared to sacrifice everything so that freedom of spirit may be saved to the world.

Such is the spirit of the Empire, of the great Dominions, of India, of every colony, large or small. From all alike, have come offers of help for which the Mother Country can never be sufficiently grateful. Such unity in aim and in effort has never been seen in the world before.

I believe from my heart that the cause which binds together my peoples and our gallant and faithful Allies is the cause of Christian civilisation. On no other basis can a true civilisation be built. Let us remember this through the dark times ahead of us and when we are making the peace for which all men pray.

A new year is at hand. We cannot tell what it will bring. If it brings peace how thankful we shall all be. If it brings continued struggle, we shall remain undaunted.

In the meantime, I feel that we may all find a message of encouragement in the lines which, in my closing words, I would like to say to you.

I said to the man who stood at the gate of the year. 'Give me a light that I may tread safely into the unknown.' And he replied; 'Go out into the darkness and put your hand into the hand of God. That shall be to you better than light and safer than a known way.'

May that Almighty hand guide and uphold us all."

1940

"In days of peace, the feast of Christmas is a time when we all gather together in our homes, young and old, to enjoy the happy festivity and good will which the Christmas message brings. It is, above all, children's day, and I am sure that we shall all do our best to make it a happy one for them wherever they may be.

War brings, among other sorrows, the sadness of separation. There are many in the Forces away from their homes today because they must stand ready and alert to resist the invader should he dare to come, or because they are guarding the dark seas or pursuing the beaten foe in the Libyan Desert.

Many family circles are broken. Children from English homes are today in Canada, Australia, New Zealand, and South Africa. For not only has the manhood of the whole British Commonwealth rallied once more to the aid of the Mother Country in her hour of need, but the peoples of the Empire have eagerly thrown open the doors of their homes to our children so that they may be spared from the strain and danger of modern war.

And in the United States also, where we find so many generous loyal friends and organisations to give us unstinted help, warm-hearted people are keeping and caring for many of our children till the war is over.

But how many more children are there here who have been moved from their homes to safer quarters?

To all of them, at home and abroad, who are separated from their fathers and mothers, to their kind friends and hosts, and to all who love them, and to parents who will be lonely without them, from all in our dear island, I wish every happiness that Christmas can bring. May the new year carry us towards victory and to happier Christmas days, when everyone will be at home together in the years to come.

To the older people here and throughout the worlds I would say – in the last Great War the flower of our youth was destroyed, and the rest of the people saw but little of the battle. This time, we are all in the front line and the danger together, and I know that the older among us are proud that it should be so.

Remember this. If war brings its separations, it brings new unity also, the unity which comes from common perils and common sufferings willingly shared. To be good comrades and good neighbours in trouble is one of the finest opportunities of the civilian population, and by facing hardship and discomfort cheerfully and resolutely, not only do they do their own duty, but they play their part in helping the fighting services to win the war.

Time and again during these last few months, I have seen for myself the battered towns and cities of England, and I have seen the British people facing their ordeal. I can say to them that they may be justly proud of their race and nation. On every side I have seen a new and splendid spirit of good fellowship springing up in adversity, a real desire to share burdens and resources alike. Out of all this suffering, there is a growing harmony which we must carry forward into the days to come when we have endured to the end and ours is the victory.

Then, when Christmas Days are happy again, and good will has come back to the world, we must hold fast to the spirit which binds us together now. We shall need this spirit in each of our own lives as men and women, and shall need it even more among the nations of the world. We must go on thinking less about ourselves and more for one another, for so, and so only, can we hope to make the world a better place and life a worthier thing.

And now, I wish you all a happy Christmas and a happier New Year. We may look forward to it with sober confidence. We have surmounted a grave crisis. We do not underrate the dangers and difficulties which confront us still, but we take courage and comfort from the successes which our fighting men and their Allies have won at heavy odds by land and air and sea.

The future will be hard, but our feet are planted on the path of victory, and with the help of God, we shall make our way to justice and to peace."

1941

"I am glad to think that millions of my people in all parts of the world are listening to me now. From my own home, with the Queen and my children beside me, I send to all a Christmas greeting.

Christmas is the festival at home, and it is right that we should remember those who this year must spend it away from home. I am thinking, as I speak, of the men who have come from afar, standing ready to defend the old homeland, of the men who in every part of the world are serving the Empire and its cause with such valour and devotion by sea, land and in the air.

I am thinking of all those, women and girls as well as men, who at the call of duty have left their homes to join the services, or to work in factory, hospital or field. To each one of you, wherever your duty may be, I send you my remembrance and my sincere good wishes for you and for yours.

I do not forget what others have done and are doing so bravely in civil defence. My heart is also with those who are suffering – the wounded, the bereaved, the anxious, the prisoners of war. I think you know how deeply the Queen and I feel for them. May God give them comfort, courage and hope.

All these separations are part of the hard sacrifice which this war demands. It may well be that it will call for even greater sacrifices. If this is to be, let us face them cheerfully together. I think of you, my peoples, as one great family, for it is how we are learning to live. We all belong to each other. We all need each other. It is in serving each other and in sacrificing for our common good that we are finding our true life.

In that spirit, we shall win the war, and in that same spirit, we shall win for the world after the war a true and lasting peace. The greatness of any nation is in the spirit of its people. So, it has always been since history began; so it shall be with us.

The range of the tremendous conflict is ever widening. It now extends to the Pacific. Truly, it is a stern and solemn time. But as the war widens, so surely our conviction depends at the greatness of our cause.

We who belong to the present generation must bear the brunt of the struggle, and I would say to the coming generation, the boys and girls of today, the men and women of tomorrow – train yourselves in body, mind, and spirit so as to be ready for whatever part you may be called to play, and for the tasks which will await you as citizens of the Empire when the war is over.

We must all, older and younger, resolve that having been entrusted with so great a cause, then, at whatever cost, God helping us, we will not falter or fail. Make yourselves ready – in your home and school – to give and to offer your very best.

We are coming to the end of another hard-fought year. During these months, our people have been through many trials, and in that true humanity which goes hand in hand with valour, have learnt once again to look for strength to God alone.

So, I bid you all be strong and of a good courage. Go forward into this coming year with a good heart. Lift up your hearts with thankfulness for deliverance from dangers in the past. Lift up your hearts in confident hope that strength will be given us to overcome whatever perils may lie ahead until the victory is won.

If the skies before us are still dark and threatening, there are stars to guide us on our way. Never did heroism shine more brightly than it does now, nor fortitude, nor sacrifice, nor sympathy, nor neighbourly kindness, and with them – brightest of all stars – is our faith in God. These stars will we follow with His help until the light shall shine and the darkness shall collapse.

God bless you, everyone."

1942

"It is at Christmas, more than at any other time, that we are conscious of the dark shadow of war. Our Christmas festival today must lack many of the happy, familiar features that it has had from our childhood. We miss the actual presence of some of those nearest and dearest, without whom our family gatherings cannot be complete.

But though its outward observances may be limited, the message of Christmas remains eternal and unchanged. It is a message of thankfulness and of hope – of thankfulness to the Almighty for His great mercies, of hope for the return to this earth of peace and goodwill.

In this spirit, I wish all of you a happy Christmas. This year it adds to our happiness that we are sharing it with so many of our comrades-in-arms from the United States of America. We welcome them in our homes, and their sojourn here will not only be a happy memory for us, but, I hope, a basis of enduring understanding between our two peoples.

The recent victories won by the United Nations enable me this Christmas to speak with firm confidence about the future.

On the southern shores of the Mediterranean, the First and Eighth Armies; our Fleets and Air Forces are advancing towards each other, heartened and greatly fortified by the timely and massive armies of the United States. Blows have been struck by the armies of the Soviet Union, the effects of which cannot yet be measured on the minds and bodies of the German people.

In the Pacific, we watch with thrilled attention the counter-strokes of our Australian and American comrades.

India, now still threatened with Japanese invasion, has found in her loyal fighting men, more than a million strong champions to stand at the side of the British Army in defence of Indian soil.

We still have tasks ahead of us, perhaps harder even than those which we have already accomplished. We face these with confidence, for today we stand together, no longer alone, no longer ill armed, but just as resolute as in the darkest hours to do our duty whatever comes.

Many of you to whom I am speaking are far away overseas. You realize at first hand the importance and meaning of those outposts of Empire which the wisdom of our forefathers selected, and which your faithfulness will defend. For there was a danger that we should lose much, and this has opened our eyes to the value of what we might have lost.

You may be serving for the first time in Gibraltar, in Malta, in Cyprus, in the Middle East, in Ceylon, or in India. Perhaps you are listening to me from Aden or Syria, or Persia, or Madagascar or the West Indies, or you may be in the land of your birth, in Canada, Australia, New Zealand, or South Africa.

Wherever you are serving in our wide, free Commonwealth of Nations, you will always feel "at home." Though severed by the long sea miles of distance, you are still in the family circle, whose ties, precious in peaceful years, have been knit even closer by danger.

The Queen and I feel most deeply for all of you who have lost or been parted from your dear ones, and our hearts go out to you with sorrow, with comfort, but also with pride.

We send a special message of remembrance to the wounded and the sick in the hospitals wherever they may be, and to the prisoners of war, who are enduring their long exile with dignity and fortitude. Suffering and hardship shared together have given us a new understanding of each other's problems.

The lessons learned during the past forty tremendous months have taught us how to work together after the war to build a worthier future.

On visits to war industries in every part of the country, the Queen and I have watched with admiration the steady growth of that vital war production, the fruits of which are now being used by every branch of our forces. We are thankful for the splendid addition to our food supplies made by those who work on the land, and who have made it fertile as it has never been before.

Those of you who are carrying out this variety of duties so willingly undertaken in the service of your country will, I am sure, find new associations, new friendships, and new memories long to be cherished in times of peace.

So, let us brace and prepare ourselves for the days which lie ahead.

Victory will bring us even greater world responsibilities, and we must not be found unequal to a task in the discharge of which we shall draw on the storehouse of our experience and tradition.

Our European Allies, their sovereigns, heads, and governments, whom we are glad to welcome here in their distress, count on our aid to help them return to their native lands and to rebuild the structure of a free and glorious Europe.

On the sea, on land, and in the air, and in civil life at home, a pattern of effort and mutual service is being traced which may guide those who design the picture of our future society.

A former president of the United States of America used to tell the story of a boy who was carrying an even smaller child up a hill. Asked whether the heavy burden was not too much for him, the boy answered, 'It's not a burden, it's my brother!'

So let us welcome the future in a spirit of brotherhood, and thus make a world in which, please God, all may dwell together in justice and peace."

1943

"And once again, from our home in England, the Queen and I send our Christmas greetings and good wishes to each one of you, all the world over. Some of you may hear me on board your ships, in your aircraft, or where you wait for battle in the jungles of the Pacific islands or on the Italian peaks. Some of you may listen to me as you rest from your work or as you lie sick or wounded in hospital.

To many of you, my words will come as you sit in the quiet of your homes. But wherever you may be today of all days in the year, your thoughts will be in distant places and your hearts with those you love. I hope that my words spoken to them, and to you, may be the bond that joins us all in one company for a few moments on this Christmas Day.

With this thought in my mind, I wish to all who are on service, good luck and a stout heart. To those who wait for them to return, proud memories and high hopes to keep you strong. And to all the children here and in the lands beyond the seas, a day of real happiness.

I send these words of Christmas greeting to all of you who dwell within the family of the British Commonwealth and Empire. I know you would wish me to send a message of hope to our gallant allies who fight with us, and to all with the loneliness of exile of a hammer of invasion, look forward to our coming victory.

In this year almost passed, many things have happened under God's providence to make us thankful for His mercies. The generous strength of the United States of America, the tremendous deed of Russia, the endurance of China under her long ordeal, for the fighting spirit of France reborn, and the flower of the manhood and womanhood of many lands which share the burdens of our forward march. All these have played their part in the brightening of our fortunes on sea, on land, and in the air.

Since I last spoke to you, many things have changed, but the spirit of our people has not changed and we will not be downcast by defeat. We are not unduly exalted by victory. While we have bright visions of the future, we have no easy dreams of the days that lie close at hand. We know there's much hard working and hard fighting, and perhaps harder working and harder fighting than ever before are necessary for a victory. We shall not rest from our task until it is nobly ended.

Meanwhile, within these islands, we have tried to be worthy of our Father. We have tried to carry into the dawn the steadfastness and courage vouchsafed to us when we stood alone in the darkness.

This is not the time for a chronicle of our progress, but there is one landmark in the somber world-embracing battlefield which I hope and I trust may endure. Wherever their duty has called our men and women, they have gained new friends and come to know old friends better. They have learnt to share the burdens and to read the hearts of their neighbours. They have laid the foundations of new friendships between nations and strengthened old ones formed long ago. As a result, there is, springing up in every country, fresh hope for that of comradeship and sacrifice so from power to restore and power to build anew.

I saw proof of this when I visited North Africa in the summer. I saw many thousands of men of the United Nations united in action in heart and mind and purpose. The only rivalry between them was in the service of a great cause. Their only aim was the defeat of a common enemy.

In the same spirit of unity, men of diverse races have come together in the council chamber and around the conference table; some to meet the stern, immediate demands of war itself, others to heal the wounds that war deals to all humanity. The feed of the hungry, shelter of the homeless, mend who are broken, and succor the poor.

So, as we see the cloud breaking on this Christmas Day, we should take comfort from our faith that out of desolation so lies a new hope, and out of strife be born a new brotherhood. From this ancient and beloved festival that we are keeping, a sacred attitude to home and all that home means; we can draw strength to face the future of a world driven by a tempest such as it has never yet endured.

In the words of a Scottish writer of our day, no experience can be too strange and no task too formidable if a man can link it up with what he knows and loves."

1944

"Once more, on Christmas Day, I speak to millions of you scattered far and near across the world. As always, I am greatly moved by the thought that so vast and friendly an audience hears the words I speak in this room, where the Queen and I and our daughters are fortunate enough to be spending a Christmas at home.

I count it a high privilege to be able to use these moments to send a Christmas message of good will to men and women of whatever creed and colour who may be listening to me throughout our Commonwealth and Empire—on the battlefields, on the high seas, or in foreign lands.

At this Christmas time, we think proudly and gratefully of our fighting men wherever they may be. May God bless them and protect them and bring them victory.

Our message goes to all who are wounded or sick in hospital and to the doctors and nurses in their labor of mercy. And our thoughts and prayers are also with our men who are prisoners of war, and with their relatives in their loneliness and anxiety. To children everywhere, we wish all the happiness that Christmas can bring.

Among the deepest sorrows we have felt in these years of strife, the one we feel most is the grief of separation. Families rent apart by the call of service, people sundered from people by the calamities that have overwhelmed some, while others have been free to continue to fight.

We have rejoiced in the victories of this year, not least because they have broken down some of the barriers between us and our friends, and brought us nearer to the time when we can all be together again with those we love.

For the moment, we have a foretaste of that joy and we enter into the fellowship of Christmas Day.

At this great festival, more perhaps than at any other season of the year, we long for a new birth of freedom and order among all nations, so that happiness and concord may prevail, and the scourge of war may be banished from our midst.

Yet, though human ingenuity can show us no shortcuts to that universal charity which is the very heart of the Christmas message, the goal is still before us, and I, for one, believe that these years of sacrifice and sorrow have brought us nearer to it.

We do not know what awaits us when we open the door of 1945, but if we look back to those earlier Christmas days of the war, we can surely say that the darkness daily grows less and less. The lamps which the Germans put out all over Europe, first in 1914 and then in 1939, are being slowly rekindled.

Already, we can see some of them beginning to shine through the fog of war that still shrouds so many lands.

Anxiety is giving way to confidence, and let us hope that before next Christmas Day, God willing, the story of liberation and triumph will be complete.

Throughout the Empire, men and women and boys and girls, through hard work and much self-sacrifice, have all helped to bring victory nearer. We have shared many dangers, and the common effort has bound us together. Yet labor and devotion, patience and tolerance will still be needed for the experiment of living as nations in harmony.

The defeat of Germany and Japan is only the first half of our task. The second is to create a world of free men, untouched by tyranny. We have great Allies in this arduous enterprise of the human spirit – man`s unconquerable mind and freedom's holy flame.

I believe most surely that we shall reach that goal. In the meantime, in the old words that never lose their force; I wish you from my heart a Happy Christmas, and for the coming year a full measure of that courage and faith in God which alone enables us to bear old sorrows and face new trials until the day when the Christmas message – peace on earth and goodwill toward men – finally comes true."

1945

"For six years in the past, I have spoken at Christmas to an Empire at war. During all those years of sorrow and danger, of weariness and strife, you and I have been upheld by a vision of a world peace. And now that vision has become a reality.

By gigantic efforts and sacrifices, a great work has been done. A great evil has been cast from the earth. No peoples have done more to cast it out than you to whom I speak.

With my whole heart I pray to God, by whose grace victory has been won, that this Christmas may bring to my peoples all the world over, every joy they have dreamt of in the dark days that are gone.

This Christmas is a real homecoming for us all – a return to a world in which the homely, friendly things of life can again be ours.

To win victory, much that was of great price has been given up, and much has been ravaged or destroyed by the hand of war, but the things that have been saved are beyond price. In these homelands of the British peoples, which we have saved from destruction, we still possess the things that make life precious, and we shall find them strengthened and deepened by the fires of battle.

Faith in these things held us in brotherhood through all our trials, and has carried us to victory. Perhaps a better understand of that brotherhood is the most precious of all the gains that remain with us after these hard years. Together, all our peoples around the globe have met every danger, triumphed over it and, we are together still.

Most of all, we are together as a one world-wide family in the joy of Christmas. I think of men and women of every race within the Empire returning from their long service to their own families, to their own homes and to the ways of peace. I think of the children freed from unnatural fears and the blacked-out world, celebrating this Christmas in the light and happiness of the family circle once more reunited.

There will be the vacant places of those who will never return – brave souls who gave their all to win peace for us. We remember them with pride and with unfailing love, praying that a greater peace than ours may now be theirs.

There are those of you still to be numbered in millions who are spending Christmas far from their homes, engaged in the East and West in the long difficult task of restoring to shattered countries the means and the manners of civilised life. But many anxieties have been lifted from your folks at home, and the coming of peace brings you nearer to your heart's desire.

There is not yet for us the abundance of peace. We all have to make a little go a long way, but Christmas comes with its message of hope and fellowship to all men of goodwill and warms our hearts to kindliness and comradeship. We cannot this day forget how much is still to be done before the blessings of peace are brought to all the world.

In the liberated countries, millions will spend this Christmas under terribly hard conditions with only the bare necessities of life. The nations of the world are not yet united as a family, so let our sympathy for others move us to humble gratitude that God has given to our Commonwealth and Empire a wonderful spirit of unity and understanding.

To the younger of you I would say a special word. You have grown up in a world at war in which your fine spirit of service has been devoted to a single purpose of the overthrow and destruction of our enemies. You have known the world only as a world of strife and fear. Bring now all that fine spirit to make it one of joyous adventure, a home where men and women can live in mutual trust and walk together as friends. Do not judge life by what you have seen of it in the grimness and waste of war, nor yet by the confusion of the first years of peace. Have faith in life at its best and bring to it your courage, your hopes, and your sense of humour.

Merriment is the birthright of young, but we can all keep it in our hearts as long as life goes on, if we hold fast by the spirit that refuses to admit defeat, by the faith that never falters, and by hope that cannot be quenched.

Let us have no fear of the future, but think of it as opportunity and adventure. The same dauntless resolve, which you have shown so abundantly in the years of danger, that the power of darkness shall not prevail, must now be turned to a happier purpose to making the light shine more brightly everywhere.

The light of joy can be most surely kindled by the fireside where most of you are listening. Home life as you all remember at Christmas is life at its best. There in the trust and love of parents and children, brothers and sisters we learn how men and nations too may live together in unity and peace.

So, to every one of you who gathered now in your homes or holding a thought of home in your hearts, I say – a merry Christmas, and may God bless you all."

1946

"This Christmas Day, surrounded by our family circle in our own home, the Queen and I are thinking of that world-wide family of the British Commonwealth and Empire. To each member of that family, the young and old, composed of so many races dwelling in so many climes, we send our heartfelt and affectionate greetings wherever you are.

Whatever your circumstances, our prayer is that this Christmastide will bring you peace and blessing. Christmas comes to cheer our hearts and to revive our faith and courage as the old year dies and the new year is born.

The year that is passing has not been an easy one. Statesmen and politicians have been burdened with the resettlement of a world that has been shattered and ruined by global war. In office, shop, and warehouse, and on the farm, men of all classes have been troubled and harassed by the shortages and economic dislocation that always follows in its wake.

All of us, instead of getting some well-earned relaxation after years of intensive work, have had to put our shoulders to the wheels of industry and agriculture with redoubled vigour. Men and women have returned from war-time service to conditions that are only slowly improving from war-time austerity, while the housewife – perhaps the most gallant figure of all – still bears many of the extra burdens which she bore so bravely throughout the war.

With all these trials to be faced, I am indeed proud that you are able to maintain that energy and cheerfulness, that courage which this difficult time demands of us all.

We cannot expect a world so grievously wounded to recover quickly, but its convalescence can certainly be hastened by our continued endurance and good will. We showed the way when the bombs were falling by our discipline, our endurance, our patience. We can show the way again.

In his own good time, God will lead our feet into the ways of peace. Though the days may be difficult, let us not forget how much we have to be thankful for.

We have survived the greatest upheaval in human history. Our hard-won liberties and our democratic institutions are unimpaired; our Commonwealth and Empire, though subject to the changes that time must bring, have not been disrupted by the stress and peril of war. We are celebrating Christmas as free men and in peace.

Christmas is the season in which we count our mercies. I know that there are many little things lacking that can add colour and variety to life, but the big things for so many of us have come back – the big things which we longed for in the Blitz, in the desert, in the lonely places of the sea or the jungle. We are back, most of us, with those we love. The guns have ceased to kill, and the bombs have ceased to fall.

Better days lie ahead. We must not concentrate too much on the difficulties of the present – they will pass – so let us rather think of the possibilities that the future may hold for us.

Our task today is to mobilise the Christmas spirit and to apply its power and healing to our daily life. The devastation and suffering everywhere, and especially in stricken Europe, must move the hearts of all of us, but the reconstruction so urgently needed is quite as much spiritual as material – it is necessary not merely to feed hungry people and to rebuild ruined cities, but also to restore the very soul of civilisation.

We cannot all think alike amid the dilemmas of a changing world. Nor is it right that we should. Opinion striking against opinion ignites the spark that can kindle the lamp of truth. But if our feet are on the road of common charity that leads to ultimate truth, our differences will never destroy our underlying unity, and our disputes will not leave us either embittered or unkind.

If the coming year has its uncertainties, it has also its promises. By God's help and by our own endeavours, let us make these brighter promises come true.

And now, my dear people, I wish you well. May the new year be full of blessing for each one of you. Welcome it when it comes with hope and courage and greet the unseen with a cheer."

Acknowledgements

I'd like to say a huge thank you to the entire ReadMore Press team — Tali, Liat, and especially Dani Zrihen—for their support, expertise, and absolute positivity about my Kingston Sisters series and for bringing their stories to life.

As I researched and wrote Tillie, Maggie, and Katie's stories in the first three Kingston Sisters books, I felt the growing need to put more focus on Christmas during wartime. There just wasn't enough space to focus on the hardships, highs and lows, endless waiting for trains and reunions, and memories of those away or lost forever.

So, I decided to write *Christmas with the Kingston Girls* to put a spotlight on this very special time of year – for those at home and those serving far away. It was fun to revisit all the characters and see their growth from the start of the war to victory and beyond. It's the final book in the Kingston Sister series:

+ *The War Twins of London*
+ *A Burning London Sky*
+ *The Code Girl from London*

Finally, this is a huge thank you to YOU, the readers, for all your support of the Kingstons and their wartime adventures. I hope you enjoy one last trip down memory lane with the brave and courageous women of WWII London.

More by Deb Stratas in this series:
+ The War Twins of London
+ A Burning London Sky
+ The Code Girl from London

Milton Keynes UK
Ingram Content Group UK Ltd.
UKHW020803031224
3353UKWH00007B/60